THE BROKEN PENNY

by Julian Symons

A country behind the Iron Curtain—a country shaped like a broken penny—is overripe for revolution. Half a dozen resistance movements are at work, but they are fighting more against each other than against the government. Only one man can unite these groups, and only two agents can smuggle him into the country. One of them is missing; the other is Charles Garden ...

"This is pure Hitchcock...[and] includes a dandy double-cross."   —Avis de Voto, *Boston Globe*

"Should keep almost any reader suitably pop-eyed with excitement."   —James Sandoe,
New York Herald Tribune Book Review

Other titles by Julian Symons available in Perennial Library:

THE BELTING INHERITANCE

BLAND BEGINNING

BOGUE'S FORTUNE

THE COLOR OF MURDER

THE 31ST OF FEBRUARY

THE BROKEN PENNY

BY

JULIAN SYMONS

PERENNIAL LIBRARY
Harper & Row, Publishers
New York, Cambridge, Hagerstown,
Philadelphia, San Francisco
London, Mexico City, São Paulo, Sydney

A hardcover edition of this book was originally published by Harper & Row, Publishers, Inc.

First PERENNIAL LIBRARY edition published 1980.

ISBN: 0-06-080480-7

80 81 82 83 84 10 9 8 7 6 5 4 3 2 1

FOR Marcus Richard Julian Symons

CONTENTS

"The thing which it is attempted to represent is the conflict between the tender conscience and the world."

ARTHUR HUGH CLOUGH in 1850

I

PLAN

1

The board in the hall said CENTRAL LIAISON OR-GANIZATION, 3RD FLOOR. Charles Garden took the self-service lift up, and stepped out into a waiting room with Cézanne and Matisse reproductions on the walls. Behind a desk sat a rather dowdy girl wearing large horn-rimmed spectacles reading a book. She looked up from it reluctantly and said, "Yes?"

"My name's Garden. An appointment with Mr. Latterley."

The girl picked up a telephone. "A Mr. Garden. Says he has an appointment with G. L. Section Three." She listened, then said without smiling, "Won't keep you a moment. Take a seat, please."

Garden leaned over the desk. "The name's Garden, not *a* Mr. Garden. And I have got an appointment, there's no doubt about it."

She said without much interest, "We get all sorts here, sometimes one name and then another. And your name, I mean Garden, well." She did not think much of Garden as a name, that was clear.

"What sort of liaison goes on here? I thought that word went out with the war."

"We're hush-hush," she said, and added generously, "Especially Section Three."

"What's Section Three?"

She stared at him through the big horn rims. "Better

ask G. L." She put down the book as if conceding a point, and took up some knitting. Garden looked at the title. It was *War and Peace*.

He walked round the room looking at the pictures and then, checked by a mirror, stared into that instead. It reflected back at him a large blunt-featured reddish face, originally amorphous seemingly and battered into some kind of shape only by the assaults of time; the nose a bit askew through untimely contact with some brick or stone, small dents and bumps over the whole rough surface testifying to distant occasions when the face had stood up reasonably well to illness, exposure or personal attack. Out of this knobbly time-beaten face looked faded blue eyes.

Now these blue eyes showed a mild surprise at the hand, well-manicured, a thick gold ring round the third finger, that rested on his shabby raincoat. The mirror, abruptly ending, left the hand disembodied. A man's voice, light and high, rippling with mockery or self-mockery, said, "Chas, my dear, it's been an age. So nice of you to come along." Now a face entered the glass, smoothly fortyish, with only a few lines of laughter round the brown eyes, thinning hair carefully brushed, delicate cheeks faintly pink. Above a discreetly expensive blue suit a stiff collar showed dazzlingly white. This was Geoffrey Latterley.

"Has La Harbottle been entertaining you? She's the dragon who guards the gate, isn't that so, Enid?"

"Oh, G. L., you really *are*." Behind the large spectacles eyes were cast demurely down.

"Harbottle," Garden said severely. "It's an improbable name." He had the pleasure of seeing Miss Harbottle blush as they passed through swing doors down a corridor with numbered rooms on either side. "She didn't like me very much, but she likes you."

In front of him Latterley checked his spring-heeled walk to look back and say ruefully, "I have a terrible

fascination for a certain kind of undesirable female. You
remember that, I expect. Here we are."

He pushed open a door leading to a tiny box of a
room, with a chair behind a desk for Latterley and another in front of it for Garden. "You don't look a day
older than when I last saw you, Chas, and that was—
how many years ago?—really I blush to remember." He
giggled. "It's true of course that you were thoroughly
looking your age then. Just come back from Spain,
hadn't you?"

Garden drew from his pocket a telegram folded neatly
into four, and opened it. The telegram said: RING ME
URGENTLY WHITEHALL 96944 EXTENSION 361 JOB FOR
YOU GEOFFREY LATTERLEY.

"Down to business at once. You haven't changed,
Chas. When was our last meeting now?"

"At your flat." Garden stirred impatiently, his foot
flickered on the carpet. "You remember it perfectly
well."

"Do I? Perhaps I do. I never could resist teasing you,
Chas. Do you remember my little sherry parties? I still
give sherry parties, but different people come to them
now. Though the young girls—really, you might think
they were the same young girls." His look at Garden was
quizzical, humorous, and in a way tender.

Latterley's sherry parties, Latterley's young girls, they
came back to Garden out of the lost world of the late
thirties. There would be a sprinkling of M.P.s who supported the Popular Front, there would be one or two
journalists who had just returned from Spain full of enthusiasm for the Republican regime, there would be
some minor figures from the Foreign Office. And there
would be the young girls, middle- or upper-class young
girls just out of their teens, their eyes blazing with a
desire for martyrdom which made conversation with
them rather unrewarding. To these young girls Latterley

was devoted, whereas he ignored the lusher feminine specimens at his parties, deep-chested women with magnificent limbs who found his jokes amusing and his insouciance delightful. The young girls, on the other hand, were deeply serious creatures who had nothing but contempt for Latterley's flippancies.

But the parties, the parties! How perfectly they belonged to their time. One of the deep-chested women would pant through a song about the iniquities of the Means Test, another would embark on a stirring piece in Spanish which was said to be a battle hymn of the Republic. During the singing of such songs faces all over the room took on that expression of respectful melancholy often to be seen in church. But Latterley, the host, was a conspicuous heretic among these worshipers. The downward look that he addressed to the sherry glass in his hand seemed to hold in it awareness of some private joke.

What was the nature of the joke? Garden never found out. And what precisely was Latterley's job? He worked during the day in some inconspicuous and mysterious way that had something to do with the Foreign Office. Or perhaps it had nothing to do with the Foreign Office, perhaps that was only one of Latterley's little jokes. He had so many little jokes that one could never be quite sure.

Out of these thoughts Garden said abruptly, "What do you do here? The Central Liaison Organization, what's that?"

"We liaise, Chas, we liaise between the people who want things to be done and the people who do them." Latterley giggled at Garden's baffled look. "Officially the C.L.O. is just a sort of government agency looking after the details of receptions for distinguished visitors here and our chaps abroad. In fact it's something between a very discreet branch of M.I.5 and a bit of the Secret Service. Supposing an unofficial meeting is being arranged between one of the big shots from the satellite countries and someone from the F.O. Such meetings do take place, I assure you. In cases like that the F.O. tell us what they want, and we arrange it. Simple stuff, but it can be ticklish sometimes. Section One handles it."

"That's not your section."

"That's not my section," Latterley smilingly agreed. "Section Three handles things that are—a little more complicated."

"And it's Section Three that's offering me a job." Latterley nodded. "I don't need a job. I've got one already."

"Goldblatt's Fur Repositories, Dingwall Road, Elephant and Castle. Night watchman. Not a very good job." Garden shrugged his shoulders. Latterley leaned across the desk. The smile had gone from his face, the brown eyes looked hurt. "We'll get on faster if you try to trust me, Chas. There's no reason why you shouldn't."

"Isn't there?"

Latterley's brow was corrugated. "What?"

"You've forgotten Peterson."

"Peterson, Peterson? That was your chum out in Spain. Believe me, Chas, there was nothing anybody could do about Peterson."

"I haven't forgotten him," Garden said.

In the Spanish Civil War Garden had gone out recommended by the wrong people, and had joined the wrong part of the army. Or that was the way it turned out. He had been a member of the anti-Stalinist P.O.U.M. militia, he was in Barcelona when the Stalinists ruthlessly repressed their nominal allies, the Anarchists and the P.O.U.M. He escaped from Spain only through the illiteracy of a frontier guard who could not read the words in his papers that showed he had served in the P.O.U.M. 29th Division.

Peterson did not escape. He was an Austrian Socialist,

a veteran of many strikes and prisons, who held the rank of captain in Garden's unit. Garden had seen Peterson in the last of his prisons, in Barcelona where he had been charged as a suspected Fascist.

Garden was young in those days. When he got back to England he went, full of indignation, to see Latterley. He was coldly received. "I told you not to mix yourself up with people like that," Latterley said. "They are no good either to themselves or to Spain."

But, Garden protested, this was a case of flagrant injustice, Peterson had fought by his side and had been wounded in the Republic's service. What about those M.P.s who had been so interested in Spanish democracy? he asked. What about the Foreign Office young men?

Latterley was cool. "My dear Chas, don't be absurd. The only people who could do anything for this man would be his own government, and from what you say they are hardly likely to help. And anyway, people like Peterson aren't interested in making a united Spain. Here's my advice, Chas. Forget your own experiences in Spain, you went out with the wrong people. Forget your chum Peterson, his fate is the misfortune of war."

It was sensible advice, as Garden found. The letters he wrote to highbrow weeklies and to important politicians received formal replies or remained unanswered. The only other news he ever had of Peterson was a rumor that he had been removed to Communist-controlled Madrid. But still Garden never forgot Peterson, and he never really forgave Latterley for his sensible advice.

"Peterson." Latterley considered the name frowningly, as if it had some connotations of which Garden was unaware. "Yes, Peterson had slipped my memory. It was all so long ago. But I have quite a lot of information about you somewhere, that our researchers have grubbed up. Would you like to hear it?" Well-washed well-scrubbed hands opened a Manila folder. In his light voice, with its undercurrent of self-mockery, Latterley began to read.

"Garden, Charles. Forty-five years old. Born Brightsand, father John Garden a schoolmaster in Brightsand Elementary School, son of Reverend Charles Lester Garden, vicar of Stoneway, Hampshire. Mother Louisa, second daughter of Charles Hancock, solicitor, of Brightsand. And so on, family background, not very interesting. John and Louisa Garden both died in air raid, July, 1941. Accurate?"

Garden said nothing. Latterley turned a page. "So much for the parents, now for young Charles. Scholarship to Brightsand Grammar School, edited school magazine the *Brightsander*. Apprentice to chartered accountants. Gave up apprenticeship after two years, became bookshop assistant, formed—ahem—association with Patricia Maguire. Joined through her left-wing organization W.L.R., or Workers' League for Revolution.

"Various jobs as railway porter, builder's mate and market gardener. Short personal associations with Lucy Smith, Eileen Braxted, Clarissa Wayne-Morfleet. Member at various times of P.F.A. (Peoples' Freedom Association), P.P.U. (Peace Pledge Union), R.C.O. (Revolutionary Communist Organization), I.L.P. (Independent Labour Party), etcetera etcetera. Then there's a list of about twenty movements you supported, arms for Spain, no more war, no conscription, and so on." The corners of Latterley's eyes crinkled as he smiled. "I say, you did go it a bit, didn't you?"

"You should remember," Garden said. "Wasn't it at an arms for Spain meeting that I first met you?"

Latterley picked a piece of fluff from the sleeve of his blue suit. "Possibly, dear boy, but times change. Wise men change with them." He continued reading. "Went to Spain November, 1936, under auspices of I.L.P. Lieutenant in P.O.U.M. 29th Division. Returned to England July, 1937, and ceased to engage in political activity. Volunteered for service at outbreak of war, September, 1939." Latterley stopped reading. "Disillusioned?" he said.

Garden rolled the word over in his mind. "Not exactly. You might say I found politics were too complicated for me."

"War record," Latterley said, and then closed the folder. "No, I think we'll leave it at that for the time being. You see we know quite a lot about you."

"Yes. Why?"

"You've suddenly become a V.I.P."

"Why?"

Latterley did not answer the question. "Tell me, Chas, you were a lieutenant out in Spain, but in the World War you refused two times to accept a commission. Why was that?"

Plucking at one of the buttons on his shabby raincoat Garden rolled this question round too. "It would have been wrong."

"What on earth do you mean?"

Slowly Garden formulated it. "The Spanish Republican army—well, the 29th Division anyway—was democratic. No saluting, the officers ate the same food as the men. The British army—that was different. It was a different kind of war." His faded blue eyes looked at Latterley, and he said without irony, "You were in the Min. of Inf. I suppose."

"Not at all." Latterley's indignation was comic, but behind the comedy was he perhaps genuinely indignant? "I was in uniform from 1940, Africa, Italy, and Normandy. Psychological warfare, you know, never less than twenty miles behind the front. Not that that was always far enough back. I ended up a colonel, and if the war had gone on another six months I might have been a brigadier." He stopped and giggled at Garden's disapproving stare. "The trouble with you, Chas, is you've got no sense of humor."

"All right. Let's get down to it. What do you want?"

"What do I want?" For a moment Latterley's brown eyes, wholly serious, met Garden's blue ones. In the stare they exchanged, there was undoubtedly a mutual antipathy; but there was something else too, some richer and more complicated emotion, hatred perhaps, or violent and destructive love. When Latterley spoke his voice was almost wooingly soft.

"I just wanted to make sure that in these cynical nineteen fifties there was one dyed-in-the-wool wrong-in-the-head idealist left in the world. You haven't changed your views, I suppose? Don't care much for the Communists, too totalitarian?"

"Yes."

"Can't approve of the Socialists, too imperialist?"

"You could put it that way."

"And of course you hate all Right-wing governments worse than poison."

"Yes."

"That's what I thought." Latterley sighed. "It does me good to meet you. And now I must take you along to meet—somebody else."

Garden stood up, shaking his head like a large and irritated dog. "I've had enough of this. If you can't say what you want, let's leave it at that."

Latterley took a beautifully brushed bowler hat from a stand behind him, put it on, and said, "How do I look?" There was something so comic about his perfect seriousness that Garden burst out laughing. "That's my Chas," said Latterley indulgently. "As a professional do-gooder you'd never forgive yourself if you missed this chance of helping Section Three. And doesn't it give you a thrill, Chas, to be engaged in something so tremendously hush-hush? It really is, I assure you. I'm only a pawn in the game."

They passed Miss Harbottle on the way out. She did not look up from *War and Peace*.

2

A five-minute journey in Latterley's bright little beetle of a car took them to a quiet street near Horse Guards Parade. Latterley used a key to open a gray-painted door that led into a small gray-painted lobby with a telephone in it. He picked up this telephone, dialed, and spoke so softly that Garden could not hear what he said. Then he suddenly disappeared, with the effect of passing through the wall. Garden went over to the gray wall and saw the thin line of a concealed door. He remembered Latterley's childish enjoyment of intrigue and secrets from long ago. In two minutes Latterley reappeared, saying, "Sorry about the spy stuff."

This time Garden noticed the small knob that he pressed. The door swung open, and closed behind them. They walked up a dimly lighted spiral staircase. At the top this suddenly brightened, as Latterley opened another door. The door led to a room in which a man was standing before a fireplace, legs wide apart, hands behind his back.

Garden had never met the man who faced him, but he still felt the shock of recognition. The heavy eyebrows beneath a dozen strands of hair plastered slantwise over the skull, the jutting chin, thick neck, and solid body—these were gifts to cartoonists which they had been quick to use. For this was the famous industrialist and one-time Minister of State whose behind-the-scenes influence had in the past been reputed enormous; who had once been shown by a celebrated cartoonist as a puppet-master dangling his party's leaders on strings and saying blandly: "But of course *I* have no influence over their actions." In the past there could be no doubt that he had influenced their actions, as any man must who voices the beliefs and hopes of masses of people, and says that they can be fulfilled. During the war his immense energy had been set to the task of increasing production of war material. He had done so with a great deal of success, but also with a disregard for the niceties of position and even at times for ordinary courtesy that had made enemies spring up like dragon's teeth wherever he walked. In opposition to these enemies he had placed his fame as a business genius, the backing of a small band of personal followers, and the great skill in debate by which he emerged triumphant again and again from the most unpromising situations. But Parliamentary triumphs may be illusory. He had made too many enemies. He could not be ignored, but in postwar administrations he found himself placed in posts manifestly inadequate to his talents. He alienated more people by the bad grace with which he took them, and by the furious lobbying through which he attempted to regain power. His influence waned, his followers fell away, and for the last two or three years he had taken little active part in politics, devoting all his time to managing his great Multiple Steel Corporation. Was he, as some said, biding his time, or had he done with politics altogether? Was he the one honest man in a crowd of time-servers and place-seekers, or the most unscrupulous politician of them all? Garden, like many other people, had not made up his mind.

They were in a square, plainly furnished room with two doors, the concealed one by which they had come up, and a big oak door for public use. Latterley said, "You know Sir Alfred?" with the merest tinge of inquiry in his voice. When Garden nodded he sat down beside the oak door, put his bowler hat on his knees and thoughtfully contemplated the knife-edge crease in his trousers. One side of the room was almost taken up by a big window that looked out sideways on Whitehall.

On another wall were portraits of Lloyd George and Winston Churchill. The great man paced up and down the length of the room, stopping to stare briefly in a belligerent manner out of the window. Garden noted that he carried himself with his head pushed out above the broad shoulders, just as the cartoonists showed him.

"Mr. Garden. Are you a patriot?" The words were spoken in the thick heavy voice, with a trace of north-country accent, that radio and Parliamentary debates had made famous.

Garden took his time to consider. "Not in the sense that the word's generally used. At least, I put my duty to other people a long way above duty to my country."

"So do I." The great head thrust forward challengingly. "But patriotism sometimes has more than its narrowest meaning. You were a patriot during the war, isn't that so?"

"Is it?"

"Volunteered for service September, 1939, served in France, 1940, Africa, 1942, Italy, 1943, twice refused a commission." Garden thought with some amusement: that's why Latterley didn't bother with my war record, he knew it was going to be recited here. "Why was that?" Sir Alfred asked. "Why refuse a commission, eh?"

Garden hesitated. Latterley stared down at his trousers. "Private reasons. Neither here nor there."

"All right. But your C.O. recognized you as a good man, recommended you for a special task. The switch, Geoffrey." There was a click, and a light showed above a map of Europe on the wall. A long pointer was in Sir Alfred's hand. "In 1943 you were dropped—*here*." The pointer's tip rested on the country where Garden had lived and worked as a partisan for the last eighteen months of the war, and for a little while after the war ended. "There are moments when nationalism and internationalism meet, when our duties to our country and to our fellow men point the same way. You felt that during the war, didn't you?" The pointer tapped insistently on that country shaped like a broken penny, the break making a jagged edge of coastline. "Am I talking your language. Do I make sense?" The small eyes beneath the thick brows considered without condescension, even with friendliness, Garden's battered face and old clothes.

"It makes sense," Garden admitted. "But what's it got to do with anything here and now?"

"This, Mr. Garden. You've reached another point in time where patriotism and internationalism pull the same way. You can help the government, you can help your fellow men, and you're one of the few people who can. There's something you haven't noticed about that map. It's out of date. Look now upon this picture—and on this." He lifted the map and flung it back on the wall, to show another. Here were the same countries, but now instead of being in variegated splashes of green, brown, and red, they were all a single color. "Before the war Central Europe was split into a dozen semifeudal states whose rulers plotted against each other and tagged along at the coattails of any important power who would give them protection and back their claims in borderline squabbles. That's all over." Sir Alfred's voice was booming now, striking against the walls and bouncing back into the room. Lloyd George and Churchill looked down appreciatively on him. "Central Europe has been unified by the Communists, artificially and by force. Free speech has gone, the right of assembly no longer exists, all heresies, whether religious or social, are punishable by disgrace or death. As an internationalist, does that seem to you a thing you can approve?"

"No. But what's it got to do with me?"

Sir Alfred pulled a chair near to Garden, and straddled it back to front. "This new map of Europe may be changed soon. The regime in power in at least one country may fall. Can we enlist your help in bringing about that change?"

"Which country?" But Garden knew the answer. Sir Alfred merely tapped with his pointer the country shaped like a broken penny.

From his place by the door Latterly laughed. "Don't look so disconcerted, Chas, to find yourself on the side of the angels."

"The country is overripe for revolt." Sir Alfred was talking more quickly now. "It's economic position, as an industrial country with a relatively high standard of living derived from export trade, has made it peculiarly vulnerable to exploitation. We have agents at work there, and they report that the abrupt drop in the standard of living has caused intense anger. Half a dozen resistance movements are working against the government and they could overthrow it tomorrow if they worked together instead of independently. As it is, they waste a good deal of their time in fighting against each other. There is only one influence that could unite these warring groups."

Garden sat back in his chair with an exhalation of breath that could hardly be called a sigh. "Arbitzer."

"Professor Jacob Arbitzer, yes. I see that you are beginning to understand me."

Almost sulkily Garden said, "I still don't see what Arbitzer, here and now, has to do with me."

"Come now, we needn't engage in dialectics." Sir Alfred pushed his chair forward so that it was within a foot of Garden. Craters were visible in the powerful nose; the whole skin, seen thus close, had a coarse strength; hairs sprouted plentifully from nose and ears. "Let's consider in a little more detail the history which Geoffrey dug out for me. In 1943 you were dropped by parachute into the country, which was German-occupied. The mission to which you belonged was assigned to make touch with Arbitzer, find out if his all-party resistance group was really fighting the Germans, and if the report was satisfactory to get help to them. Colonel Hallam, who headed the mission, was killed by stray shots from a German plane. The other officers, Captain Mackenzie and Lieutenants Jones and Pollock, were killed in an ambush. You took charge of what remained of the mission, got to Arbitzer, and became friendly with him. Personally friendly, so that when someone else was sent out to take charge of the mission, Arbitzer insisted on dealing with him through you. After the war you stayed on when Arbitzer formed his broad-based Provisional Government, including the Communists. What happened then is an old story. The Communists gained control, Arbitzer was demoted to Vice-President and then suddenly accused of treachery to the workers. He got out of the country just in time, with your help, getting his head grazed by a bullet wound as you crossed the frontier. After he left, there was a general round-up of politicians favorable to him. You were featured in the Communist press as the English agent-provocateur, Garden." Sir Alfred permitted himself a brief baring of yellowish teeth.

Garden's battered red face had not changed its expression. "Well?"

Sir Alfred jumped up suddenly. The chair clattered to the floor. Latterley drew himself up stiffly as though he expected some kind of physical assault to be made on him. "Well, well—it's not well at all." Six long paces took him to the window, from which he stared angrily out. "He must go back, he must go back at once, do you understand? In the years that he has been away Arbitzer has become a legend. He need only show himself and the country will rise to him. And you must go with him. Do you realize what it would mean to Britain, to Europe, to the whole free world, if we had a footing— there." Again the pointer tapped the broken penny.

"I see that, but I don't see why I must go with him.

Suppose I told you that I have had enough adventure, that I want a quiet life."

Latterley spoke from the door. "Now my dear Chas, do you really expect us to believe that?" He began to laugh on a delicate, high note. Sir Alfred joined in with a gusty bellow that shook his solid body. After a moment Garden laughed too.

"Another point," Sir Alfred said when he had stopped laughing. "The Garden mission—shall we call it that—must be absolutely unofficial. If anything goes wrong we will try to help you privately, but we must disown you publicly. You must not in any circumstances get in touch with any of our few remaining officials in the country. The position is difficult enough at present. We can't afford an international incident on your behalf."

"I understand that. I still don't see why you want me at all."

Latterley shook his head in a kind of despairing mockery. "I said we should have to tell him, chief."

The great head nodded indulgently. "You did, Geoffrey. When Arbitzer came to England, Mr. Garden, you were responsible for finding him a home. How long is it since you have seen him?"

"About three years."

"Yes. We have seen him—unofficially, you understand, always unofficially—more recently than that. Last week, in fact. He is not the man he was. Fortunately that is not important. The point is that Arbitzer is willing to go back only if you accompany him."

"You mean he makes that a condition?" Garden asked incredulously.

"Not exactly. How shall I put it? From what Geoffrey tells me, you will understand things better when you see Arbitzer." The hairy hand went up to stroke the great chin. "I suggest at least that you go down and see Arbitzer—acting, of course, through the proper channels, which Geoffrey will tell you about. From what Geoffrey says, Arbitzer needs a staff to lean on, and you can be the staff. In fact, we are relying on you, Mr. Garden."

Garden thought of the cool-minded idealist whom he had known so well and admired so much, who had been grateful for help but had certainly not needed a staff to lean on. "There's no doubt that he wants to go back?"

"None whatever. He wants help, that's all. Are you going to withhold it from him?" The whole great head was thrust forward menacingly.

From the doorway Latterley began to chortle. "You've done it, chief, you've done it."

"Be quiet." There was a look of anger on Sir Alfred's face. The look changed slowly to a smile as he saw Garden's expression. He came forward with hands outstretched to clasp Garden's shoulders: "You'll do it. I knew you would, and I know you'll do it well. You don't say much, but I'll lay it's a good man that can shift you when you've made up your mind." The hands tightened on Garden's shoulders, the great face, magnificent in its seriousness and power, was inches away from him. At the doorway Latterley wore his characteristic smile of self-mockery.

3

"So it's a holiday you're taking," said little Mr. Goldblatt. "I got to find myself another night watchman, that's what you're telling me. I tell you what now, let me make a guess, is it money you're interested in?" Garden shook his head. Mr. Goldblatt took no notice but went on talking, peering sharply at Garden now and then through his gold-rimmed spectacles.

"Five pound ten a week it is you get, isn't it? Now, that's not a bad wage. A man can live on five pound ten a week—"

"Barely," said Garden. They were talking in the office

next door to the night watchman's room in Goldblatt's Fur Repositories, near the Elephant and Castle.

"I know, I know, don't tell me. You look at all the lovely furs coming in here, you look at Goldblatt who's got all the money in the world, Goldblatt who's getting fat because he eats so good because he's got so much money and can't find any other way to spend it, and you say to yourself 'Garden, I'm underpaid.' Ain't I right now, ain't it a pistol you're holding at poor old Goldblatt's head to make him put up his hands?" And here Mr. Goldblatt did in fact put up his hands.

Garden began to laugh. "No, it's not money, though it's true enough you'll never get another honest night watchman for the money you're paying me."

"Don't I know it," Mr. Goldblatt said disarmingly. "I tell you what I'm going to do with you. From today it's six pound a week, how's that?"

"No."

"And I pay your insurance stamp, the whole of it. That ain't legal, mind, but I do it."

"No, it's no good."

"And two weeks' holiday I pay for," said Mr. Goldblatt in desperation. "You think yourself hard done by you don't have a holiday in three years, well I ain't had one in ten years. I don't complain. But you want a holiday. All right, I pay for it, two weeks. What more do you want?"

"Nothing," Garden was laughing again. "But I tell you it's no good. There are some things I've got to settle up, and I don't know how long they'll take."

"Oh, ah, things to settle up, that's different. Family affairs, eh?"

"Not family affairs."

"Personal is it, a girl you've been hiding from me. Ah, before I had my ulcer, believe me I was a boy for the girls."

"No, it's not a girl."

"Pity. A good-looking boy like you should have a girl."
Suddenly Mr. Goldblatt's head nodded up and down in
horror. "I know you're a bit of a politician. Don't get
telling me it's politics you're going in for."

"In a sort of a way, yes."

"You're not standing for Parliament."

"No no."

"Thank you for that. But politics now, it'll never do."
Mr. Goldblatt, a second generation Polish Jew who was
a pillar of his local Conservative Association, frequently
indulged himself in long political arguments with Garden. "Setting the poor against the rich is it, burning
down respectable people's houses, turning the old pal-
aces into rest homes, homemade bombs to blow-up the
banks—eh eh." Mr. Goldblatt clasped his stomach with
his hands, as though in pain.

"Nothing like that."

"Believe an old man, it's always like that. However it
begins, it always ends like that when you say politics like
you say it. And it never does any good in this world. I
tell you what now, you collect all the money in the
world together and divide it all equal, weigh it out with
scales you can, and in ten years you know what happens? The same people have got all the money again
and the poor ones are starving. It's a sad thing, my boy,
but you know what the old song says—the rich get richer
and the poor get children, and that's the way of the
world."

"Not for ever." Garden got up to go. "Good-by, Mr.
Goldblatt."

"Good-by, good-by. And believe an old man, if it's
politics you're going in for, it'll do no good to anybody
in this world."

4

Garden walked into a big white office building, took the lift to the third floor, went twenty yards along a corridor, and stopped outside a door with an opaque glass panel. Words on the panel in fresh black lettering said THE NEAR-EASTERN, EUROPEAN AND BRITISH GENERAL SECURITY COMPANY LIMITED. Below them, in smaller black lettering, appeared the name COLONEL CHESNEY HUNT. Garden opened the door and stepped into a small passage where another door faced him. He pressed a bell which said PLEASE RING. A small wooden panel just by the door shot open, a woman's head appeared for a moment, fair and small, the face rouged and doll-like. The Cupid's-bow mouth also opened and shut like the mouth of a ventriloquist's doll. "Mr. Garden? Come in."

The room was small and warm. There was a window which looked down to the street, and another door with an opaque glass panel and gold lettering, which said this time COLONEL CHESNEY HUNT, D.S.O. There were four new steel filing cabinets. There was a new desk on which stood a typewriter and small telephone switchboard. The little woman who had opened the panel sat at this desk in a tip-back typist's chair, and smiled. "My name's Fanny Bone." Her hair was bleached almost white, and drawn back to show very white ears. Rouge had created a patch about the size of a crown piece on each of her cheekbones. Her lips and fingernails were the same color red.

Garden sat down.

"You're coming to work with us, isn't that so?" Miss Bone fluttered her eyes at him, and then slowly cast her gaze down to the desk.

"I don't know about that. I have an appointment with Colonel Hunt." Garden eyed her curiously. Miss Bone

was hardly the kind of secretary that he expected to find
in an organization used by the Minister and Latterley.

"Oh, he wants you, no doubt about that." Miss Bone
pressed down a switch on the board in front of her, and
sang rather than said: "Mr. Garden is here, sir." She said
to Garden, "He won't keep you a moment." Then she
got up and made a journey across the office to one of the
steel files, brushing past him as she did so, skirts almost
touching his trousered knee, hips swinging and buttocks
turning in the wind of her own passage. She consulted
a paper and made the voyage past him again to her desk,
smiling triumphantly when she had returned, rather like
a visitor to the zoo who has tempted a wild animal behind bars with no untoward result. "The Colonel's aw-
fully nice, and Mr. Bretherton too. You'll like them."
This seemed to Garden not to call for any reply. Miss
Bone pursed her Cupid's bow of a mouth in disapproval
of such sullen silence, smartly swung in her chair a
quarter-turn to the left, took writing paper, carbon sheet
and copy paper from three separate drawers in her desk,
and began to type a letter. She had typed only two or
three lines when the outside bell rang again. With a
bright doll's glance at Garden Miss Bone reached toward the panel from which she had inspected him.
Before she could open it a man's voice called, "It's only
little me," and the handle of the office door was turned.

The man who came into the room was hardly more
than five feet in height, and although he did not walk
exceptionally quickly, the high heels that he wore and
his black bird's eyes that did not rest on any person or
object for more than a second or two, made all his movements seem both rapid and slightly unpremeditated. He
wore a fawn trilby hat which he took off as soon as he
entered the room, a double-breasted fawn overcoat, a
well-pressed brown suit discernible under the overcoat,
and light tan shoes. His small face was round and fresh
as a little apple, and when he took off his hat his hair

was revealed as lightish in color and parted exactly in the center. He carried in his hand a neatly rolled umbrella, which he poked playfully at Miss Bone.

"And how's Fanny?" he asked. "How's the delectable Miss Bone? Excuse me." He skipped daintily past Garden and walked with little tip-tapping steps over to an umbrella stand. He placed the umbrella in the stand, sat down, pushed his small legs out in front of him, hitched up his brown trousers to show gaily patterned socks, and regarded Miss Bone with a cocked, inquisitive eyebrow.

Miss Bone positively chirruped at him. "I'm very well, thank you, Mr. Hards. And how have you been keeping? You're looking very spick and span, I must say."

Mr. Hards took out a cigarette, placed it between plump cherry-red lips, and lighted it with one twitch of a gold lighter. "How have I been keeping? Mustn't grum, my dear, mustn't grum. Is the boss in?"

Miss Bone fluttered. "He's engaged. And then he has to see this gentleman. I'm afraid you'll have to wait."

"And what better company could I wait in?" He leaned forward and twinkled at Miss Bone, who twinkled gaily back at him. "I tell you what, Fanny. I haven't taken any pretty girls like you to the pictures lately. No indeed. I've thought about you a lot, my dear. Would you believe it?" Mr. Hards twinkled now directly at Garden. "Fanny pretends to be afraid to go to the pictures with me. Afraid of a little chap like me. I ask you." Now Mr. Hards laughed outright, but discreetly, showing neat white teeth.

Miss Bone tossed her doll's head. "It's not that. I told you that I have a gentleman friend."

"A dozen, I expect." Mr. Hards's eyes twinkled more brightly than ever. "One damned man after another, I'll bet. The more the merrier, *and* they're all alike, ain't they? But I'd lay odds I could name *your* one particular friend, Fanny my dear, and he's a very big boy indeed, ain't that so?"

"Not at all." Miss Bone obviously did not care for the turn the conversation was taking. A bell rang, and she put on her earphones. With a sweet doll-smile at Garden she said, "Colonel Hunt will see you now." She got up, opened the door into the Colonel's office, and Garden went inside. Mr. Hards twinkled very merrily as Garden passed him, a twinkle of commiseration perhaps that he should have had to wait so long; but when Garden had gone by the expression of Mr. Hards's face changed so that its look of lecherous good nature was replaced by a very stiff and ugly sneer. A friend of Garden's (if Garden had had any friends) might have been excused for thinking that the little man bore Garden some personal ill-will. But the hypothetical friend would have been wrong, for Mr. Hards had never heard of Garden three days before, and had never seen him until that morning.

In the room a big man with a bald red head got up from behind a light oak desk. "How de do, Garden. I'm Hunt." They shook hands. "Meet our secretary, Bretherton." A man about thirty years old, who was sitting in a corner of the room, nodded without rising. He was neatly dressed, his hands were small and white, his face also was white, his lips thin, and his complexion bad.

Colonel Hunt's hands moved across his bald head frantically searching for patches of missing hair. His face was seamed with deep lines that twitched and changed position as he talked.

"Happy to have you working with us, Garden. Know your job, eh, know your assignment?"

"I had a talk with Latterley, but he left me in the air—"

"No names, no names. Walls have ears, eh, Bretherton?" The secretary, who was surreptitiously picking his nose, said nothing. Quickly the Colonel ran the long nails of his left hand over his pate, scratching furiously.

"Expressed myself badly. Know the terms of your job as our agent, do you?"

"No."

"Twelve pounds a week and expenses. We specialize in all forms of foreign insurance—marine, ordinary commercial, other jobs like insurance of livestock going overseas. You're one of our fully accredited agents. Understand?" Garden nodded. "Sometimes send our agents abroad with an important shipment to keep an eye on it. Got it?" Very deliberately the Colonel closed one small eye in a wink. Garden winked back. "Let's have a drink." From a drawer in his desk the Colonel produced a bottle of whisky with an unfamiliar label on it, and two dirty glasses. He poured a generous measure of whisky into each glass, and gestured at Bretherton. "No good asking him. Doesn't drink, doesn't smoke, never touches a girl. Must have some real vices, eh? Well, cheerio. No water, no heel taps." Garden raised his glass and drank. The liquid ran raw and rasping down his throat, and lighted a fire in his stomach. For a moment he thought he might have been poisoned. Then he saw the Colonel laughing. "The real McCoy, eh, Garden? You're a man after my own heart. Now let's get down to cases. Your first assignment takes you to Brightsand. Check."

"Check."

"There you make contact with our agent, Floy. Check."

"Your agent?" Garden raised his head in surprise. "Nothing was said to me about anybody else. They only told me to make contact with Arb—"

"No names, no names." The colonel scratched his head vigorously, flaked away dry skin, and nipped it from under his nail. "Thought you were the only pebble on Brightsand beach, eh?" He let loose a guffaw in which neither Bretherton nor Garden joined, then wiped a little mist from rheumy eyes. "Seriously, Garden, this isn't

a job to be tackled singlehanded. And anyway you belong to us from now on. Receive orders, carry them out,
leave the headwork to us. Check."

Garden stiffened. The hectoring tone, however jovial,
and the comic boozy militariness of Colonel Hunt,
represented what he had most disliked in the army.
"Check."

"Right. Expect they told you we'd made contact already with your assignment? Good. Name of our man is
Floy."

"Floy?"

"Floy, right. A good fellow, one of the best. Arranged
a date with him for you. No good using telephone, you
never know who may have it tapped." He glared at the
hand microphone on his desk. "Bloody thing. Now the
appointment is—is—what is it, where is it, Bretherton?"

The little finger of the secretary's left hand was still
ferreting in his nostril. He took it out reluctantly. "Do
you know Brightsand?"

"Yes." These people, obviously, lacked the knowledge
of his childhood possessed by Latterley and Sir Alfred.

"You're to meet Floy at two o'clock by the third seat
along from the far end of the pier, on the jetty side. Be
looking over the rail. He will ask you for a match. You
can discuss the situation with Floy and he will tell you
how to proceed."

Fiercely the Colonel raked his bare head. "Recognition, Bretherton? You don't know Floy?" he asked
Garden.

"No."

Bretherton took a small photograph from a drawer in
his desk and gave it to Garden. With a shock of surprise
Garden saw the face of Hans Peterson.

Garden had respected Peterson more than any man he
had ever known. He had gone out to Spain an enthusiastic boy, mentally innocent in a way possible only for

an Englishman, an inhabitant of a country where politics for a century has been conducted peacefully, and where violent minority movements are not a threat but a joke. To watch Peterson, to listen to Peterson, had been an education for him. In Peterson's detachment there had been practically no desertions, there was never any shortage of volunteers for patrol duty. Yet Peterson exercised no apparent authority over his men, and would argue patiently for five minutes if necessary to get an order obeyed. That, he said, was an essential part of democracy.

"But what will happen when the Fascists are attacking us?" Garden asked. "There will be no time for argument then."

Peterson spat reflectively. "And then there will be no need for argument."

Peterson had been wounded in the assault on Huesca, and then sent back to Barcelona. There he had been arrested at his hotel when he had been about to set off for the front again. There Garden had seen for the last time his narrow head and humorous face. He had taken the occasion of Garden's visit to him in prison to enlarge his friend's political education.

"Lesson number one, Garden. This is the kind of thing that is always happening. We know our opponents, we know what weapons they will use against us. Very likely I shall be shot. Or perhaps I shall be lucky, it does not much matter. What matters is this. Lesson number two. Do not let things like this destroy your faith in man, Garden. Do not think because there is treachery on both sides that the two sides are equal. Do not be angry, or indulge feelings of betrayal. Above all, Garden, do not hate. Believe me, I do not hate anybody." Looking into Peterson's deep-set eyes, seeing the calmness of his bearing, Garden realized that this was true. "Now you must go. There is nothing whatever you can do for me or for Spain any more. Go back to England. Good-by." Quite deliberately Peterson turned his long narrow back and walked into the darkness without so much as a wave of the hand.

That was Peterson, whom Garden had thought dead, who was now suddenly alive.

In comparison with his recollection this photograph was Peterson seen, as it were, through a mist. The face that had been thin was here almost emaciated, the mouth that had once been wide and generous was drawn together in a tight line with the ends curving downward, the hair had greatly thinned.

While Garden looked at the photograph the telephone rang. The Colonel picked it up and barked a Hallo. Then his voice became muffled, his replies monosyllabic. He gestured to Bretherton who picked up a watch receiver, listened for a few moments, and then left the room. The Colonel continued the conversation, in which his share was limited to saying "Yes," "No," and "I see." Finally he said, "All right, our man will be down at two," and replaced the receiver. He hummed tunelessly beneath his breath. Garden, looking up from the photograph, saw the little bloodshot eyes staring at him. "Somebody wanted to know when you were coming. Told them you'd be there at two."

"Yes."

Garden handed back the photograph of Peterson. The Colonel pushed it under his blotting pad without a glance, and said almost absently: "Now, money. Said you were on the pay roll. Want some?"

"I can't go far unless you give me some, and that's a fact," Garden said with composure.

The Colonel hitched up the waistcoat of his suit, and selected a small key from a chain that ran to a pocket inside his trousers. He opened a wall safe across the room and took out an envelope full of pound notes. He laboriously counted out forty-eight of these, and pushed them over to Garden. "Four weeks in advance. Let me know expenses. If you run short tell Floy, he'll fix you up."

During the counting of the notes Bretherton had glided palely back into the room. He sat down again now in his corner, staring at nothing. Garden carefully tucked away the notes in a shabby wallet. They made a slight bulge inside the right-hand side of his jacket.

"That's the lot, then." Colonel Hunt abandoned head scratching. "We'll keep in touch, Garden, don't worry about that. Telephone if it's very urgent, not unless. Better not make a note of the number, remember it." And he gave a Mayfair number. "Good-by. And good luck."

"Good-by and good luck," Bretherton echoed. He stepped forward, a pallid ghost. His hand, as Garden held it, was cold and apparently boneless.

In the outer office there was no sign of Mr. Hards. Perhaps he had got tired of waiting. Fanny Bone sat primly at her desk, rattling on the typewriter. She flashed a smile at him and then lowered her eyes demurely to the sheet of paper in front of her. The lift took Garden down.

5

Walking down Station Road Garden sniffed nostalgically the salt sea air. He passed the Railway Hotel and stopped a moment at the stationers that sold comic postcards, many of them remembered from his childhood. The striped-trousered manager, the girl assistant on top of the ladder, the customer gleefully gazing at a fine expanse of leg. "Show this gentleman something a little higher up, Miss Jones." Or the man in a shop full of parlor tricks balancing three balls on three fingers and saying to a prospective purchaser, "You should see the trick I played on the wife last night."

With a feeling of melancholy Garden walked down the street that ran straight for a hundred yards and then plunged steeply rightward to the sea. Here was so much that had been commonplace in childhood, so much to which time had lent glamor. The tall narrow houses still had short lace curtains across their triple bow windows. In the middle bow a card said, as it had done long ago, "Bed and Breakfast," and another time-dishonored card in the left- or right-hand window announced "Vacancies." Toy shops displayed hopelessly buckets and spades on this cool day of early autumn. Sweet shops offered confectionery in the shape of sea shells. Beach shoes and swim suits were in the shop windows, as they would be even in February fill-dike weather.

At the corner where Station Road turned sharp right to the sea and the pier, Garden looked at his watch. He had twenty minutes to spare. He turned left into the more discreetly prosperous part of Brightsand, where lived the stockbrokers and chartered accountants who commuted daily from London, the rich bookmakers and doctors who liked to live by the sea, the retired army officers and maiden ladies who watched their lives drain away year by year in the stuffy lounges of small genteel hotels. Down wide roads full of detached villa residences he walked, most of them with a side entrance for the garage, a strip of green in front, and a larger square of lawn at the back. Here were Byron Avenue and Scott Road and Wordsworth Crescent, and leading off them other glimpses of a literary Elysium, in streets named for Arnold and Moore and Patmore, Rossetti, Meredith and Morris. In Rossetti Gardens, which was a little shabby but still genteel, he stood for a moment looking at a typical small seaside villa of the year 1910. In this house he had passed his childhood and schooldays.

How the past overwhelms us as soon as it comes washing through any gap in the high wall we have made to keep out the seas of memory, what a mistake it had

been to turn left instead of right. With painful clarity
Garden saw himself as a mop-haired schoolboy pushing
open the slightly squeaking gate, heard his feet on the
asphalt drive, halted at the sound of his father's and
mother's voices raised in angry dispute. What were they
quarreling about? She had spread butter with a ruin-
ously lavish hand upon toast, she had bought a new
dress without telling him, she had overspent her household allowance and was asking him for money. Garden's
father was a schoolmaster who combined a Wellsian belief in the betterment of mankind through education
and scientific enlightenment with a cramping personal
meanness. His mother was a feckless, gentle woman who
was quite incapable of adding up a column of figures
correctly, or of resisting bargains at sales. One day she
had bought three umbrella stands and a dinner service
for twenty-four persons, a pair of very old armchairs, sets
of the works of Bulwer-Lytton and Charles Lever, a
shooting stick and a large bird bath. Garden, a boy of
twelve, was appalled to find her carefully dusting the
books and arranging them so that they should be the
first things his father saw. Inevitably the storm broke
over her. "But they were so *cheap*," she pleaded.

"Junk," said Mr. Garden. He had come back from
a meeting of the Rational Religious Society where,
through some trickery, he had been voted off the committee. "Filth. Rubbish. Take it away, get it out." He
gave the set of Lytton a kick and sent half a dozen books
flying. One of them smashed a plate from the dinner set.

"Oh," wailed Mrs. Garden. "Look what you've done.
The set's ruined."

"Don't be a fool. What does it matter whether we
have twenty-four or twenty-three dinner plates, there are
never six people here to eat. It won't hurt to break a few
more of 'em." Mr. Garden picked up a volume of Lytton
and threw it at a gravy boat. His aim was bad. The book
struck his wife over the right eye. She staggered back-

ward against an umbrella stand which tottered, and then
fell onto the dinner service, reducing its numbers con-
siderably. Young Garden rushed at his father, hitting
out wildly. Mr. Garden, who was in principle a man of
peace, caught him by the arms. "Now young feller me
lad, no fisticuffs. Remember it's the reasoning faculty
that distinguishes man from the brute creation."

Mrs. Garden's eye was undamaged, but her sensibili-
ties were deeply wounded. She sank back into one of
the newly purchased armchairs, the springs of which
squeaked beneath her, and held out both arms to her
son. "Charlie, Charlie, you're the only one who under-
stands me."

Looking back through the years, as he stared at the
very front window behind which many such scenes had
been enacted, Garden saw his mother and father as
wholly ludicrous figures, and their lives as fragments of
Dickensian fantasy. To live through such a fantasy, however, is to experience reality in its most painful shape.
Garden was wholeheartedly on the side of his mother
against his father, and he fought for her in the most
effective way possible, by expressing contempt for his
father's ideas. When Charles Garden was in his teens
his father was a man in his middle fifties who believed
himself to be in the forefront of advanced thought. Had
his son been a Conservative or a mild Liberal he would
have felt able to condescend amiably enough to the ig-
norance of youth. But to be told, as he was, that Wells
was an outmoded writer whose mental outlook was as
antiquated as his novels about feminine emancipation,
to have his elaborate commentaries on the factual in-
accuracies of the Bible dismissed casually with the remark that since every thinking person was an atheist
nowadays all that was so much wasted ink, was a harder
fate than any he had expected to bear. Nor, indeed, did
he feel inclined to bear it, for this apostle of pure reason
was a choleric man, strikingly intemperate in his expres-

sion of a sweetly reasonable point of view. "There's no use arguing with you," he would say to his son. "It's like arguing with a lunatic, a crazy man. Pure materialism indeed, I call it pure bilge water. Do you mean to tell me," Mr. Garden shouted at his son, "that you don't believe in a Life Force controlling everything?"

Garden laughed provokingly with one leg over the old horsehair sofa. "Certainly. Individual life has no purpose. The only meaning in life is that given to it by social change."

"Blasphemous rubbish." Mr. Garden tugged at his frayed collar. The whole of his life outside school had been occupied in a delicate flirtation with different religions, comparisons of the ideals of pure Christianity, Zen Buddhism, and Mohammedanism, a quest for the ideal in thought which had been utterly denied to him in the life that had made him a tired and impatient teacher of small boys. "Do you mean to tell me you believe in nothing?"

"Not at all," said Garden. "I believe in man."

Many years ago those words had been spoken. In 1941 a stray bomber off its course had dropped its load on Brightsand, and one of the bombs had fallen with pleasing accuracy two yards from the air raid shelter in which Mr. and Mrs. Garden spent their nights, as became logical people who knew that an air raid shelter was safer than their beds. The two old people were killed outright, while the house remained almost undamaged. Garden, who was serving in Africa at the time, felt the deaths to be merely ridiculous until, some weeks afterward, he received a few pages of manuscript that had been found in the shelter. He recognized them as fragments of the textual commentaries on the Gospels that had occupied so many years of his father's life. Looking at the pieces of paper, slightly burned and then well soaked, in which a few words and phrases were still discernible in his father's neat, clear hand, Garden had a sense of the pathos and futility of human effort. Yet in the presence of those pieces of paper he could still say, "I believe in man." And now, when the years had turned a fresh-faced arrogant boy into the battered man who passed this villa with a wry smile on his way to the pier, many more years of deceit and treachery had left those words unblurred in his mind.

At the end of Rossetti Gardens you are confronted at once by the sucking, lapping greenish-blue sea. A hundred and fifty yards of small restaurants and teashops, with two amusement arcades and half a dozen sellers of Brightsand souvenirs brings you to the long finger of the pier that points more than half a mile into the sea. Along here Garden walked, looking at two boys skimming the water with stones, sniffing up memories with the ozone. The deck chairs had been put away, the front was almost deserted. Beside a beach photographer's hut a man lounged with a camera strapped round his neck. Garden paid his twopence toll and stepped onto the wooden boards of the pier. The time was just before two o'clock.

As he walked up the pier it seemed to him that he caught a glimpse of somebody hurrying the other way, a figure for some reason vaguely familiar, but when he turned to look the figure, if it existed, had passed through the turnstile and out of sight. Passing the idle Brooklands Skooter Race Track, looking casually at the people who sat reading newspapers on the sheltered side of the pier, Garden shook off the distant past that seemed here to surround him, and thought again of his coming meeting with Peterson. What would they have to say to each other, he and this ghost who called himself by the ridiculous name of Floy? How had Peterson got out of prison, what had he done during the war, what above all was he doing now in some kind of secret Government service? There was a kind of assurance of integrity and truth for Garden in the knowledge that

Peterson was his companion in this affair. Vivid in his memory was that day in the prison and the words: *Believe me, I do not hate anybody*. And then Peterson abruptly turning away. This time there would be no need to turn away.

Garden had reached the end of the pier. Nobody was standing by the third seat from the end on the jetty side, but near to it there were two men fishing. As he watched, one drew back his line and cast out to sea. Garden walked round the dance pavilion, an empty wooden blob topped by an onion dome. He did not see Peterson. Iron steps led down to the platforms underneath the pier, almost washed by water, which were used in summer as landing stages. Garden made a circuit of the pavilion, walked back to the third seat on the jetty side, and stared out to sea. He looked at his watch. The time was ten minutes past two.

Twenty minutes later he had made another circuit of the onion-domed pavilion, and had returned to his position by the seat. Nobody had spoken to him. The two men were still fishing, and now one of them, a thickset figure with a handlebar mustache, showed for the first time some sign of animation as he began to reel in. He beckoned to the other man, a green-jerkined figure, who carefully propped his rod and went over. Handlebar pointed downward, and gesticulated. Green Jerkin tentatively tested Handlebar's line, nodding sagely. Both looked a little askance when Garden joined them.

"Rod's caught up," said Handlebar tersely, in reply to Garden's question. "Something carried it under the pier. Don't want to break it. I'm going down." Green Jerkin took the rod and Handlebar went to the end of the pier and began to descend the iron stairs.

"I'm coming," Garden said. He clattered down the stairs after Handlebar, looking down upon good broad shoulders and a head of hair with a tonsured patch.

They walked along the stone fretwork together, the sea just beneath them.

"Don't get many people stopping up this end of the pier when there's a bit of a blow," Handlebar said. "Waiting for somebody?"

"Just taking the air."

Handlebar grunted. They were now directly under the pier, invisible from above. "Here we are." He bent down within a foot of the sea. "Got tangled round the pillar. But why—my God, what's this?"

A dark, shapeless mass had come into view as Handlebar pulled. Garden felt a premonition, that turned in a moment to certainty, about the nature of the mass. He heard Handlebar's cry, "It's a man," he knelt down and disengaged the hook that had caught in the man's coat, he helped to pull the sodden thing onto the iron stage. The thing was on its back, but sight of the face was merely confirmation of his knowledge. The body, cold and lifeless, with a little seaweed ornamenting the left ear, was that of Hans Peterson.

In one steady look Garden took it all in: the face, more terribly gaunt even than in the photograph, the long matchstick of a body, the open mouth that deprived death of dignity. Then he turned away.

Handlebar uttered an exclamation. "I know him. What do you think of that? Seen him half a dozen times in the last week. Often on the pier. And there he is now, dead as a doornail. Makes you think. Here, what's up, you look a bit greenish. Did you know him too?"

"No." Garden added with an effort, "We ought to tell somebody. You go and do it. I'll wait here."

"You look as if you've had a shock." There was no chance, Garden thought, that he would go unremembered. Handlebar's rather prominent eyes were popping forward at him. "Sure you don't know the chap?"

Garden forced himself to look down again at the

body. Water from it trickled slowly onto the stone fret-work. "I don't know him."

"All right." With one last stare at Garden, Handlebar walked away. His feet clattered decisively on the stairs.

He must go at least to the end of the pier, Garden thought, and first he will tell Green Jerkin. If he comes down here I shan't have more than a couple of minutes to spare. He dropped on one knee and turned Peterson over again. He had glimpsed the tear in the cloth when he and Handlebar lifted the body out of the water. Now the two holes were clearly visible. A dark stain showed round them in spite of the body's immersion. Peterson had been stabbed twice in the back. Thinking quickly while he turned over the body again and went through its pockets, Garden thought that Peterson must have come early to keep the appointment, or perhaps made an earlier appointment with somebody else. He had then been lured down to the landing stage, stabbed twice in the back and pushed into the water. Whether he had died from the wounds or been drowned did not seem of much importance. Then, by a queer stroke of luck, he had been caught in Handlebar's fishing line.

There was a wallet in Peterson's breast pocket. In his jacket pockets there were some papers, in his trousers only coins. Garden put back the coins, and stuffed the damp wallet and papers into his own pocket while he pondered his next move. There was no sign of Green Jerkin, who was presumably waiting at the top of the iron stairs. It seemed to Garden essential that he should get away and report to Colonel Hunt without being seen or questioned. He walked to the end of the landing stage and looked contemplatively at one of the pillars that propped the pier. The pillar was covered with green weed, and looked uninviting. On the other hand it was not very far away, and if he could climb up it he would come up well out of Green Jerkin's view. There was, in fact, no other way. Garden looked back once at the body of his friend, then gathered himself at the edge of the platform, and jumped.

He clasped the pillar tightly and tried to inch up it, but it was like climbing a greasy pole. Twice he almost slipped back into the water, then he was able to tear and push away some of the weed to get foot and hand-holds. After an unpleasant couple of minutes he was on one of the ornamental iron struts below the pier, desperately cleaning rust and weed off his old raincoat. He climbed the strut, waited to make sure that there were no onlookers and swung himself over onto the pier. He took off the raincoat, folded it over his arm and walked off the pier. He did not see Handlebar.

The first thing to do was to look at Peterson's papers. Garden paused uncertainly for a moment, took the first turning right off the promenade and then the first left, and went into a teashop called The Chinese Lantern. This was a teashop of his youth, and he half expected to see old Mrs. Brewis or her pretty daughter come to take his order. But the waitress who came was a placid, solid, square young woman who merely shook her head when he asked about Mrs. Brewis. Garden ordered a pot of tea and some bread and butter. His hand was in his pocket to take out Peterson's papers when something hard jabbed him in the side. A voice said, "Well, what a coincidence." Garden looked up to see the neatly rolled umbrella—which had just poked his ribs—the apple-red face and black bird's eyes of Mr. Hards.

6

"Make that pot of tea for two, miss," said Mr. Hards to the cow-eyed waitress. "And mind it's hot and strong."

"Anything to eat?"

"Toasted tea cake, and a little something sweet in the

way of pastries. I like to get my teeth into a little something sweet." And here Mr. Hards showed his small reg-
ular white teeth in a merry smile, and raked the waitress's solid figure with a glance that seemed to include
her among the sweet things he would like to get his
teeth into. He eyed her broad retreating back. "A fine
figure of a woman. I like 'em buxom. For that matter I
don't mind 'em skinny. There's always something about
the sea air that gives me the old rodeodo feeling if you
understand me. It's the ozone." With no change of tone
he added, "I'm afraid our friend wasn't able to keep his
appointment."

How much did Hards know? Garden seized upon the
one fact of which the little man must certainly be igno-
rant, that Peterson's body had been found. "What
happened?"

"Don't ask me. Transferred to another job very likely.
They asked me to come instead." The waitress brought
the tea and food. While she bent over the table to put
down the pastries Mr. Hards, his eye fixed greedily upon
them, deliberately gave her ample buttock a great pinch.
Horrified, Garden watched the expanse of black material gathered up by bony thumb and finger, the pinch
carried out. He watched for the effect, but the expression on the waitress's placid face did not change. She
walked away apparently unaware that her person had
been rudely violated. Was her rear covered by a rubber
pad, Garden wondered? Mr. Hards, in high spirits,
poured out his tea and drank it while steam rose from
the cup. He disposed of the toasted tea cake in three
powerful bites, and selected a sickly pastry.

"It seems very odd that they should have changed
their minds at the last moment, when it was too late to
let me know."

"Often happens. I expect they've got their reasons."
With a sudden reptilian gulp the little man finished the

pastry. "I waited at the entrance to the pier. You stayed a long time. See anyone?"

"Two people fishing. There was nobody else at the end of the pier." In his pocket Garden could feel the wallet. He added carefully, "Nor on the landing stage."

The black eyes stared hard at Garden. "Why the landing stage? What's that got to do with it? You weren't meeting him there."

"I just said nobody was there. Why didn't you come up to the end of the pier and meet me? I should have been saved half an hour's wait."

"I was coming, then I spotted a couple of lads who know me. Decided it wouldn't do. Waited at the entrance and followed you in here."

"What do you mean, lads who know you?"

Mr. Hards carefully selected a cream bun. "There are quite a lot of people who'd like to stop us carrying out this little job. I saw two of 'em today, though they didn't see me." He bit into the bun. Cream spurted out over his cheek.

"What do we do now?"

There was no reply. Garden stared idly at the little man's coat, hat and umbrella that hung on a stand. Some kind of recollection struggled for acknowledgment at the back of his mind. Then he realized that there was something odd about the silence. Mr. Hards was staring with peculiar fixity at Garden's raincoat which, flung carelessly over the chair beside him, showed marks of damp, and green slime from the pillar. On the little man's cheek there remained a blob of cream. His bony hand shot out, fingered the raincoat, and picked off a green fragment. As Mr. Hards looked consideringly at the fragment of slime, Garden knew what he had been trying to remember. The slightly familiar figure hurrying off the pier as Garden walked on it had been Mr. Hards. He had been lying, then, when he said that he waited at the end of the pier. For what purpose?

"Not exactly seaweed," the little man said. "Slime. Wonder where that came from."

"I had a few minutes to spare," Garden said easily. "I used to know Brightsand quite well. I went up to Cliff End and scrambled about among the rocks there."

"You'll catch a cold," Mr. Hards said mildly. "Cliff End, that's where we've got to pay our call. Sure you didn't look in and see Arbitzer on your own?"

"Quite sure."

"That's good. I shouldn't have liked that, I mean the big boys wouldn't have liked it when I sent in my report." He put the scrap of slime on his plate.

"You've got cream on your face."

The little man picked off the cream with a fingernail, put it beside the slime, and frowned at the two as if they were irreconcilable elements in a jigsaw puzzle. Then he abandoned them and called, "Here, Josephine, let's have the bill." The waitress came over. Mr. Hards eyed her hungrily up and down and returned to what Garden had begun to regard as a kind of professional patter. "And what do you do when the washing up's done and the blinds are pulled down, eh, Josephine? As if I didn't know. What do you say we bat it around together some dark corner some dark night? Say the end of the pier at eight o'clock?" His eyes twinkling merrily, Mr. Hards glanced covertly at Garden.

"All right. I'll bring my husband. He's a policeman."

"Good. And I'll bring my wife, she's a coal-heaver." He cackled with laughter and rose from the chair, two inches shorter than the waitress and a head below Garden. As the girl turned away, however, his laughter turned to a ferocious scowl. He took out a threepenny piece, bit it, and put it down by his plate. "That's enough for *her*," he said, and tried almost angrily to refuse any help in putting on his coat. Garden, however, already had the coat in his hand. As the little man slipped into it Garden noticed upon the right sleeve of the coat, near the cuff, three new reddish-brown spots. They might be some kind of rust or stain. They might also, Garden thought, be blood.

7

Cliff End lies on the west side of Brightsand. The residential villas have given way to bungalows, the bungalows have lessened in density and increased in size, so that they are single spots on the road that rises sharply upward with the chalk cliffs at one side falling steeply to the sea. When you reach the top there is sharp air, a fine view over rolling downs, and the rose pink stucco Cliff Top Café with its chromium-armed chairs and glass-topped tables. After two hundred yards the road begins to descend again until it reaches the outskirts of Brightsand's rival resort of Pallersea.

Here Jacob Arbitzer lived in a bungalow named Mon Repos, which Garden had rented for him after their escape from Arbitzer's country. The bungalow belonged to Garden's stockbroker uncle, George Monk, who with a flat in London and a house in Hampshire used it very rarely and was pleased to let it furnished. Later he had agreed to sell the place and Arbitzer, who had been able to get most of his money over to England, bought it. Here Garden had last seen him some three years ago, when the former Professor seemed to have settled into a placid domesticity. He had expressed little interest in British politics or in the possibility of his own return to power—all that, he seemed to imply, was done with. He talked instead about the fine air at Cliff End, and was particularly enthusiastic about the vegetables he had been able to grow in the sheltered patch of garden at the back of the bungalow. Garden found the visit dis-

heartening, and did not go down to Brightsand again.
His last news of the Professor had been that a young
niece of his had joined the household, and that he had
taken up chess. But that news was two years old and
now, with the prospect for Arbitzer of a return to his
own country, things must be very different.

"Have you met the Professor?" Garden asked. They
had come up the hill in the bus. Nobody else had got
out at the Cliff Top Café, and Mr. Hards had seen nobody he knew.

Mr. Hards shook his head. He looked in incongruous
figure in his neat town clothes and tightly rolled umbrella. "Don't know the old boy from Adam. Seen his
photograph, of course. I say, devilish windy up here,
isn't it? Shouldn't care for it myself, but everyone to his
taste as the young man said when he got into bed with
the female sea serpent. Here we are."

Garden saw that the bungalow's name had been
changed to Distant Prospect. Then his companion lifted
the latch of the little wooden gate and they walked up
the path. The bell sounded clearly inside the house. For
perhaps a minute there was no sound. Then the door
half opened and a girl stood there, with her hand on
the collar of an Alsatian dog. "What do you want?"

"Come from Mr. Floy to see the Professor," said Mr.
Hards cheerfully.

"Oh, all right," she said ungraciously. "You'd better
come in. Quiet, Nicko. Friends."

She let them into a small square hall, and at sight of
it the past came rushing back again to Garden, as it
had done so often in these last hours. Here he had
stood, a gangling nervous boy uneasily turning school
cap in hand or winding and unwinding his red and white
scarf, in the moment before entering the room full of
roaring, laughing people brought together by Uncle
George because it was Christmas or because it was Aunt

Ellen's birthday or simply because he liked to have a good time.

These thoughts he put resolutely away as he stood in the square hall looking curiously at the girl who, now that he saw her clearly, was not a girl at all but a sullen-looking young woman. She stood there now, slim and small-breasted, with straw-colored hair combed carelessly over her ears, arms hanging down at her sides with a certain helplessness or hopelessness about them, exposing herself indifferently to the bright eager gaze of Mr. Hards. She was wearing a scarlet sweater and a gray skirt, and she somehow had the air of a juvenile delinquent who neither expects nor wishes to change her way of life. She paused with her hand on a door to the right. In her gaze there was nothing friendly. "Where is the other then, Floy? I don't know you."

"He couldn't manage it," Hards said briskly. "May I?" He took off his overcoat, laid it carefully over a chair with hat and umbrella, and fingered his neat tie. "You're Miss Arbitzer."

"Ilona Arbitzer, yes."

"My name's Hards, Samuel Hards. Pleased to meet you. I'm only a little chap they tell me, but I always say little and good." Her limp hand was pressed tightly by his bony one. She opened the door. For a moment Garden seemed to hear distinctly the back-slapping shouts and laughter of the past. Then this was washed away in a sea of silence, to the actuality of two people sitting in a rather badly lighted room. A small woman with faded gray hair and a certain distinction in her features sat by the window working on a hand loom. This was Madame Arbitzer. A man sat close to the fire, with one leg stretched out on a footstool. This was Jacob Arbitzer himself, the man of legend. Madame Arbitzer came over to greet them at once. Arbitzer more slowly hoisted himself to a standing position with the aid of a stick.

Madame Arbitzer clasped Garden's hand warmly in

both her own. "My dear dear Charles, it is so long since you have been to see us. But no matter, for here you are. Your friend though, where is he?" Madame Arbitzer spoke English well, but rather slowly.

"Couldn't come." Mr. Hards stepped forward, bowed gallantly over her hand, and kissed it. "I've replaced him —temporarily, only temporarily. Hards is the name, Samuel Hards at your service."

"That is a pity. We liked him very much, and he was looking forward to seeing you again, Charles." Garden saw Mr. Hards's little head rear like a cobra's at this word *again*, and then hunch inside his shoulders. Madame Arbitzer smiled. "My manners are bad. We are pleased to see you also, Mr. Hards. It is good of you to come."

"Jacob," Garden said. The figure by the fireplace had moved over to them slowly, leaning on his stick. Garden was shocked by the change in Arbitzer's appearance. The features, always ascetic, now seemed almost ghostly in their white refinement, some kind of cloud had misted the brightness and keenness of the eyes, the once upright shoulders sagged sadly forward. There could be no doubt, however, of Arbitzer's pleasure in seeing Garden, and the voice in which he spoke had at least something of the resonance and firmness that Garden remembered.

"So here is another one come to persuade me against my better judgment. I am very happy to see you, Charles, and you too, sir. Sit down, sit down." Mr. Hards gave Arbitzer's hand a cautious shake, and sat down on the edge of a chair. "Where is our friend Floy?"

Now Mr. Hards was rather curt. "Couldn't come. Shouldn't be surprised if headquarters has transferred him to another assignment."

"Why?" said Garden.

"Don't ask me. Maybe Floy was—" He paused and looked slyly at Garden. "Friend of yours, was he?"

"I knew him for a month or two," Garden said. "But that was a long time ago."

"You know as well as I do a lot of people want to stop the Professor here getting back home. Communists who've got hold of his country don't want him back, they tell me. They got their agents. Could be Floy was one of them and our H.Q. found it out." Mr. Hards had been looking at his fingernails. Now he stared at Garden, and Garden remembered the spots of blood. "I don't say it is, I say it could be."

Madame Arbitzer expostulated. "That I cannot believe. Floy—that was not his real name I think—had told us his story. The Communists had treated him shamefully, oh shamefully. In Spain they put him in prison, he escaped, they caught him again. He was working in Poland and they took him to the Soviet Union. There he was in a labor camp until the end of 1940 and then, oh it was beastly, how can human beings commit such beastliness, such cynicism, they handed him to the Germans because he was originally an Austrian. He was in Dachau until the war ended."

The little man had listened to this with bored politeness. "Could be true, could be a good story. Anyway, as far as I know he's been transferred. Have to put up with me, I'm afraid."

There was a silence which Garden, at least, felt to be uneasy. Arbitzer broke it when he addressed the girl, who had been leaning by the door looking indifferently at Garden and Hards. "Ilona, my dear, tea for our guests." She nodded and left the room. Arbitzer sat down in the chair by the fire, and again propped up his leg on the stool. "This weather gets into my bones. Arthritis, I have arthritis in the winter very badly, I can always feel the cold weather coming on. In the next week or two the weather will change, I can feel it." Looking into the fire Arbitzer said, "So you have come to persuade me to go back, to be the man I was in the old days. And you will be by my side, eh, as you were in the old days; that's it, isn't it?"

"Yes," said Garden.

"Ah, I was a man and a half in those days, isn't that so? I had something then, some dynamo inside here." Arbitzer touched his chest.

"You still have it." Garden said what seemed expected of him. "May be a little rusty, that's all, needs use."

"You are flattering me." Still Arbitzer stared into the fire, never once raising his eyes to look Garden in the face. "But tell me, there is something I often think about, Charles. I was a man and a half then, you were with me, we had devoted and intelligent friends. And yet we failed. Why was it that we failed?"

"We were tricked. We made mistakes."

"Those are the simple answers. But I often wonder now—was it all decreed that it should be as it was? The barbarians conquered the civilized, but who knows, perhaps it was the decree of history that the barbarians should conquer. It has happened before, it will happen again."

Garden moved uncomfortably in his chair. He began to understand what Sir Alfred had meant by saying that he might find Arbitzer changed. "You used to believe," he said, "that men could control their history."

Looking into the fire, rubbing his hands, Arbitzer went on talking as though Garden had not spoken. "You tell me I should go back. The papers tell me about riots in my country, crowds in the streets shouting my name. The exiles, the dispossessed, come down here and talk —how they do talk, to be sure. They say I have only to show myself and the country will rise. The army is on my side, half the Air Force. There will be little bloodshed, no bloodshed. Your friend Latterley told me that when he came to see me. Floy also. He is an idealist that one, a good man, but he understood little of my country's problems. Would it be enough for me to go back?

Perhaps, perhaps. But shall I tell you what three-quarters
of those who talk to me are really thinking? The exiles
think I shall be a puppet whose strings they can pull,
that when I am there again they will get back their big
estates, they will recreate their old world of dances and
parties, good manners and polite corruption, law for the
rich and a whip for the poor. That is what they think.
And what does this Latterley think who comes down
and talks so smoothly, Latterley and whoever is behind
him in your Government? He thinks: when we have
put him back into power, he is bound to show his grati-
tude for our help. Indeed, if he does not show his grati-
tude, we can soon make him. Trade concessions, military bases—oh yes, I can see clearly enough what he is
after. I shall be in the hands of these people, Charles.
Is it for this I should return?"

Garden gripped one hand with the other. When he
spoke there was no sympathy in his voice. "You pity
yourself too much."

"What do you mean?"

"You don't really believe that your return is impossible. You know it can be done. But you know it will
mean hard work after you are back. When we were in
the hills together such things didn't worry you. We
fought the Germans with one hand, the native profiteers
and bloodsuckers with the other. But now you think,
'I am an old man, I cannot go through all that again,
they had their chance of decent government, honest
elections, a liberal regime, and they didn't take it. Let
them stew in their own juice, I have done enough for
my country. I—'"

"Tea," the girl said. She handed a cup to Garden. He
put it on a table without looking at her. "I have earned
the right, you think, to sit back now and live out the
rest of my life in peace." The teacup rattled as Garden's
hand struck the table in front of him. "Let me tell you,
Jacob—it is something that in the past you have often

told me—there is no such right. The cause for which we are working, you said to me, is one which far outweighs the value of our individual lives. I have not forgotten those words, Jacob. Have you?"

Arbitzer stirred and held out thin hands to the fire. His wife clacked at her loom, eyes downcast to her work. Mr. Hards sipped his tea, bit into a homemade scone, and allowed his eyes to travel leisurely down Ilona from straw-colored hair to flat-heeled shoes. The girl herself sat stiffly in her chair.

"You make me ashamed," Arbitzer said. "I am not the man I was, perhaps I was never the man you thought me. I was Arbitzer, you say, the guerrilla leader, quick witted, able to make speedy and right decisions. Be Arbitzer again, you tell me. But who was this Arbitzer, who had been a meek, reflective professor of history? Was he not made up of all his friends and supporters, you Charles, and Pantek, Granz and that young Russian Volkhovsky—we thought differently about the Russians in those days—Paltchev, Cetkovitch, Tranin and others? It is the conditions and the supporters that make a guerrilla leader. Take them away and you have—a professor of history again. Without a Chair," Arbitzer added with a faint smile. "Summon up again all those others, those ghosts, who are dead or who have compromised with the regime, and you might have again—a guerrilla leader."

The silence that followed this speech was broken by three sharp knocks. In a moment little Hards was on his feet. "I'll get it. Pardon me." He brushed by the girl and out of the door. There was a sound of voices, and then the little man reappeared. "Surprise, Professor," he cried, and stood aside. A man came in, a man so tall that he had to bend a little through the doorway, a man with a face granitic and handsome, thick black eyebrows, angry dark eyes, and a hard mouth.

Arbitzer stood up, his stick forgotten, a slight flush on his thin cheeks. "Theodore," he said.

8

"Theodore," Arbitzer repeated wonderingly. "I thought you were dead."

"But I am not." Theodore Granz spoke in German. His voice was heavy and sounded, as the man looked, dependable if a little slow. He embraced Arbitzer and his wife, clasped Garden's hand, looked questioningly at the girl Ilona, and said to Hards, "You are the man from headquarters?"

"What's he say? Tell him I don't know the lingo."

Granz's English was halting but intelligible. He repeated in it, "The man from headquarters."

"That's right. Pleased to meet you." Hards looked round with a birdlike gaze. "This is where I skedaddle. I told you I was only standing in for Floy. Now Granz here has all the details sewn up, or so I'm informed, and you won't want me any more."

From his great height Granz nodded smilingly down at the little man.

"So long, everybody. Is there a back way out? I'd better use it if there is. Don't want too many comings and goings at the front."

"I will show it to you." The girl got up and they left the room together. A moment later there was a sound like a crack, and then a muffled cry. Garden, who was nearest to the door, jumped up. From the square hall a passage turned left to the back door. There he found the girl, a hand clasped to her cheek, and Hards with a sneer on his face. The girl turned on Garden angrily.

"Your *friend*," she said. "He touched me—here—and when I pushed him away he struck me. *An English gentleman,*" she added ironically. She took away her hand and her cheek showed red.

Hards leaned forward and prodded at her with his umbrella in a manner less comic than menacing. "No man or woman pushes Sam Hards around, girlie. Remember that."

The girl slammed the door as Hards skipped away down the garden path. "Your friend," she said again. "An idealist, I suppose, like you."

"Not like me." Garden was remembering the three spots and wondering whether he should have let Hards go. But had there been an alternative?

"And what are you doing to Uncle Jacob?" she said fiercely. "Why don't you let him live out his life decently? To be killed in a stupid argument about whether the Communists or your Social Democrats are going to be bosses, what good will that do him?"

They stood and talked in the narrow passage where years ago Uncle George's guests, hooting with laughter, had played sardines and murder. "There was a time when he did not think the argument stupid," Garden said. The words were perfectly true, but spoken they seemed unpleasantly priggish.

She mocked him. "There was a time—when are you going to realize that the clock has moved on, that you don't live in that kind of world any more? Shall I tell you something? There was a time—"

The sitting-room door opened, Granz's voice called "Garden." They went back into the room, where Garden was aware of a change in the atmosphere. Granz and Arbitzer were leaning over a green baize card table with maps on it. Arbitzer straightened up as Garden came in. There was a new brightness in his look, and a kind of radiance showed under the pallor of his skin. "Charles," he cried. "Theodore has told me of the preparations that are made. I begin to think we can do it."

"It would be madness not to do it." Granz held out a

big hand, open. "The country will fall into our grasp—like this." His hand closed.

Theodore Granz had been a watchmaker before the war, with no political convictions. During the war he became a pilot, and when his country was occupied by the Germans this watchmaker left his home town of Lodno and joined the guerrilla forces. He quickly became a commander, noted particularly for fearlessness, good humor, and ruthless treatment of enemy prisoners. He was one of Arbitzer's ten group leaders, but took little part in discussions. "I am not strong up here," he used to say, tapping his head. "You decide the policy, I carry it out." His chief weakness was a mercurial temperament which made his views of events at times unreliable. Yet his optimism could have a tonic quality, and in fact that appeared to have been its effect on Arbitzer.

"Theodore escaped a year ago," Arbitzer said exultantly. "He has been in hiding since then."

Granz had last been heard of when, with typical overoptimism, he had headed a feeble revolt a few months after Arbitzer had left the country. The revolt was crushed in two days, the leaders captured and sentenced to various terms of imprisonment. Granz had got fifteen years, and Garden had thought him dead long ago. Now this very live Granz wagged an admonitory finger. "Not so much in hiding, Jacob. Last week I walked openly in the streets of Lodno and bought fruit in the market. I tell you they have lost control now of the whole south. Our men visit the towns at will. We are only waiting for the right moment."

"What about the north?" Garden asked. In the north was the country's capital, and most of its industry.

"The north too," Granz said happily. "In the north they think they are strong, but our men are in every regiment, every Air Force unit. I am not a planner, you know that, I carry out orders, I have been carrying out orders all my life. And look what bad company it has brought me to," he added with a laugh so joyous and free that both Arbitzer and Garden joined in. The sound of Madame Arbitzer's clicking on the loom had stopped. She was looking out of the window. Ilona joined her.

The door opened and the apple-red face of Mr. Hards appeared round it. His words broke up their laughter. "There's a man watching outside."

"What man?" There was a kind of dignity about Arbitzer as he said, "Why should a man be watching my house?"

"One of the agents of the people who want to stop you getting away," Hards said. "Saw him earlier today, but thought I'd given him the slip. He's round the side, with an eye on both exits. Now listen to me. I'll stall him as long as I can, but I can't do it for ever. Get out of here inside a couple of hours, understand? And watch your step when you're going."

"How are you going to stall him?" Garden asked.

"That's my business." There was a suppressed excitement about the little man. "I'll manage. But look out when you go." His head disappeared like a Jack-in-a-box. They heard a door close.

"A funny little man," Granz said tolerantly. "Not surely the man Floy I was supposed to meet."

"Floy is dead." With these decisive words spoken, there seemed no reason why Garden should not tell them all he knew. He told them of the body picked up by the fishing line, the stab wounds, the spots on Hards's sleeve. Finally he took from his pocket the wallet and the papers. Arbitzer listened with his finger tapping the map. Granz's face was impassive. When Garden had finished he said merely, "Let us look at the papers."

They looked first at the loose papers. There was an envelope addressed to H. Floy, Poste Restante, Brightsand, with a London postmark. There was a letter with-

out address or opening, written in German and signed
"Rosa." Water had made the ink run, but a few phrases
were decipherable. Garden, who read German better
than he spoke it, translated: "The weather here is very
good . . . if you are able to get away for a holiday with
your friend we . . . the sooner the better . . . do not fa-
vor our original idea . . . air on the coast is milder . . ."
The other words were unreadable.

"I was the friend, the holiday our return, yes?" There
was a note of authority in Arbitzer's voice. "Air on the
coast milder. Rosa favored a landing on the coast,
agreed?"

Granz shook his head. "If she did she was wrong. On
the coast there is less political feeling, and the coast
towns are well guarded."

They unfolded a map of Brightsand, and then turned
to the wallet. It contained a British passport in the name
of Harold Floy, with a photograph similar to that Garden had seen in Colonel Hunt's office, several pound
notes, and a tiny diary containing several sheets of what
looked like blank tissue paper. "Lemon juice," Granz
said. "But whether it will show after being in salt water—" He held it before the fire, and slowly writing appeared on the top three sheets. The first was a list of
half a dozen names and addresses in Granz's country.
He shook his head over them doubtfully. "Not our people. At least I do not know of them." The other two
pages were headed CHARACTERS. There followed what
were obviously brief notes on people, indicated by initials. Garden remembered that Peterson had always
liked to make such brisk assessments, which he then filed
away neatly in appropriate pigeonholes of his mind.
Here the listing was alphabetical, the comments cryptic:

Ar. Can a mouse make history? Perhaps, if we dress
him up as a lion.

Br. Jackal.

Ha. Cobra with rabbit appetites. Dangerous.

Hu. Bullfrog undoubtedly.

La. Always the straw that shows which way the wind blows. Garden identified the characters: Arbitzer, Bretherton, Hards, Hunt, Latterley. Clearly, Peterson had held no high opinion of his associates.

There followed a fable:

A fox, a tiger, and a lion conspired together to overthrow the rule of man. The fox suggested that mantraps should be set, baited with a sweet smelling piece of woman's flesh. This was done, and many men fell into them and were devoured by the partners. After a time, however, the lion began to claim the lion's share of the spoils, and was inclined to treat tiger and fox with contempt. The fox, who had thoughtfully obtained some poisoned darts from pygmies destroyed in the traps, shot these at the lion, and killed him. "I always knew lions were rather stupid," he said to the tiger, who looked at him thoughtfully and then agreed. After this, fox and tiger lived amicably together, until one day the fox found that the rest of his poisoned darts had disappeared. After this the tiger's treatment of the fox was markedly less courteous. The fox, however, managed to dispose of his friend by entering into an alliance with some hornets who made a concerted attack upon the tiger, and stung him to death. "I am most grateful for your assistance," said the fox as he sprayed the hornets afterward with a newly discovered and deadly insecticide.

The fox now reigned supreme. But alas, one of the few remaining men was the possessor of a pack of hounds, which he set upon the fox's trail. These, as the fox said to himself, were very inferior animals; the lion would have disposed of them with a roar, the tiger would have crunched up a dozen of them before breakfast. Nevertheless, the hounds caught the fox and tore him to pieces.

Moral: Fox must combine, with tiger or lion. History is a record of checks and balances.

"Too much for me," Granz said. "Is that first page a code?"

Arbitzer shook his head. "I recognize myself as the mouse dressed up as lion. It is a shrewd stroke. Floy never spared me when we talked. He tried to stir me to action, sometimes by insult. Today he would be happy."

The girl Ilona stared at him. "You mean you are going?"

"I am going, yes."

Garden slipped back the papers into his pocket.

"Then you are a fool. You are all fools. What do you think you can do? The Communists will kill you, and I wish them good luck. Or you will kill the Communists, and then you will preach about liberal principles. Isn't that it?" She pointed at Garden a finger that shook slightly with rage. "And you are the worst of them, the biggest fool, because you are the blindest. Shall I tell you something? I was married to a man who thought like you. We had a son. After Jacob left—after *you* left, Mr. Garden—my husband stayed. He had some mad idea that there was something to be done, he thought parties did not matter, he talked about a great social experiment. We could have got away. I implored him to leave—for his sake, for my sake, for the sake of our son. He was like a deaf man." Her thin shoulders shrugged in the scarlet sweater. "And what happened? What anyone in their senses knew would happen to people connected with Jacob. A man came from the secret police one day, a smug man, round-faced and smiling. He pulled the ear of my son Peter, and the boy cried because it hurt. The man said to me: 'Do not worry. We shall see that he grows up in forgetfulness of the fact that his mother and father were traitors.' Paul, that was my husband, made all sorts of fantastic confessions.

When they had got what they wanted from him he was shot."

"You escaped with your son?"

"I got away, yes. My son caught diphtheria and died while I was in prison."

"Hatred is no good," Garden said. "You must try not to hate the Communists."

"The Communists!" Her blue eyes were like stones. "It is not them I hate. I cannot forgive the fool I married."

"Ilona." The voice was Madame Arbitzer's.

"I hate him, and all fools like him. All fools and all cant. That is why I hate you, Mr. Garden, because you are full of cant."

"Ilona," Madame Arbitzer said more sharply. The girl sank into a chair by the window. "You will forgive her, she has not been well." Madame Arbitzer got up slowly, came over to her husband and put her hands up to his shoulders. "You are going, Jacob."

"Yes, my dear."

"You will do what you believe to be right. My heart goes with you." The words, and the brief embrace that followed them, had a surprising dignity. "Now you will have much to arrange. Come, Ilona." She left the room with her arm round the girl.

Arbitzer sighed. Then he said: "Now my friends, let me tell you my own position, then you can say what you have to propose. Some weeks ago Mr. Latterley came to see me. He tried to persuade me that the moment had arrived for my return to my country. He said that he was a mere agent for other and more important people, that the British Government itself was behind the scheme. I can see that it would be of great advantage to them to replace the Communists by a government more favorable to them. But as I said to this young man I am old, I feel worn out, my day is over. I am content to live out the rest of my days in the country that has generously given me asylum. He would not accept such an answer. He insisted on remaining in touch with me through the man Floy.

"I liked Floy. He too was persuasive, but in a different way from Latterley, who had presented the positive benefits to me of my return. Floy stressed that it was also my duty. Indeed, he seemed hardly to think it possible that I should refuse. He became often angry with me, and at times I was angry with myself. But to him also I felt bound to say that I am an old man and worn out, and that my country's future does not rest with such as me. He would reply that I was less interested in my country's future than in eternally debating about it. He had a sharp tongue, that one. I liked him, although there was about him always—what shall I say? —a something strange. I had always a feeling that he was occupied by some inner struggle that had little to do with what he was saying to me. In any case, he did not finally convince me. What is past is past, I told him. The man I once was is dead. There remains only an exile who potters about his garden, has a stiff leg, and feels the wind from the sea."

Garden said without conviction, "Nonsense." Granz shifted impatiently.

"Perhaps. I had mentioned your name to Latterley, Charles, as a man who had once been at my side. He told me that he would find you and persuade you to join me—and he has. Now he has sent you to me also, Theodore. You tell me all is ready. You urge me, both of you, to go." Arbitzer smiled, and his smile was one of singular sweetness. "You are my friends. You are risking your lives. How can I refuse to risk mine?"

"Keep the speeches for when you arrive, Jacob," Granz said. He added apologetically, "You know I am not much for speeches, always fidgeted through them. Remember that Theo means no harm. Now to business. I have not come alone. I have brought Marinka." An immense smile passed over his face at their mystification. "She will seat four and she rides comfortably at two hundred and fifty miles an hour."

Garden slapped his knee. "I'd forgotten you were a pilot. But when did you land here? Is the plane safe?"

Granz put a finger to his nose. "Quite safe, our friends have seen to that. I landed last night less than thirty miles from here. Tonight we go back, the three of us."

"Tonight!" There was such a shocked note in Arbitzer's voice that Granz paused in surprise.

"The sooner the better. Our friends here can't keep a plane out of sight indefinitely, and at home they are waiting for my return. They do not know positively that I am bringing you back with me. Much rests on that."

"Yes, yes, of course." Arbitzer's hand was shaking.

"Cigarette?" Granz said, staring at him. Arbitzer took one of the strong black cigarettes of their country. Peterson was right about this, Garden thought. He's frightened. It will be a mouse dressed up as a lion that we take with us. Aloud he asked: "Where do we go to?"

"Lodno. My plane came from there, and the airfield there is ours. The committee will meet us. Then tomorrow we act. You know what tomorrow is, eh? Seven years ago to the day you left the country, Jacob. They have made it a holiday, a day of national rejoicing. It is a good day to act on, yes?"

"Very good." Arbitzer's laugh was shaky.

Granz's enthusiasm mounted as he talked. "We are organized in cells of five members, so that betrayal by any individual is not important. Twenty cells make a group, every five groups has a committee member in charge of it. We have relied very much on the committee members. They are all tried men. In the north things have been handled by Peplov. He has seen to it that the 23rd Regiment is quartered in the capital. They are ours, from Colonel to mess orderly. He is a great brain, that Peplov. He will be there tonight, as well as others that you know—Cetkovitch, Volnich, Udansky."

"I look forward to meeting him," Arbitzer said with a kind of trembling dignity. "We shall see if a place can be found for him in the administration."

"*See* if a place can be found." Granz spoke half-incredulously, then burst into a countryman's guffaw. "After we have taken power Peplov will name his own place."

"I see. You do not want me, you want my name. I suppose I should have understood that."

Granz caught his arm. "Jacob, I am a fool and my tongue often says what it does not intend. You know that we want you, we cannot do without you. Believe that." He shook the thin arm almost angrily.

"My beliefs or disbeliefs, what do they matter? Do not be afraid, Theo. I have been given a part to play and I shall play it. I don't doubt that Peplov has done much, and will deserve a high place. It is simply that all this means violence, and I feel more and more doubt of . . ." His voice died away as he walked over to the fire and stood staring down at the dully burning logs.

Granz looked at Garden, and then tapped the maps. "Jacob."

Arbitzer looked up. "The plans, yes, of course. But not just now, Theodore. Leave me alone for a little while. I wish to think, to compose myself." He smiled faintly at the look of alarm on Granz's face. "Don't worry. These are not second thoughts, though perhaps they are last thoughts. How soon do we need to leave?"

"Half an hour."

Arbitzer bowed his head in a gesture of dismissal about which there was undoubtedly something Presidential. Garden and Granz left the room and stood in the passage. "He has changed," Granz said.

"We've all changed." Even to himself he could not admit how great was the change in Arbitzer. In the bedroom to the right he could hear the sound of muffled sobs. The little hall stifled him with its weight of memories. "Breath of air," he said, and opened the front door. Granz joined him on the porch. Outside was a clear moonless night with stars, and the wind blowing in cold from the sea. In his thin clothes Garden shivered. "I wonder what's happened to the man Hards was talking about. He said the side of the house. You take left, I'll take right."

Granz murmured something, and moved away. As silently as possible Garden moved round the hedge that skirted the house. His eyes grew accustomed to the darkness, made out the positions of trees, avoided a flower bed. Hards had said the man could watch both front and back entrances. If so he must have been somewhere about here. . . . At the side of a bush Garden almost tripped over something bulky. He knelt, could not find a match, and groped with hands. They touched the cloth of trousers, a coat, a face. When Garden called for Granz his hand was warm, and felt wet. The big man was with him quickly. Garden was surprised to find his own breath coming faster than usual. "Torch, match, lighter, quickly. Someone here." The finger of light from a torch with Granz's protective grasp over part of it showed the bright red stain on Garden's hand and moved on to the crumpled figure who stared open-eyed but sightlessly at the night sky. The torch played on the body, moved up to the blood-covered collar, lingered a moment on the wound in the neck, and stopped on a dark thin face that was strange and yet somehow familiar. Granz's voice said harshly: "Who is he?"

"I'm not sure," Garden said. "I've seen him recently. Run the torch over him again, will you?" He exclaimed sharply as the light showed a green jerkin. Now he could see that this man also had been stabbed through the body. "He was one of the two fishing on the pier this afternoon. I told you about them." With a decisive click

Granz snapped off the torch. Garden rubbed his bloody right hand on the grass and stood up. "This is what our friend Hards calls stalling. He stabbed this one twice, neck and body. I wonder how he got near enough to do it. I told you about Floy."

"Yes," Granz said indifferently. He dropped to his knees, ran his hands over the body and straightened up. "You have a revolver? Then take this one. Perhaps we shall need it."

Garden's hand closed on metal. "Hards must have surprised him. Why didn't he use this?"

In Granz's voice there was a note of impatience. "How should I know?"

"Who was he, and what did he want?" Garden shivered again suddenly. "That man Hards is a killer. For pleasure."

"For pleasure or not, what does it matter? You have seen dead men before. Is there something about this English air that makes men timid? You know the struggle we are engaged in, you say you believe in it, you know there is no time for sentiment, wondering this and fearing that. At times like these some people die unjustly, some who should have a rope round their necks get a medal." This was a long speech for Granz.

"I know all that," Garden said hesitantly. "But—"

"If you know it, good. It is time to go."

Garden stood by the side of the body, staring down at the dark mass. How was it possible to explain what he felt? How, indeed, could he be quite sure of what it was he wanted to say, what truths struggled for expression within him? Did it amount to anything more than a certainty that Floy or Peterson was one of the best men he had ever known, and that there was something evil about Hards? He remembered Peterson's note with the initials Ha.: "Cobra with rabbit appetites. Dangerous." Was it mere sentiment that made him dislike finding himself on the side of such a man? He walked slowly after Granz into the house, and washed his hands frantically in the small bathroom. Red stain came off them and flowed down the waste.

Outside the bathroom door he met the girl. She said to him calmly, "Katerina and I are going with you."

Garden thought quickly. If the two women were left in the bungalow they would certainly have awkward explanations to make. "I thought you never wanted to go back."

"I have changed my mind. If it is all as you say, if *he* is going back, perhaps I shall meet the gentleman who came to arrest us that day and pulled Peter's ear. I should have something to say to him." One finger curled round in her fair hair and tugged it. "You don't understand that I might want to see him, do you? Or what I should like to do to him? That is beyond you."

He stood there looking at the childlike face set into its mold of sullenness. "I can understand it, yes. I don't like it. But perhaps you ought to come back."

He was glad of the words when for a moment the sullenness vanished and she ran to the door of the front room, pulled it open, and cried like a child who has been given permission to go to a party: "He says we can go."

In the room Katerina Arbitzer was stuffing things into a large suitcase, Arbitzer and Granz were talking in low voices. "Does he?" Arbitzer said. "We had reached the same conclusion."

The girl pointed at Granz. "But I thought *he* said—"

On the rocklike, reliable, but slightly stupid face of Granz there was a look like that of an ox who is being pestered almost beyond the limits of docility: "It is all nothing to me. Bring everything, sewing machine, loom, anything, as long as your uncle comes too."

"That means Nicko can come," she said eagerly.

"Who is Nicko?" The Alsatian came into the room and stood by the girl's side. "The dog. Yes, let us take along the dog by all means. He will not object to the airplane?" Granz asked with heavy sarcasm.

"It may be a good idea for them to come, in view of all the circumstances," Garden said to Granz, who shook his head in disgust.

"Bah. You behave like children. But if we are going, let us go. My car is on the back road."

Katerina Arbitzer stood up, an old woman flushed with bending. "I have shared his fate so long, Theodore, you can understand that we do not wish to be separated now." She looked speculatively at the loom in the window. "You said the loom. I have a carpet there half-finished. I do not suppose—"

"No, *no*," Granz cried. There was something pathetic about him. "This is ridiculous. I came here to take back the leader of a revolution. I am saddled with a pack of women and dogs, and the leader himself—"

He stopped. Arbitzer was rubbing his knee gently. "Yes, Theodore, what about the leader himself?"

Granz pushed his hand through his hair like a schoolboy. "He is fine. I give you all five minutes to get into the car."

9

The car was an old Daimler. They got in, Arbitzer in the front with Granz, Garden between the two women in the back. The dog settled at Ilona's feet. At the last moment Katerina Arbitzer cried out something unintelligible and hurried back into the house. She came out again with a rug which she carefully tucked round her husband's legs. "His leg gets stiff if it is not wrapped up," she said apologetically, and then to Arbitzer: "Have you got your stick?" His reply was lost in the sound of the engine as Granz started the car.

They drove for a few miles along the coastal road, and

then turned inland. Garden soon gave up trying to follow the direction they were taking. Ilona's thin knee pressed against him, he could smell the faint fresh odor of the scent she used. They did not speak. In the front Arbitzer and Granz carried on a conversation audible only as differing voice tones, Arbitzer's light and faintly petulant, Granz's a bearlike roar. Garden was jerked from remembrances of his childhood at Brightsand by some words of Katerina Arbitzer's.

"What was that?"

"I said where are we going?" With her lips pressed almost to his ear she whispered, "Is he altogether to be trusted, this Granz?"

He was shocked. His instinct was to answer with an immediate "Yes," but the words sowed in his mind the smallest possible seed of doubt. Katerina voiced exactly the nature of this doubt when she whispered again, "He is somehow so changed from what I remember. He was always so respectful to Jacob."

He is somehow changed, Garden thought, it is what we are all saying. Perhaps we should have changed as Granz has done if we had lived through years of imprisonment and conspiracies. And have not we changed more whose minds have lost the flexibility, whose wills have lost the courage, that Granz still possesses? He gave an encouraging pressure to Katerina's arm at the same moment that she whispered, "I am glad you are with us, Charles."

The Daimler, which had just passed through a small village, now swung right up a hill, then right again into a big asphalted courtyard. The car stopped and Granz got out. Peering out of the window Garden could see buildings in front of them, black masses untouched by light. In the car's headlights he saw Granz advance toward a door ahead of them and knock, two short, one long, two short. Shutters rolled up ahead of them to reveal a garage. Granz got back into the Daimler, drove them in, and got out of the car again.

"Here we are then," he said with recovered cheerfulness. "Now, where are the others?"

Electric light suddenly illuminated the garage, revealing it as a big, bare, and very high shed, with wooden steps at one end leading to an upper room. The door of this room opened and a voice said: "Hello hello. Done the first lap in good time, eh." Colonel Hunt clattered down the wooden stairs, beefy hand outstretched. "How are you, me boy," he said to Garden. "And this is the Professor. Greatly honored to meet you, sir." Arbitzer got out of the car leaning on his stick, and allowed his hand to be pumped up and down.

A voice from above said, "Who else is in the car?" Katerina and Ilona got out. The Alsatian stood quietly by the girl's side. Garden looked up and saw the narrow figure of Bretherton.

Granz said disgustedly, "Jacob's wife and niece. He insisted that they come."

The Colonel goggled with surprise. His hand quickly ran up to his bald head. He seemed at a loss for words. The voice from above spoke again: "They'd better come up."

Upstairs there was a large room with a table, uncomfortable wooden chairs and a map of England on the wall. A small electric fire gave a little warmth. The Colonel sat down heavily behind the table. "Unexpected," he said, "certainly unexpected. Always delighted to see the ladies of course, but—well dammit, this is a man's job." Apparently at a loss he looked at Bretherton.

The secretary looked down at his fingernails. "You realize, Professor Arbitzer, that no guarantee of your safety can be given. Everything possible has been done to ensure that things go smoothly, but you have powerful enemies. They are active even in this country, which they would like to stop you leaving."

Garden leaned forward. "But Hards can be relied on to deal with them, isn't that so? Like the man watching the bungalow. Was he an enemy?"

Bretherton stared at Garden speculatively, but did not reply. Arbitzer said, "I don't understand. What—"

"There was a man watching the house, Hards told us that. Somebody killed him."

The Colonel said in his plummy voice, "Unfortunate that was, unfortunate but necessary. Can't have things going wrong now. Sammy told us about it. Impetuous boy, but his heart's in the right place."

"Let us get back to the point," Bretherton said, and again Garden interrupted him.

"That is just the point. We could not leave Madame Arbitzer and her niece to face a police investigation."

"So that was why you agreed we should come," the girl said scornfully. "I should have known it was not simple generosity."

"We can keep the two ladies in hiding. I can assure you that they will be perfectly safe. They can join you in a few days when the movement has succeeded. It is hazarding everything—the success of the movement and their own safety—to take them with you now." There was a faint but penetrating note of irony in Bretherton's voice as he added, "And to take a dog as well, that makes it perfect. What do you think you will be doing, playing a parlor game?" The Alsatian pricked up his ears at the word "dog." The girl patted his head.

Both Bretherton and the Colonel looked at Garden, but it was Arbitzer who answered them, speaking with some of the force and incisiveness that Garden remembered.

"I have not met either of you gentlemen before today. You are showing your interest in our cause, and I am grateful for it. Nevertheless, our interests are not identical and our risks are not equal. If we fail you will say, 'Well it was a pity.' But we—you know very well what

will happen to us. When I talked to Mr. Latterley and
Mr. Floy"—here a glance impossible to interpret flashed
between Bretherton and Colonel Hunt—"I asked them
if your government could not give me some official
backing. They both told me that it was absolutely out
of the question, that I must be content with unofficial
blessing and private help. I realize the reasons for that
decision, and I bow to them. The fact remains that the
risks are being taken by me and my friends. Accordingly
the decisions are ours, not yours. Theodore, the plane
can take these extra passengers." Granz shrugged and
nodded. "Very well. The ladies will go. There is no more
to be said."

"And the dog?" Bretherton was sarcastic.

"And the dog."

The Colonel looked at Bretherton. Bretherton
pushed at the cuticle of a fingernail and nodded almost
imperceptibly. With a great outrush of breath and a
quick scrabbling at his jaw the Colonel said, "My word,
Professor, you're a man after my own heart. Come right
out and say what you mean, no beating about the bush.
You want the ladies to go, right you are then, they're
going. Nuff said. Let's have a little drink on it, success
to a mission." He was interrupted by a light showing
on the desk. The Colonel pressed a button and a telephone swung out from the wall. He barked monosylla-
bles into it and then slammed down the receiver. "No
cause for alarm, but no time for that drink. One of our
boys from Brightsand—not Sammy, Sammy's got himself in enough trouble, he's lying low like Brer Rabbit.
But they've found that feller in the Professor's garden
and they're headed this way. Don't know this place as
far as I know, got a perfectly good reputation as a warehouse of Multiple Steel Products—but better be on the
safe side."

Garden leaned forward. "Colonel, who are *they?*"

The Colonel's bloodshot eyes stared at him blankly.

Then he guffawed. "They want to keep you from getting away, want to stop the old mission. Plain enough, eh? No prizes for guessing who they are."

"It is plain enough," Arbitzer said. "Not plain to you, Charles? Not satisfied?"

"I suppose so." What, after all, was in his mind but an obscure uneasiness, a tangle of doubts and hesitations? And was this uneasiness anything more than an acknowledgment of the fact that he was no longer by any means the man who had been Peterson's companion in Spain, not even the man who had been dropped into the country shaped like a broken penny during the war? Was it mere age that made him find something ludicrous about this adventure undertaken by two middle-aged men, two women, and a dog? And, of course, Granz. A little reluctantly Garden admitted to himself that Granz seemed efficient enough. But Granz was younger, perhaps Granz was the only one of them who felt a really whole-hearted enthusiasm for what they were going to do. This is dangerous thinking, Garden told himself, this will never do. "Satisfied," he said.

"We're wasting time." Bretherton led the way downstairs again into the garage. The Colonel pulled down a switch at the top of the stairs and the wall at the end of the garage rolled up to reveal a silver airplane.

"A hangar," Arbitzer said in surprise. The Colonel chuckled.

"No, Professor, a warehouse. Pull down another switch, make it two rooms as shutters roll down from the roof, pull down another make it four. No room for a plane then, eh? Never heard such nonsense, a plane indeed. Then take the shutters up, got a ready-made hangar. Fine flat meadow outside, good landing field. Useful, eh?" The Colonel scratched his bald head. "Uncommon useful sometimes for our friends."

"You talk too much," Bretherton said. The doors that opened onto the landing field rolled up. Slowly and silently they rolled out the plane and then stood in darkness lightened only by Granz's torch. This disappeared abruptly as he jumped inside. He reappeared wearing a helmet. "Come on." The women got in first. The Alsatian Nicko gave vent to one protesting howl, and jumped in. Arbitzer followed, and then Garden. "Good luck," the Colonel shouted hoarsely. Garden waved an invisible hand and slammed the door. Inside he struck a match, sat down opposite Arbitzer and listened to the throbbing engines. From in front Granz shouted, "All right." The plane taxied along the ground for what seemed an interminable time. Shall we never rise? Garden thought, and realized that they were in the air.

It has often been remarked that there is something about air travel which offers a release to the spirit. So Garden now, emboweled in this great insect buzzing meaningfully over the earth, felt doubt and distrust washing away from him, leaving pure and free the spirit of adventure that a few minutes ago he had been lamenting as lost. He put away from him the thought of Peterson's body as he had seen it on the pier, his doubts about the organization headed by the Colonel. All that appeared now to belong to the past, to be unimportant, and in a way absurd. Danger, excitement, and the chance of death lay ahead of them and he could face them now, as he had done long ago, with a calm and even happy heart.

From the seat beside him Arbitzer's voice said, "Charles."

"Yes."

"Are you worried for our mission? About me? Do not worry."

"I'm not worried," Garden said truthfully.

"Katerina does not believe me, but I feel in myself a passion and strength more than that of an old man. It is good to be going back."

"Yes."

"Whatever happens I shall not regret it. For you it is different. You have much to lose, little to gain. I want you to know that I am grateful. And glad you are with me."

"Don't be a fool," Garden said. "People do what they want to do. If we succeed this is the kind of thing I've wanted to do all my life. And if what Granz and the papers and everybody else says is true, there's very little danger."

"Granz was always an optimist."

The lights came on and made them blink. Ahead of them Granz held up a thumb. Arbitzer was looking with mild earnestness at Garden. His wife presented pathetically slumped shoulders with a little dandruff on them. Across the aisle from her Ilona stared out of the window into darkness, one hand smoothing the fur of the dog Nicko.

Garden walked up the aisle, squatted behind Granz, and shouted, "How long?"

"About three hours." Granz turned round and grinned like an overgrown boy. "Time for a little sleep. How do you feel?"

"Fine."

"Jacob?"

"He's fine too. You're sure everything's laid on at the airport, there won't be any trouble?"

For answer Granz stuck his broad thumb into the air again. On the way back to his seat Garden stopped by Ilona. Nicko put up his head and growled.

"What did you really come on this trip for?" he asked.

"I told you. I might meet the man who took away my husband and my son."

"I don't believe you want revenge as badly as that."

"Believe what you like, why should I care? I am not going back because of those fine words you used, that is what you would like to believe, isn't it? It's not so." The hand that was stroking the dog bunched into a ball.

The hand was thin, the fingers long and narrow. "The world is not like that. Force and weakness. What else is there?"

"I don't understand you."

She shook her yellow head angrily. "Of course you do. There are those who use force and those they use it on, nothing else. Not only in the Communist countries, everywhere. Stand up and talk about the brotherhood of man, somebody puts a bullet in you, where's the brotherhood of man then? You talk cant about your ideals, other people's totalitarianism. What does it really mean? They shoot their enemies, you put yours in prison for twenty years and call yourselves humanitarian. What have you had in England the last few years but the poor robbing the rich? Let them rob them then, but do it honestly, not as if it were an honor to be robbed. What is it but cant? I hate it."

"That's not what your husband believed."

"He was a fool. If he hadn't been a fool he and my son would be alive today."

"You don't like me, you make that very plain."

"I don't dislike you." She stared out into darkness. "Or like you. I think you're a fool."

"But that doesn't explain why you're here."

"Because I'm a fool too." She spoke with a note of finality.

Garden returned to his own seat and closed his eyes. Now we are over Europe, he thought, over the melting pot where the violence of men's hope and suffering has simmered down in the last decade to hopeless acquiescence in what is done to them. Can we flutter that acquiescence, change it to some kind of action? Will people open their papers in two or three days' time and read about changes that give them some hope for the future? Hope for the future, he thought comfortably, hope for the future, hope for the, hope for, hope . . . He slipped a hand into his jacket pocket and felt the comforting bulk of the revolver. Then he fell asleep. The next thing he knew was a shout from Granz, "Ten minutes." He opened his eyes and sat up. Arbitzer and his wife were talking together. The girl had taken out her bag and was making up her face. She said to him, "You were snoring."

II

FULFILLMENT

The plane landed like a feather. Garden opened the door and jumped out. A light rain was falling. Three men, two short and one tall, advanced toward them over the shining tarmac. Granz got out and stood beside Garden. His voice bubbled with excitement. "Cetkovitch, the one in the middle is Cetkovitch, you remember him, a good man. The others, Udansky and Matchek, I don't know if you remember them, were they in your time? Good men anyway, all good men. Let us go to meet them." Arbitzer was with them now and Granz pulled his arm, as though prepared to propel him along by sheer exuberance. Garden dropped behind, and followed with the two women and the dog. The airfield was perfectly quiet except for the sound of their feet on the tarmac. Lights showed in the control tower and the reception hall.

"Not many to receive us," Ilona said to Garden. Her voice was not loud, but Granz heard her. He turned his head and snapped, "Did you expect the whole committee to come?"

A moment later the two groups met, and Cetkovitch stepped forward to embrace Arbitzer. "Welcome home again, Mr. President. On behalf of the National Liberation Committee, I greet you."

"Thank you, Cetkovitch."

"May I present committee members Udansky and

Matchek." It was all too polite and formal, Garden thought. Udansky was a little barrel-like man with a gigantic smile. Matchek was thin and dark. There was an all-round shaking of hands. Garden remembered Cetkovitch. He was a handsome man with curling gray hair, by profession a lawyer. He said to Garden, "Very happy to see you, Charles. It has been a long time." They walked toward the reception hall. "It is perfectly safe here, only our men are on duty, the commandant has seen to that. But still it is better not to linger. We have two cars outside. That is just as well I see. We were not expecting such a large party." He glanced at the two women.

"It was difficult."

Cetkovitch took off the scarf he was wearing and gave it to Arbitzer. "Put this round your face as we go through the hall. We must not take chances." Arbitzer obediently wound the scarf round the lower part of his face.

There were three men in the reception hall, wearing the light blue uniform of the national airways staff. They straightened up as they saw Cetkovitch and Granz, looked curiously at the others. Cetkovitch merely nodded, and in two minutes they were out of the building and in the cars. Cetkovitch drove one, with Granz, Arbitzer, and his wife and Garden in it. Matchek drove the other car. He said to Ilona as the dog jumped in, "You are very fond of this dog, yes?"

"Yes."

"I am touched. Are not you touched, Udansky?" The little barrel of a man merely chuckled and slammed the door.

"Come now, tell me how things are going," Granz said to Cetkovitch as they drove off. "There have been no suspicions, no accidents, no trouble? Everything is ready for tomorrow?"

"Everything is ready, Theodore. Nothing will go

wrong." Cetkovitch's voice was calm, with a slight note of superiority. "We have been waiting only for you, Jacob, your presence makes things certain. You sleep tonight at my house. Tomorrow morning at nine o'clock we move to take control of all radio stations, telephone exchanges and public buildings. That is all arranged. Peplov has done wonders with the organization in the north—"

Arbitzer murmured, "Peplov. I shall not forget that name."

"All leading figures in the government will be placed under arrest. The army is on our side, and they will look after the People's Police in case of fighting. But I do not think there will be fighting when we are able to announce the President's return."

Unexpectedly Katerina Arbitzer spoke. "They love him. They all love him. Jacob, my dear, we were right to come back."

Garden had been peering out of the window. "The streets are very quiet."

Granz chuckled. "They are preparing for the—national holiday. What's that?"

They had passed out of the town center into one of the western suburbs. Four men in the black coats and stiff caps of the People's Police were pulling a fifth man into a car. The fifth man's face was covered with blood. A woman was tugging at the coat of one of the policemen and as they passed he struck her head with his blackjack. Garden saw her fall, almost in slow motion, to the pavement. Under the blue electric moons of the lamp standards the street was silent, except for the purring of the long black car at the curb, and the sound of their own car passing it.

"Stop," Granz cried. He pulled at Cetkovitch's arm. "That was one of our men. Stop, Cetkovitch."

Cetkovitch accelerated a little. "Don't be a fool. Do

you want the President to be involved in a street brawl tonight?"

"How long are we going to let those bastards—"

"Until tomorrow morning."

"All right, I know I am wrong, I am always wrong. I have nothing in my head but sawdust. I know that, but when I see them—" He left the sentence unfinished and then said meditatively, "They've been too frightened to do any strong-arm stuff for a long time now. Why should they start again tonight, that's all I want to know."

Nobody answered him. Five minutes later their car ran into the garage of Cetkovitch's house, with Udansky's just behind it.

Cetkovitch's house was that of a prosperous lawyer who, Garden remembered, had made his peace with the new government quite early, at a time when they had been anxious to keep the professional classes on their side. The lighting was indirect, the carpet luxuriously thick, the furnishings delicately opulent. A tall woman with a fine aquiline nose and a firm chin waited for them in a wide, high hall. This must be Cetkovitch's wife, Garden thought. The woman embraced Katerina Arbitzer and led her upstairs. The girl followed, trailing behind them with the dog at her heels. A murmur of voices came from a room at the right.

Arbitzer suddenly said to Cetkovitch, "No."

"What is it?"

"Katerina has shared my journey. There is much more that she will have to face. She should be at my side when I meet our friends."

"Come now, Jacob, this is serious business." The women had paused on the stairs.

"For a few minutes," Arbitzer said with a kind of old man's obstinacy. "Let her come in for a few minutes."

The diplomacy of Cetkovitch's voice was wearing thin. "This is a revolution, Jacob, not a reception."

"For a few minutes," Arbitzer repeated. Cetkovitch began to say something and then stopped. Katerina came slowly down the stairs again, and put her hand on her husband's arm. Ilona, as before, trailed behind them with the dog following her. Udansky hurried forward and opened the door. In the room a dozen people stopped talking as the door opened. Arbitzer and his wife went through it together. It was all, Garden thought, much more like a reception than a revolution. A yard inside the door Arbitzer stood still and said in a firm, clear voice: "My friends, you have asked me to come back. Here I am. Let us work together for the good of our country."

Now people were crowding round the visitors, talking and laughing. Garden was introduced to half a dozen people as "the Englishman who has come to help the fight for freedom." It was all like old times, wasn't it? Perhaps. Yet there was about the whole thing—this room with the Impressionist paintings on the walls, the porcelain shepherdesses on the mantelpiece—something of a dreamlike absurdity, something so removed from Garden's past experience that he felt as if he were taking part in a musical comedy. In an effort to shake off this deepening impression of unreality he said to Granz, "Which is he, this famous Peplov?"

Granz was looking over heads. "Yes, where is he? Cetkovitch, where is Peplov? What can be keeping him?"

"Don't disturb yourself, Theodore," Cetkovitch said with his calmly superior air. "Peplov said he would be a little late."

Matchek sneered a little. "He wishes to show his importance. To be a little late, that is a good tactic."

Garden found Ilona by his side. "Are you disappointed, Mr. Garden? It is not romantic enough for you, I expect. You like meetings in cellars." She bent down to pat the dog's neck. "Nicko is hungry."

"Ah, here he is," said Granz.

The door opened and a man walked in with a quick, slightly nervous step. He was of medium height, perhaps in his late thirties, with a plump friendly face, a pleasant color in his cheeks, and a thatch of dark hair. He was dressed in a neat dark suit, and looked like the keeper of a small grocer's shop dressed up for some specially important occasion. A man who would smile readily, Garden thought, although his face was wholly serious now as he advanced across the room to Arbitzer, who stood leaning slightly on his stick.

Just behind Garden Ilona Arbitzer screamed, a thin piercing sound that cut through the thin wave of conversation. Her words, perfectly clear and coherent, appalling in their sense and implications, followed close upon the scream. "That is the man who took away my husband and my son. He is an agent of the police. You have been betrayed."

They stood frozen into attitudes of passivity, staring at Peplov. The round-faced man himself stopped, for what may have been one or two seconds, but seemed an endless length of time. Then, with surprising speed, he moved for the door. Ilona cried, "Get him, Nicko," and the dog sprang after the man. Peplov pulled out a pistol, fired once and missed. Then the dog was on him, and they rolled together on the floor.

What followed was, like almost all scenes of violent action, extremely confusing. There were sounds of beating on an outer door, then shots. Two or three men had joined with the dog in tackling Peplov on the floor, with the effect of a Rugby scrum. Peplov got free of the dog and struck it on the head with the butt-end of his pistol. The dog yelped once, a high cry of pain, and by Garden's side the girl cried out also. Garden pulled Cetkovitch's arm and said, "We must get Jacob away. The car."

Cetkovitch pointed to a door across the room. "Out

there, down the stairs to the cellar. At the end of the cellar a pile of wood. Push it aside, a passage leads to an empty house in the next street. There's a garage with a car in it. You may be lucky. We will try to cover you. Take Granz."

"What about you?"

"If you get away try to get to Baritsa and rouse our friends. While Jacob is free we have a chance."

"What about you?" Garden asked again.

"Jacob is our chance." The assumption of superiority had fallen away from Cetkovitch. "We shall manage. Now go."

There was a tinkle of glass as a bullet came through the window and buried itself in the ceiling. A voice outside shouted something unintelligible. A woman was screaming. Arbitzer seemed dazed. Garden seized his arm and pulled him toward the door. Katerina Arbitzer followed. "Granz," Garden shouted, "Granz." The big man had been helping to push a sideboard against the door. Now he ran over to them.

"I trusted him, Garden," he said and kept repeating it. "I trusted him, I trusted him."

"Come on." Granz followed the two Arbitzers through the door. There was an irregular but continual patter of shots. Cetkovitch had organized the men in the room remarkably quickly. Two or three guarded the door, the rest took cover and fired out of the windows. They all seemed to have revolvers. Glass from broken windows lay about the room, but nobody seemed to be hurt, although one of the china shepherdesses had been hit. Garden found himself pushed aside by Katerina Arbitzer, who was crying, "Ilona, Ilona."

The girl was on the floor, holding the dog Nicko in her arms. "Killed him, he killed him," she said. Peplov lay on the floor, dead or unconscious. The girl got up, drew back her foot and kicked him feebly in the stomach with a gesture that was a kind of parody of the brutality seen in Hollywood films. There were more shots. Where were they all coming from?

Garden pulled the girl, not gently. Would they never get out? Katerina Arbitzer put her hand to her breast with a look of extreme surprise, and dropped to the floor. A red stain spread quickly over her dress. She smiled up at them and said, "Not hurt." The red stain grew larger. Her eyes closed. Garden dropped to his knees beside her, felt for a pulse, lifted her eyelid, searched vainly for her heartbeat.

Cetkovitch came over, his face contorted with rage. "Why the devil haven't you gone? We can only hold out here because they want us alive."

"She's dead."

Cetkovitch looked at her briefly. "Right, she's dead. She is a few hours in advance of most of the rest of us. Now get out."

Garden took the girl's hand. She did not resist him. They went out through the door and down a flight of steps. Just before he closed the door Garden heard a soft plop and a hiss, and caught for a second the smell of tear gas. They ran through the well-lighted cellars, which were full of pieces of furniture, pottery and pictures, all carefully labeled. The wood pile had been hastily pushed aside to show a dark hole ahead. They groped up stairs here. Once the girl stumbled and Garden felt her body warm against him. Invisible above them a voice said, "Hallo."

"Theodore? Garden."

"About time." A beam of light came down the steep stairs. "Jacob is in the car. Where's Madame Arbitzer?"

Garden told him. Granz said nothing. The garage at the side of the house was a broken-down affair, but the car inside was long, sleek, and gleaming. Arbitzer was huddled in a back seat, looking white and ill. Garden put a finger to his lips and Granz nodded. They opened the garage doors and Granz started the engine. "In the front," Garden said to the girl and she got in. Garden opened the back door and sat beside Arbitzer, who did not even look up. They slid smoothly out into the empty road and away from Cetkovitch's house.

Garden glanced quickly at Arbitzer who remained in his corner, looking straight ahead. Then he leaned forward and talked to the back of Granz's neck. "How much did Peplov know about the organization?"

"Everything in the north. He controlled it."

"The classical touch," Garden said. "The agent-provocateur who is half in sympathy with the movement he betrays. Down here?"

"Not so much, but enough. He could have found out." Like a man in agony Granz cried out again, "We trusted him."

Half a dozen of the People's Police were guarding a house while one knocked thunderously on the door. This time Granz said nothing about stopping, but simply swore fiercely to himself. As they came nearer the town center there were more black-coated police in the streets. Little squares of light showed in houses where the police stood at the door or hustled protesting pajamaed figures out to waiting cars.

"Keep away from the square," Garden said. "We don't want to be questioned."

Even as he spoke a black-coated figure waved the car to a stop. He came to the window and revealed himself as a very young man with a fair mustache that was carefully curled upward. He spoke in a dialect strange to that part of the country. "You are out late."

With surprising fluency Granz said, "These are English comrades, come to attend the Cultural Congress for the outlawing of Imperialist warfare. I have been instructed to take them to the airport."

"The airport is closed," the young man said.

Granz leered at him. "You are smoking out some of

the counter-revolutionary assassins, eh? There are too many of them in this town."

"Our mission here is of the first importance," the young man said proudly. "That I can tell you."

Garden said in English, "Jacob and I have papers, but not the girl."

"What did the English comrade say?" the officer asked.

"He said that even in a short stay he has seen too many of such gentry, who like sewer rats have poisoned the pure rivers of our town. Other towns too, they tell me." Granz put the car into gear.

The young officer stopped twirling his mustaches. "I have no knowledge of that. Your papers, comrade."

"Papers, yes." Granz fumbled in his coat. "Here they are." He leaned out of the window and swung viciously at the young officer's head with the butt end of the revolver in his hand. The blow caught the man absolutely unprepared. He staggered and fell, but his hat broke the blow's force. Garden heard two shots as they drove away, and a ping on the glass window at the back.

"Bulletproof glass," Granz said happily. "They should have shot at the tires. He won't follow us without instructions, but he'll report back. They'll be after us."

Arbitzer moved like a man rousing himself from sleep. "Katerina, where is Katerina?" The car was moving fast now, and they had reached open country. Arbitzer put a hand on Garden's arm. "Where is Katerina?"

"We left her behind." In the darkness he could not see Arbitzer's face clearly.

"Left her behind? Nonsense, we must go back."

"Why don't you tell him?" the girl asked harshly.

"Katerina was struck by a stray bullet," Garden said. "She came back to comfort Ilona, who was upset about the death of her dog. Katerina is dead, Jacob. She died at once."

Arbitzer showed no sign of having heard these words.

He sat bolt upright, a spectral but commanding figure. "Go back, Theodore. Go back at once." The road vanished underneath them, an endless ribbon stretched ahead. "Theodore!"

"It's no good, Jacob. She died at once." Garden put a hand on one thin shoulder. It was impatiently shaken off. "We must go back and fetch her, she will think that I left her behind. She must know that I would never do that. Katerina!" Absurdly Arbitzer tried to stand up, bumped his head and fell down sideways on the seat.

"Listen to me, Jacob. It's no good going back, we can't go back, Katerina is dead."

"Lies, all lies. Where are you taking me in this car? You have kidnaped me." Arbitzer began to shout at the top of his voice, "Help, help." There was a rattling sound. He was trying to get the car door open.

"The light, Theodore, quick." Arbitzer turned as the light came on in the back of the car, revealing wild eyes enlarged in a white anguished face. Garden brought up his right fist the short distance to the old man's chin. Arbitzer grunted, his eyes closed, and he slumped down to the seat. Garden covered him with the rug.

Granz switched off the light. "Our President," he said bitterly.

"Why do you sneer at him?" the girl said. "He has risked his life to come back. His wife has been killed. Can you do nothing but sneer at him?" She spoke so quickly that Garden could hardly follow her.

"You had better be quiet," Granz said. "What do you think we should do, Charles? Twenty miles to Baritsa. Shall we go there now?"

"I think so. Remember that we have one small advantage. If everything had gone as Peplov planned it, we should simply have walked out of Cetkovitch's house into the arms of the police. We should not have known the identity of the informer. As it is we know it is Peplov, and we know their plans. The revolution was arranged to begin tomorrow morning, they suppress it the night before. Was Peplov killed?"

"Don't know."

"It's an outside chance that we can do anything in Baritsa, but worth trying. After all, Lodno was the focal point of suppression. They may not have arranged things so well elsewhere." Through Garden's veins there crept a warming stream of assurance and excitement. "If we are stopped again, Theodore, I am one of the party's foreign friends on a tour of inspection. We know all about what is going on, and Peplov has sent us to see how things are progressing in Baritsa. Ilona is my girl friend, Jacob is a friend who has got tight. We shall have to muffle his face so that they don't recognize him. We may get away with it, eh, Theodore?"

"We shall be lucky if we are alive tomorrow morning," Granz said gloomily. The car drank up the road with hardly more than a purr to tell that they were moving. This wide highway running two hundred miles from the southern provinces almost to the center of the country was, Garden remembered, one of the Government's principal achievements. It had been made by that odd kind of voluntary principle on which those who do not volunteer are deprived of rations and get a black mark in their occupation. Nonetheless, it was a fine road. Houses, fields, toy villages rushed past them like a screen backcloth.

The girl turned round. Dimly Garden saw her yellow hair and her pale face. "Now you're feeling happy, isn't that so? This is what you came for." Garden thought, How well she knows the secret injury, how cleverly she touches the inner core of doubt. He did not reply. "I do not enjoy it so much. Why should I pretend to be your piece of local skirt?"

Granz muttered angrily. Garden said, "All right. If you want to destroy your uncle and the rest of us, it is simple enough. If we are stopped, tell the People's Police who we are. Granz and I will be shot. They will shoot you, too, but they may pin a badge on you saying that you are a heroine. Your uncle will be preserved for a public trial. If that's the kind of thing to make you happy, we can't stop you doing it."

"Oh, you're so smug." Her voice was high. "What do you care about my dog?"

Granz spoke with heavy brutality. "Speaking for myself, I do not give a damn for your dog. Or for you either."

"I don't mind about you. You don't pretend. I am talking about him, I am talking to him. What does he care about Nicko, what does he care about Katerina? All he wants is the chase, the excitement, the violence. He does not care if any of us live or die. Why do you pretend?" she screamed. "Why don't you answer?"

Garden leaned forward and smacked her face hard twice, once on each side, with an open palm. As he felt the warm contact of flesh against flesh he knew that the action was in a way a triumph for her, a betrayal of himself, and that this was something she would understand, perhaps without ever being able to put the thought into words. For the moment, however, the action was effective. She sank down in her seat with a cry which expressed astonishment and indignation as much as pain. The toy villages were replaced by ghostly limewashed houses, mildly modernistic in appearance. They were in the suburb of Baritsa.

Garden remembered Baritsa from two short visits to it, once on a raid during the war and once when the war was over. It was a small town whose inhabitants were dependent for their living on a large tobacco factory which made half of the country's bitter-tasting cigarettes. There was an enormous and once-luxurious hotel which on Garden's visit had lacked running water or any kind of room service. This was a democracy, people were saying. It was not fitting for one man to wait on another. The result was exhilarating but uncomfortable. No doubt that had all been changed. What could not have been changed so easily was the semi-Moslem atmosphere, the houses with their projecting upper storeys full of windows, the onion-domed churches. They had come to Baritsa the second time, he remembered, to rename Wilson Square. It was to be called in future Arbitzer Square. Cetkovitch—yes, of course, Cetkovitch—had made an easy and graceful little speech. It had all been polite, but it had been enthusiastic too. And what was the square called now?

"What is it called, Theodore, the big square here? You remember we named it for Jacob." In his corner Arbitzer stirred.

"What do you think? Who is Number One?"

"Number One? Oh yes. It is not one of your own people."

Granz chuckled. "They would have to change it too often. You remember we have had two new Presidents and three new Foreign Secretaries in the last five years. Now we shall see. Round the corner one of our men lives." Their headlights played on a narrow cobbled street that had about it an unnatural stillness. "The third house down. I don't see anything—oh yes." From the darkness of the doorway two figures emerged wearing familiar long coats and stiff caps.

"Stop the car," Garden said. "What was the man's name here?"

"Trajko. But—"

"Stop." Granz stopped the car. Garden got out and walked up to the two men. "I am from headquarters at Lodno, on a tour of inspection. Is everything under control here?"

"No trouble at all," said the taller of the two men. Garden recognized again the northern dialect. "We dragged the rats out of their holes one by one. Respectable citizens stayed indoors." He winked and spat.

"You have taken the man Trajko?"

"Took him in bed. There was some trouble though—resisting arrest."

"What do you mean?" Garden made his voice sharp.

"He had a gun under his pillow and one of our chaps got hurt. So—" The man grinned, put his finger to his head and clicked.

"Didn't you receive orders that all suspects were to be taken in for interrogation?" The man continued to grin foolishly. "Comrade Peplov of the Central Committee will take a serious view of this. Have there been other cases of men shot while resisting arrest?"

The other man spoke for the first time, in a treacly, wheedling voice. "Now have a heart, comrade. Mistakes will happen."

"Come to attention when you speak to me." The man, startled, sprang to attention, and as he did so his cap fell off, revealing cropped fair hair and a youthful face. Why, he's no more than a boy, Garden thought with a sudden, sharp, unidentifiable feeling. "In a workers' state, mistakes do not happen. Who is your officer and where shall I find him?"

The wheedling voice had become frightened. "Lieutenant Knapp, the Central Hotel in Josef Stalin Square. That is our headquarters."

Naturally the Central Hotel would be the headquarters of the security police—that, of course, was the inevitable. Garden snapped, "Return to duty. I shall investigate this and whoever is responsible will be punished." He went back to the car. "Trajko is dead. Drive in the direction of the square when you leave here, but turn away from it. Get out of the town as quickly as you can. It is hopeless here."

They drove down the cobbled street, then turned sharp left and left again. Beyond its small center of square, solid Government buildings, Baritsa was a town of steep cobbled streets with houses that bent toward each other clifflike, alleys at the openings of which in daylight children sat begging. Down these twisting streets Granz guided the great American-style car. No glimmer of light showed in any window. The only figures to be seen in the streets were People's Police who stood on street corners in bunches of three or four. They paid no attention to the car. Obviously anybody out in a large car on this particular night was thought automatically to be a member of the ruling oligarchy.

About these utterly silent streets there seemed to Garden something terrible, something that told of an awful conformity of the human spirit. Was it awful, however, or merely contemptible? Draw the curtains close, turn out the lights, pretend that the knocking at the house next door does not exist, put cottonwool in your ears against the screams, be thankful above all that it is not your turn, perhaps it will never be your turn. Contemptible? Garden asked himself. And answered, no, it is merely human. Looking at the broad back of Granz he thought, few are what we call heroes, and those few are so most often because they have denied social responsibilities. "Are you married, Theodore?" he asked.

Granz hesitated.

"No. Why?"

"Nothing."

Granz stopped the car. They were out of the town now, and in the countryside. Garden turned the handle of the window and drank in the soft, rich air. It was no longer raining. He looked at his watch. The time was five minutes past eleven. Four hours and five minutes ago he had been in England.

Granz shook out a packet of cigarettes and offered them to the girl and to Garden. "Is the old man awake?" He snapped a switch and the back of the car was illuminated. Arbitzer was sitting up staring straight in front of him, with his eyes wide open. He seemed not to see the packet of cigarettes.

"Lodno no good, Baritsa no good," Granz said. He sounded hopeless, like a child looking for guidance. "What are we going to do now?"

"Go back." They were all surprised to hear Arbitzer's voice. "We must go back to fetch Katerina. That man Peplov is keeping her prisoner. He should never have been trusted. I should have handled things myself. . . ." His voice died into murmurs.

"Jacob." The girl's voice was softer than Garden had heard it. "Katerina is dead. There is no use in going back."

"But in that case—" Arbitzer passed a hand across a forehead as white as wax. He seemed to have forgotten what he was going to say. Suddenly he began to talk very fast, as though some dam between himself and normal speech had been suddenly broken. "You are accusing me, Ilona, that's so, isn't it, you are all accusing me, you think I should not have brought her. Vanity, vanity, it was vanity that made me come over here, an old man fit for nothing. And Katerina would never have come, never wanted to come but for me."

"Dear God," Granz muttered.

Garden said, "Jacob, remember when we were in the car. She said you were right to come back."

"She said that, yes. But she is dead."

Granz threw his cigarette away. "She is dead, yes, and I am very sorry, Jacob. But we are alive, and I want to know what we are going to do. We have till daylight if we are lucky. Then, if we are seen in this car—finish."

In his dull voice Arbitzer said, "What does it matter? There is no chance of escaping, and if there were what is there to escape for? I am ready to give myself up now." He looked vaguely round as if in search of a captor.

"Ah, you don't know what you're saying."

Garden said, "Listen to me, Theodore. Your leading

figures in the towns are all known, and unless they're
lucky they will have been arrested. Is there any organization in the mountains?" *The mountains*—as he remembered the months he had spent there, the efficiency of
their communications, the speed with which news had
been filtered through to them, he longed for Granz to
say yes.

"None." Granz's voice was bitter. "Two years ago, yes.
Peplov persuaded us to abandon it, to concentrate on
the towns. He said you cannot make a revolution by
little raids, ambushes, we must work among the people.
We came down, not all at once you understand, a few
at a time. Everything seemed all right, we found many
friends, there was no trouble. Oh, he fooled us cleverly,
that one."

"Yes. We can try the mountains. We can reach them
in two hours, three hours, in the car. But we have no
food, no friends, one of us cannot walk long distances.
It doesn't seem a good prospect."

"It is suicide," Granz said simply.

"I think so too. Now, Theodore, is there anywhere
near here a friend who would hide us? I don't mean an
active member of your organization who will be on the
police list. I mean some rich secret backer, or a political
boss who has promised you support, or his mistress, or a
General who has a grudge against the regime—somebody who can help us without much risk to himself."

"There are such people, perhaps, a few, but nobody I
could trust." Granz sounded dispirited. "Such people
will work with the regime in power, they have no sense
of loyalty, there is no personal link to bind them." Suddenly he threw back his great head and roared with
laughter. "A personal link, yes, that is good. There is
somebody, I have thought of, somebody who has helped
me before, not once but often."

"Reliable?"

"I think so, yes." Granz began to laugh again. "She is

certainly not a Communist. Anyway it is a very good chance, the best chance."

"A woman."

"Very much so, very much so. Oh undoubtedly a woman." Granz glanced at Ilona and burst out laughing again, apparently in the highest spirits.

"And she is not openly identified with your people?"

"This woman is identified with nobody but herself. She is a friend of my boyhood." Granz rocked with laughter. "We must go. There is no time to waste."

"I don't understand."

"It is not at all necessary that you should understand." Granz turned the car back in the direction from which they had come. "Back to Baritsa."

2

The house stood in one of the three streets that run off the central square, a long narrow building which from the outside looked as dead as the rest of the town. Granz drove round to the back, where a narrow street was flanked on one side by the River Molna that straggled through the town. He said to Garden, "You come, the other two stay." They went through an iron gate and up half a dozen worn steps. Granz rang a bell.

"Back and front entrances," Garden said.

"Yes. The front is for public customers, the back for particular friends."

"Public customers." Garden understood. "A brothel."

"Have you any objection? You think the little bitch out there will be shocked, eh?"

Garden was surprised. "Why should I worry about that?" Granz did not reply.

The door opened, and a man's figure appeared in it. The light that glimmered behind him was faint, so that

Garden could see nothing more than the outline of a short, thickset man. The man said, "Yes."

"I wish to see Madame Sophie."

"Madame is engaged." The door began to close.

"Tell her it is Theo. Hurry."

The man did not reply, but merely closed the door. Granz muttered something and pressed the bell again. This time the wait was a little longer before the door opened and a woman stood there. Again Garden could see nothing more than a mass of hair and a blurred white face. Her voice when it came was remarkably rich and deep. "Theo," she said. "It's been such a very long time."

"Let us in, Sophie." Granz fairly pushed past her in his eagerness and Garden, moving after him, found himself brushing against a silk dress. The contact, in the semidarkness of this passage with its one dim light at the far end, was oddly disturbing. Granz was talking now in an urgent whisper. "Somewhere to stay, Sophie. The room at the top. Not for long, a few days at most."

She threw back her head and laughed. Garden saw the whiteness of her throat. "I might have known you wouldn't come without wanting something. I suppose I should be complimented you ask me to provide bed and board, but the black boys have been doing a good job tonight from all I hear. There's no one left but Sophie, is that it? And you know I have always been a fool for you. What about your friend—you want me to take him too?"

"There are two more outside, a young woman and an old man." Granz still spoke in the whisper and now for the first time she whispered back.

"Four is too many. What are you trying to do to me, Theo? The assistant police chief here, you know Baltnik that little rat of a man, was in last night. He told me something big was coming off in the next few days. I can't get mixed in too far, I've got my reputation to think of." She gave a throaty chuckle. "Now listen, I'll take you two here, the two others find somewhere else."

"There is nowhere else. They've made a clean sweep of our people here. If you don't take us we're done for."

Garden was standing so close to the woman that he could feel the bodily warmth that came from her. He heard her heavy breathing and then she laughed again, almost gaily. "I said I was a fool, Theo. I've never let you down, have I? You've let me down, but I've never let you down, that's the way I am."

Granz's voice at once matched this jocularity. "You've never let me down, Sophie."

"All right. Bring them in."

Almost conversationally now Granz said, "There is another small thing. The car, big, black, American style. It is a danger to us."

"Milo will see to it." She said ironically, "Is that all?"

Granz chuckled. "That is all, Sophie. I will get the others." When he came back with them Arbitzer's head was almost completely hidden in the scarf.

"Come," the woman said. They passed the squat man and she murmured something to him. She led them up three flights of thickly carpeted stairs, opened a cupboard door and pushed aside some books to reveal another door inside the cupboard. She opened this door and pressed the light switch. A small bare room was revealed, with two truckle beds in it. There were two hard chairs, a small table, a washstand, and a tiny window. A trapdoor led to the roof. "Two of you on the beds, the other two on the floor." She looked at the girl and added, "Unless, of course, there's any sharing going on. You'll be safe enough. Nobody will come up here except Milo and you can trust him."

"If he or anyone else asks questions—" Granz began. She checked him.

"Nobody asks questions of Sophie." In the light she was revealed as a bony woman in her late thirties, with

the remains of beauty. Now her dyed red hair showed
dark at the roots, her mouth had a bitter downward
curve, her black dress was slit deep in front to reveal
the swell of breasts. She was loudly and deliberately vul-
gar, yet Garden seemed to sense behind the vulgarity of
her assurance, and the sharp calculation of her glance as
it moved from Granz to Garden, rested thoughtfully on
the girl for a moment, and flicked past Arbitzer, an inner
recklessness that was eager to find expression, a generosity kept, perhaps for years, under unwilling control.

"Is this the best you can do?" the girl said to Granz,
and the red-haired woman burst out furiously:

"Yes, my girl, this is the best he can do, the best I can
do. And I am not doing it for you, believe me. There is
nothing I should like better than to see you downstairs
with my other girls. Except that I doubt if you would
earn your keep. Most of the men like something with a
bit of flesh on it."

Granz was looking gloomily down at the floor. "Sophie, Sophie," he muttered. "This is not like you. The
girl means nothing, she is tired, we are all tired."

"But grateful," Garden said, and smiled.

"You are not one of us?"

"English."

"An Englishman, eh. I once had an Englishman hiding here in the war for three months. The Germans
looked for him everywhere else, but not here. Shall I
tell you why? Because I am sensible, I co-operate, I am
on their side, you understand. I have no politics. Politics
is all—." She used an impolite word. "Some people I do
not like, then I am on the side of the Germans, or today
on the side of the Communists. Some people I like, and
then nothing is too much to do for them. I like Theo.
He used to like me."

Granz looked up. "Sophie, you are talking too much.
The car."

She snorted contemptuously. "I spoke to Milo as we

came up the stairs. He is out of the town by now. He will drive near to Kotsin ten miles away, abandon it, and stay with friends in Kotsin. Tomorrow morning he will come back. You see I don't forget things. Now, are you hungry? What do you want—sandwiches, coffee?"

When she had gone Ilona said, "What did she mean about the girls, about being with her other girls?" Granz told her. She blushed deeply, but said nothing.

Granz said, "Jacob, get into bed, cover yourself up. I don't want her to see your face. It is good to be able to trust somebody, but better to have no need for trust."

With a kind of mild, bewildered obedience the old man began to take off his clothes. Then he stopped. "Where are my pajamas?"

"Our bags were lost when there was that trouble at Cetkovitch's, uncle. Perhaps you can sleep without pajamas for tonight. Just take off your trousers and get into bed."

"But Katerina packed them," Arbitzer said fretfully. "I know she did, it is not the kind of thing she forgot. How very careless to leave them at Cetkovitch's. I shall certainly say something when she brings them tomorrow."

Ilona sat by him and put a hand on his forehead. "You must pull the things up over your face. It won't do for you to catch a chill."

Arbitzer looked up at her slyly. "Are you sure that you don't want to stop the people from seeing their President?" Nevertheless, he allowed her to pull up the bedclothes so that only a small fraction of his face was showing. When Sophie came back with a tray of sandwiches and a pot of coffee he presented to her only the back of his head. She put down the tray on the other bed.

"Listen to me, you heroes. This part of the house is mine. Clients and girls hardly ever come into it, but we cannot afford to take chances. Wash in here—I will

bring you towels. There is a lavatory on the half-landing
below. Be very careful when you use it. Trust me and
Milo, nobody else. What are your plans for getting
away?" Granz and Garden looked at each other. "You
are relying on Sophie for that too? What a valuable
woman she is to be sure. You will be safe here for a day
or two while we think of something. Now Theo, and
you Englishman, come with me."

They followed her downstairs to a bedroom with pink-
striped wallpaper, a mushroom-colored carpet, an enormous double bed with red tassels hanging from each of
the four corners, a dressing table covered with make-up
jars and bottles of lotion, and a large mirror above the
bed. Sophie stopped just inside the door and surveyed
the room with candid admiration. "Nice, eh? I don't ask
Theo, he remembers it too well, but don't you like it,
Englishman? Don't be afraid, I'm not going to eat you.
Bedclothes you wanted, here they are." They went
through into a bathroom where she unlocked a great
cupboard. The top shelves were full of monogrammed
and colored sheets, and damask tablecloths. Below
them were wonderfully soft blankets and eiderdowns.
They stood and gaped. "You wonder how I got them?
I will tell you. I kept my eyes open and my mouth shut.
I never put my hand into the fire and I never played
with politics. I was always on good terms with the men
who matter. I gave them what they wanted and listened
to the things they said—oh, not when they were being
clever and trying to make a fool of me, but at those
other times when they were relaxed enough to tell me
real secrets. Once it was about the stock market, then
about troop movements, now it is spies, conspiracies.
Such information turns itself into these things. Well,
Englishman, why are you looking at me like that?"

"I was thinking that you are a dangerous woman."

She was delighted. "The Englishman knows how to
pay a compliment, eh, Theo? It is a pity you have for-

gotten. What else? Mattresses, yes." She opened the door of another cupboard which contained half a dozen mattresses. They took one each and, staggering under their loads, went up the stairs again. From below Madame Sophie watched them, hands on hips.

When they got back Ilona put a finger to her lips. "He is asleep." She bit into one of the sandwiches.

Granz stood scratching his head. "What do you make of him?"

"Shock. He'll be all right in the morning," Garden said with a confidence he did not feel. He began to eat a cold pork sandwich, and realized that he was hungry. "Now, when was the last time I tasted real cold pork? I can't remember. Certainly your friend Sophie lives off the fat of the land."

"Yes. Will he ever be any good again, do you think?"

"He will never lead a guerrilla movement again or fight in the mountains, no. For him those days are over, Theodore."

"And our revolution, the seizure of power, you think that is finished too?"

"If they have acted as efficiently everywhere as they did tonight in Lodno and Baritsa, yes, it is finished. For the time being."

Granz put down his coffee cup on the floor. "Where did it go wrong? For years we have worked and prepared, and now all that has gone. One enemy agent sticks his dirty nose among us and ruins it all, is that possible? The best of us taken or killed, and our President, the symbol of our movement, our great asset—" Granz cast a look of mingled scorn and pity at the figure on the bed with its head turned to the wall. "But even today three-quarters, seven-eighths of the people are on our side. They are on our side—and what can we do about it?" He sat with arms hanging loosely, a picture of despair.

"Time to go to bed," said Garden. He spoke to the

girl: "We will stand outside the door. Call us when you are in bed." She nodded. The two of them stood outside the door without speaking, in the small cupboard, until they heard a murmur from inside the room. Ilona was in bed, her hair as bright as metal on the pillow, her face turned away from them. They made up the mattresses on the floor, and took off jackets and trousers. Garden turned off the light. As he groped his way in darkness the girl spoke.

"Open the window. We shall all stifle in here." He found the tiny casement window and opened it. She spoke from a place just at his side. "Garden?"

"Yes."

She said in English, "I am sorry if I have been a nuisance. I am not a very nice girl, I am afraid. I will try to be better in future."

"Future is a good word," Garden said. He bent down to a bright patch and kissed it under the impression that it was her head. His lips touched the bar at the end of the bed. He heard a laugh, quickly suppressed. A hand caught hold of his arm and drew him down. Her lips as they met his were soft and cool.

3

At half-past nine on the following morning Sophie brought up breakfast, and an hour later she came up with the newspapers. At this second visit she said nothing, but looked thoughtfully at Arbitzer, who was sitting on his bed with his hands clasped together. Granz read the paper and Garden looked over his shoulder. It was, of course, a State-controlled newspaper, since no others were permitted. The girl was making up her face with things from her handbag with as much care as if she had been getting ready for a dinner date. "What does it say?"

The whole of the front page was taken up by thick black headlines. Garden read:

ANGLO-AMERICAN PLOTTERS ARRESTED
ATTEMPT TO SABOTAGE SOCIALIST RECONSTRUCTION FOILED
PRESIDENT WARNS "ON GUARD AGAINST WOLVES AND
HYENAS OF REACTION"

Granz muttered indistinctly and turned to the inside pages. Here there were pictures of the attack on Cetkovitch's house. Matchek, Udansky, and some others were being led away by the People's Police. There was a long report describing the arrest of the conspirators who were called "Trotsky-Imperialist-Titoist-Cosmopolitans" in the pay of the Western powers. Brief biographies followed. Cetkovitch was described as "a well-known shyster lawyer who had wormed his way into the confidence of unworthy officials." Other descriptions were equally pungent. Matchek was "a notorious receiver of stolen goods and associate of criminal elements," Udansky "a so-called critic, companion of the lowest riffraff of Western decadents and spies." There seemed to be little that they did not know. Cetkovitch was dead, and so were some of the others. The captured plotters were said to have admitted that their plan was to kill the President and the leading Ministers and then conclude a treaty binding the country to the Anglo-Americans. Peplov was not mentioned. There was nothing about Arbitzer or Granz, but there was an indirect reference to Garden, which did not mention him by name. "Incontestable proof of the fact that the saboteurs were backed by the Anglo-American brigands is given by the presence of a certain well-known English Trotskyite, who had flown over specially to direct the plot." There followed an account of this figure's activities as a wrecker in Spain and his career as a spy giving information to the Germans when part of an Allied mission during the war. There were brief notes on the arrest of plotters in other towns, and a quotation from the President promising a thorough investigation of the whole State apparatus. Telegrams from the chiefs of all the armed forces pledged their loyalty to the regime.

Reading the newspaper raised Granz's volatile spirits immensely. "You see what it means, eh, Charles? They do not mention any of us by name. They are still afraid of us, afraid of what we can do. If they once admitted Jacob was in the country the people would rise."

"Come now, Theodore, be a little realistic."

"We must get away from here." Granz began to pace the room with long strides. "Somehow, I don't know how, we must get down further south. There we have many fine contacts, we print thousands of leaflets, Jacob shows himself, the President has returned. When the match is struck it may yet light the fire."

"You're living in a dream, man. What about the army?"

"The army would never move against a rising led by Jacob. The army belongs to us." Noting the expression on Garden's face he added, "Potentially at least."

"Come here," the girl called. She was standing at the casement window on tiptoe, peering out. Standing beside her they could look out along the road into the square. The day was overcast, but it was not raining. Far below them, looking like toys, a hundred or so soldiers were being harangued by an officer. What was he saying? They could not distinguish words, but plainly the officer was speaking with some passion. A sprinkling of townspeople stood watching and listening. Words of command were barked. The troops divided into four columns and marched away down each of the four streets. They passed below the watchers at the window, efficient-looking and neat in their gray uniforms. "They do not look as if they belong to you," the girl said.

"Potentially, potentially." But Granz was a little

shaken. "At any rate we must get out of here, this is no good."

"The river at the back of the house," Garden said. "What's its name? The Molna. Where does it go?"

"One way twenty miles up into the mountains, the other down to Dravina on the coast. But the coast, I don't like the coast. I told you we have not much support there."

"Dravina. Wait a minute." Garden pulled out Peterson's wallet from his pocket—was it really less than twenty-four hours ago that he had found it?—and read the top name on Peterson's list: "Joseph Lepkin, Street of the October Revolution 14, Dravina."

Granz rubbed his chin. "I don't know this Lepkin, I don't know that I should like to trust him. But perhaps from there we could get further south. I will speak to Sophie."

Arbitzer had been sitting on the bed reading the newspaper. He had seemed perfectly normal this morning, and by general consent they had said little to him. Now he spoke to them in a sharp, thin voice. "You told me that Katerina was dead. It says nothing about that here, it does not mention her."

"It doesn't mention any of us by name," Garden said. "Don't you see why? Theodore puts it too strongly when he says they are afraid of you, but it is true that they can never admit a failure or an error. They want us alive, Jacob, for specimens at a State trial, and they will say nothing about us until we are caught."

There was a knock on the door, and it opened to reveal the squat figure of Milo. He was a little brown-faced man with slanting eyes that made him look like a Mongol, and a perpetual smile. He answered their questions readily, and even eagerly. The car? He had driven it to some woods near Kotsin, poured petrol over it, and set light to it. Whoof! He grinned with remarkably fine teeth. Then he had ridden off on his bicycle, which had

been put inside the car, to Kotsin. On the outskirts of
the town he had been stopped by the People's Police,
who asked if he had seen anything of a big black car
with three men and a woman in it. He had told them
of the burning car and—here Milo could hardly contain
his mirth—told them also that he had seen four people
very much like those they wanted, in a big gray car
headed north. They had thanked him and he had gone
on to spend the night with his friend in Kotsin, coming
back this morning.

"What's it like in Kotsin?" Granz asked. "What are
they saying, what do they think is going to happen?"

"They are saying it is no good. They wish it were some
good, but it is no good, the others are too strong for
you." Milo's smile did not falter as he said to Garden,
"You are the Englishman they talk about in the paper, eh?"

Garden hesitated. "Yes."

"I can always tell an Englishman." The little man was
delighted with himself. He peered past the three of
them at the figure on the bed. The look on his face did
not change, but he said, "Jesus Christ."

"What's the matter?"

"I do not think you should have brought him here.
Does Sophie know who he is? You do not have to deny
it, I recognize him. So will she—so has she, perhaps. So
will others." He said to Granz, "You are trying her very
high. There are rumors that they are searching the
town."

"They would never search this house. Sophie is in a
special position."

"But this is a special case." The little man was shaking his head.

Garden felt a sudden curiosity. "Who are you?"

"He is Sophie's fancy man," Granz said with a shade
of contempt. "He has been hanging round her for years."

The little man's smile grew broader. "You see, your

question is answered. Sophie is a remarkable woman. She has been very good to me. I am her fancy man. I was also at one time Count Milo Bondi, a representative of our country's effete aristocracy. In the war I picked the wrong side. I thought the Germans would win. I am still astonished they did not." He broke into an outright laugh. "Do not look so shocked, you who are an Imperialist agent and a Trotskyite saboteur. When the war ended I was lucky. I was deprived of my estates and sentenced to three years' corrective labor. After that I met Sophie and—there you are."

"Why should you help us?"

"I do not love you, you are right. But I hate the others. If you were in power—a prospect against which in the days when I had my estate and was a betting man I would have laid about a thousand to one—one might talk to you reasonably. You might be inclined to return his estates to a man who wanted nothing more than to live peaceably until the end of his life."

"Never," said Granz.

"Never is a big word. But why should we argue about something that will not happen? Say only that you are men in a trap, and I am a man who has been trapped in my time."

"We mean to get out of the trap," Garden said. He leaned forward. "What do you think of a boat down the river?"

"Down the river, yes, that might be managed. At any rate it is a chance. Then to one of the coastal islands and back to England."

Garden assimilated the casually spoken words with a shock. Back to England, a confession of defeat—was that what he intended? He had thought no further than Dravina and the address written by Peterson. "Perhaps," he said. "Anyway, a boat and a pilot. Can that be done? Tonight."

"For money anything can be done. You have money?"

Garden looked at Granz, who nodded. "Then I will talk to my friends. We former aristocrats, you know, still have friends. That is our advantage over the Communists, who have only comrades."

He had hardly closed the door behind him when Granz began to reproach Garden for putting them in the hands of such an unreliable and reactionary figure as Milo. His harangue was broken by Arbitzer saying, "I shall give myself up. I have decided."

Granz said angrily, "You cannot mean what you are saying. You are a symbol of our resistance. More than that, you are now our only hope."

If Arbitzer yesterday had seemed a mere shadow of the guerrilla leader Garden remembered, Arbitzer today was very much like the aging, pedantic figure who had talked in the seaside bungalow of peace and freedom. His hands twitched, and he had not bothered to shave. His appearance had that peculiarly degrading shabbiness that is apparent only in neat men who neglect themselves. His soiled collar was particularly noticeable because yesterday it had been so perfectly clean, the badly knotted tie revealing his collar stud was conspicuous because it was of such good quality. Yet there was still something likable about the wavering smile with which he responded to Granz. "You have made it very plain that I can be no kind of symbol to you today, Theodore. I do not complain, it is simply that I am out of date. I have no longer strength for the struggle, nor any desire for it. There is only one thing I can do for you now. If they have me perhaps they will not want you, perhaps you can get away."

"But don't you see that it's just what they want," Garden said. "A State trial, all the apparatus they use for extracting confessions."

"They would not make me confess," Arbitzer said with feeble obstinacy.

"How can you say that? Can you stand up to interrogations carried out in relays by people who are prepared to argue for days on fine philosophical points? Are you stronger than Bukharin, Zinoviev, Rajk, Mindszenty, Slansky? Think what you are saying, Jacob, think how the facts could be represented. You come here to try to overthrow the government, that's true, isn't it? You had British assistance, correct?" A grim smile showed on Garden's battered red face. "Even if the English Trotskyite Garden is not caught his reputation and career will be useful to them. Behind all spies and saboteurs stand their governments, isn't that so? And wouldn't the effect of your policies have been to bring your country within the Anglo-American orbit? When you have agreed to all these things, which after all are very near the truth, what do you think the effect will be on the people of this country?"

"If you think these things are near the truth, what are you doing here yourself?" Arbitzer asked in a tired voice.

There was something faintly heroic about Garden as he replied. A light shone in his boiled blue eyes, he wore his shabby clothes like a badge of honor, his voice rang with conviction. "Because there is something more important than all this, because it is a quarter truth and three-quarters lie to say that we must be in the Anglo-American or the Russian camp. Because the world needs more than anything else the example of men fighting for a nation's freedom, of a nation fighting for real social equality and liberty. By the side of that example, our lives are not of much importance."

"Bravo, bravo." Granz was enthusiastic. "It's a good job they haven't got you in the dock." Arbitzer smiled faintly. The girl said nothing. Garden turned on Granz almost savagely.

"Do you really think I should say those things in the dock? Comrade Peplov, or whoever has taken his place would take care I didn't. That is why we owe it to ourselves not to be captured, not to let our weaknesses as human beings betray us."

"Very fine." There was no sarcasm in Ilona's voice. "But Jacob's weakness as a human being is not what you think. He believes Katerina is still alive, and he wants to see her. Isn't that so, Jacob?" She went down on her knees and took the old man's hands.

"The papers, you see, said nothing." He whispered the words.

"I swear to you, uncle, that I saw her dead, that Garden and Cetkovitch saw her also, will you believe me?"

"You had only an instant. You might have been mistaken." Now they could hardly hear him as he said, "We have been together for so many years, you see. I could not leave her to face things alone."

"I saw her too, Jacob," Garden said. "I looked at her closely, I am ready to swear she was dead. What do you say to that?" Arbitzer said nothing to it, but looked down at the floor and would not meet Garden's eyes.

Ilona waved a dirty pack of cards at them. "I found these outside in the cupboard. Let's play."

They settled down to play *skon*, a national game which is a cross between brag and poker. The game can be exciting when it is played for money, but they were not playing for money. After half a dozen hands Arbitzer shook his head. "You must excuse me." He began to read the paper again.

"He is right. Queen of spades, king of hearts, what have we to do with kings and queens?" Granz took out a toothpick. "I still think you were mistaken to trust that Milo. He cares for nothing but his skin."

"Don't you see that we are already committed to him? If he wants to tell the police where we are he can do so at any time."

"I don't like it. But we must do something, you are right about that. I shall speak to Sophie when she comes up at lunchtime."

But at lunchtime it was Milo who came up with food on a tray. His inevitable grin broadened when Garden asked if he had made contact yet with his friends.

"I have spoken to them, yes. Nothing is decided. You must be patient."

"But we want to leave tonight."

"If it is possible, yes. If not"—the little man hesitated—"we shall think of something else."

"What do the—the girls think about all this?"

"What do you expect? To them it is all the same who wins, who is in power. For them things do not change. Once it was the monarchy and the aristocracy, then the Germans, now the Communists. Perhaps they do not love the Communists, but they do not wish for change. Change is always bad for business."

"I thought there was a decree abolishing prostitution."

"A decree, ah yes, but the big Party officials are not worried by decrees. They are much concerned for the morals of the workers, you understand, but their own morals they are prepared to endanger. It is very brave of them." His beaming smile broadened, and then he became grave. "They are searching the town, the soldiers and the black boys."

"Is there any resistance?"

"Resistance?" Milo looked as if he were about to spit. "The people are sheep. They say the black boys have found many weapons, mostly rifles. If they had come to take my rifle, I should have used it."

"You have a rifle?" The little man nodded, grinning at Garden. Garden grinned back at him. "Let us look after it for you. If they come to take it we will make sure it is used."

Milo pulled his lower lip. "Can I trust you?" Garden burst out laughing.

"Isn't the boot on the other foot? A few minutes back Theodore was asking if *we* could trust *you*."

"Ah yes. I will bring you the rifle." He left the room

and came back with a Mannlicher rifle, in beautiful condition. He handed it to Garden, who put it under the mattress of Ilona's bed.

Granz stopped eating a stew of meat and beans to ask, "Where is Sophie?"

"Madame Sophie is out."

"Tell her when she comes back that I should like to see her."

When Milo came up half an hour later to take away the plates he said in answer to Granz's question that Sophie had not come back yet. The afternoon passed away. Arbitzer lay on his bed and closed his eyes. Granz picked his teeth, bit his nails, and looked out of the window. Garden taught Ilona how to play piquet. She held astonishingly good cards. When she had scored three repiques and he had been twice rubiconed they stopped playing. "You are too lucky."

She protested. "No no, I am a good player. Today I feel happy, very happy. I feel that everything will come right."

"A queer time to be happy," Granz growled from the window.

"Why do you stare out of the window? What is happening?"

"Nothing at all. Nobody on the streets. Soldiers, police, beggars, that's all. You'd think everybody was dead."

They crossed to the window and stood looking out. The street, certainly, was deserted. By craning their necks they could see the soldiers standing at the door of the Central Hotel. Little busy military figures scuttled in and out. A beggar sat in a doorway, carefully picking at his dirty feet. A woman hurrying along with a child almost directly beneath them was challenged by two soldiers. There was a long altercation between them, with much production of documents. Then she was allowed to pass on.

"The day of national celebration," Garden said. "The day of our revolution. And how do they make a revolution? By staying indoors."

"Are you out in the streets?" asked Ilona. Then her breath was indrawn sharply. "Look."

Out of the Central Hotel came two smart-looking army officers. Between them walked a man with a bandage round his head, who moved with a quick, slightly nervous step to one of the waiting cars, bent to say something to the driver and then jumped in while one of the officers held open the door. The officers got in, the car moved slowly out of their range of vision.

"Peplov," Granz said. "Just one shot while he was talking to the driver. So simple. What a pity. But it is bad that he is here, eh? Where is Sophie, I should like to know, what is she doing?"

The day grew darker, more overcast. A big fly buzzed lazily round the room. Garden and Ilona played German whist and then Japanese whist. Granz put a chair in the middle of the room, pushed open the trapdoor leading to the roof, and levered himself up until only his waving legs were visible. Then they too disappeared, and they heard his voice. "Very fine up here. You can see a long way."

"Be careful," Garden called.

"Don't worry, I am hidden behind chimney pots. I am exploring, that's all." They heard footsteps, but Granz's voice died away. Above them was a square of gray sky. They finished their hand of German whist before the footsteps returned. Granz's long legs appeared, then his body. He dropped lightly on to the chair and closed the trapdoor.

"Well?"

"Very well. We go across this roof which is almost flat, over the next which has a little slope, and to the next which has—what do you think—a fire escape. Al-

most the whole time we are under cover. Useful perhaps. But where is Sophie? What has she arranged?"

Garden played another hand of German whist with
Ilona, and lost it. "Hopeless," he said. "It's hopeless to
play against you."

4

The day grew darker still, outlines in the room became indistinct. Arbitzer lay staring up at the ceiling
with his eyes open. Granz walked up and down, went
out to the lavatory and came back, sat on the other bed,
and looked out of the window. Garden and Ilona sat
one on each side of the small table, the cards lying dis-
ordered between them, and talked in murmurs. Garden
told her about the bungalow and his Uncle George. She
talked about her childhood in the north of this country,
and recreated for him a picture of the assured, calm material prosperity that he had never known. Arbitzer's
brother, her father, a successful doctor, had been killed
in a German air raid on the capital; but still he had left
a considerable fortune, the Germans had really behaved
rather well, Ilona and her mother were able to keep the
big house in town, the officers quartered on them were
polite, people had little to complain of.

"People," Garden asked, "or just rich people?"

"I don't know, perhaps it was only rich people. I was
not much more than a child, you understand, it seemed
to me nobody who came to our house suffered, there
were inconveniences of course but things would have
been much better if only the others had not made so
much trouble. They were always talking about Uncle
Jacob, the officers, more as a nuisance you understand
than anything else. 'That terrible uncle of yours has
been up to his tricks again,' they would say, but they
didn't seem to take it very seriously. I could not under-

stand how anybody could be so foolish." Then things had changed with the German retreat from Russia, the Second Front in Europe. Allied air raids became frequent. The officers were a little less polite, they spoke of Uncle Jacob as a traitor to his country, a man who was determined to wreck the New Europe. The air raids got worse, and in one of them her mother was killed. Strangely, although she had been as fond of her father as of her mother, Ilona felt much more bitterness over this second death. Coming after the first, it made the whole of life seem meaningless to her, a feeling that persisted after the Allied victory. She was not really converted to the new regime, even when she fell in love with a young man named Jan Kapelik, who had been fighting with the guerrillas for two years.

She seemed to expect him to know the name. Kapelik, Kapelik? Garden shook his head. "He was dark, thick hair, a low forehead, very young. He talked fast, always enthusiastic. He had great enthusiasm," she said sadly. "He worshiped Uncle Jacob, and sometimes spoke of you."

Kapelik, a dark young man with thick hair and a low forehead, very enthusiastic, how many such had there been? He said apologetically, "It was so long ago."

"Yes." It was almost dark in the room now. Her fingers moved over the surfaces of the cards. When Arbitzer and Garden left the country and the others took power, Jan Kapelik was distressed, but he never thought of getting out himself, never dreamed that a loyal supporter of the revolution could be in danger. When he found out his error it was too late. "My son was fair like me," she said suddenly. "He would be a big boy now. We have not been lucky, my mother and father and Jan and I and my little boy. The Germans kill one, the British another, the Communists kill others. Does it matter who has the power, since they all use it to kill?" With her fingers moving over the grain of the cards on the table she said, "But you see I am lucky at cards."

Does it matter, Garden asked himself, and tried to answer the question honestly. But it was far too late, he knew, for him to make such reconsiderations and revisions, and he found himself saying the words that he had used so many times before about the hard fate of the individual in our day. Did he believe the words any more? It was too late, also, to ask himself that question, but he felt some sympathy with her when she asked fiercely if he thought that what he said was any consolation.

The door opened, and Milo said, "All in the dark." Granz pulled the curtain across the window. There was the flick of a switch and they were blinking at each other in yellow light. Then they were all staring at him, a little nut-brown man with a face as wrinkled as a walnut. For a moment he relished their dependence on him, and then he spoke. "It is all arranged. At exactly seven-thirty there will be a boat under the bridge. You go out through the trapdoor, over the roofs, down the fire escape of the Government Land Revision offices—"

"Saw it today," Granz said.

"Good. The offices are shut today for the holiday. The boatmen will take you to the steamer *People's Pride* which lies half a mile up the river. The captain will expect you. He has a cargo of hides for the tannery at Dravina. It is all arranged." He paused. "Except for the money."

"We pay him," Granz said bluntly. "We do not pay you."

"You do not trust me, eh." Milo's smile broadened. "That I expected. I arranged that you pay the captain. He does not help for love, you understand, but for money. He is not interested in our currency. He asks four hundred American dollars. You have dollars?"

They looked at each other. "No," said Garden.

"A pity. Then he wants two hundred English pounds. You have that?"

Garden remembered the advance given him by Colonel Hunt. "Fifty." Granz shook his head. "I have only our money." Milo suddenly looked very serious. Then Arbitzer said, "I have the money."

He got off the bed and fumbled in the lining of his coat. "We always kept money in the house, Katerina said we might have urgent need of it one day. She distrusted banks. Right in that as in so many other things. She sewed it in before we left the house, though what use I said to her, what use do you think English money will be when we are back in our own country." There was a tearing sound. Arbitzer took out three neat bundles and put them on the table. "One hundred in each. Take them."

"But you heard Milo. We don't pay until we are on board."

"Take them, take them. They are of no use to me any more."

Garden stuffed the three packets carefully into an inside pocket. "One more thing," he said to Milo. "How do we know that this Captain—what's his name?"

"Kaffel."

"This Captain Kaffel won't simply take our money and hand us over?"

"That is a risk you must take. I do not think it is great. He will not wish to explain how you got onto his boat." Milo seemed about to say something more, but he did not.

"Are we all satisfied?" Arbitzer and the girl said nothing. Granz had been frowning. Now he thumped his fist on the table.

"No. Where is Sophie?"

"I told you before, she is out. She has not yet returned."

"I believe she's down there. I'm going down to see her."

In a moment Milo was at the door. "Believe me, it is better that you should not go down."

"Then she's here. I knew it." Granz brushed Milo out of the way with the gesture of a man brushing off a cobweb, and opened the door. Garden ran after him, closed the door of the little room and the cupboard, and followed him down the stairs. Granz was standing at the door of the bedroom, with an expression on his face that was quite unreadable. Garden came up by his side.

Sophie lay on the bed in a pink dressing gown. Her mouth was slightly open. She was snoring. On the table by her side was a half-empty bottle of whisky with a "Johnny Walker" label on it.

"Sophie." Granz went over and shook her shoulder. "Sophie, wake up." The shaking became more violent. Reluctantly she opened her eyes. She stared up at Granz's face that bent darkly above her. Then her gaze moved slowly to Garden, who still stood by the door.

"Ah, the Englishman," she croaked. She sat up for a moment, and fell back with a shudder. "Give me a drink, Theo."

"You've had enough."

"Don't be a fool." Her hand groped for the bottle and found it, while she still stared at the two men. She put the bottle to her lips, drank, and sank back again onto the pillows. There were heavy shadows under her eyes and her face, without make-up, looked tired and old. "What do you want?"

"Milo told us you were out. I came to see for myself. You are here—and in what a state." Granz's voice was full of disgust. "Is this the way you help us?"

Milo was standing beside Garden in the doorway, his brown face calm but, for once, not smiling. "Can I be of any help?"

"What? No, no, Milo, I don't want you. Go downstairs." She spoke in the tone some women use to an overaffectionate dog. As silently as he had come there, Milo disappeared. With a slight effort she returned her attention to Granz and Garden. "Get away, eh? I said I'd help you get away. Well, I'm not saying I won't even though the Englishman is a saboteur."

"I don't understand you," Granz said stiffly.

"You don't. Perhaps the Englishman will understand me. Come over here, Englishman, I want to tell you a story." She patted the bed. "Sit down. It's a very sad story. What do you think of me? Tart with a heart of gold who turned into a good old madame out for herself and no one else, eh? Think I'm attractive? Give me that whisky." She took another drink. A smell of whisky clung to her as if she had bathed in it. She stretched out a hand for the looking glass. Garden handed it to her and looked dispassionately at the pasty face, the red hair with its dark roots, the sagging neck line. Sophie looked at them too, and shuddered.

"I look terrible. And do you know why? Ask him." She pointed to Granz. "If he'd been a man, any kind of ordinary man, we'd have been married, had kids. Little curly-haired kids growing up, going to school, calling me mother." She began to weep alcoholic tears. Granz made a movement of dissent and impatience. "Shut up, it's the Englishman I'm talking to, he's interested, isn't that so?"

"Very interested." Garden began to play with one of the red tassels at the foot of the bed.

"You're interested, all right. Now this is what I'm telling you, Englishman, that there was a time when I was a girl. You can understand that at sometime or another we were all girls and boys. And girls and boys grow up to be tarts and politicians, you can understand that too. And I was beautiful, do you believe that? Put me beside that little bitch upstairs and it would have been an arc lamp by a night light. Do you believe that? Never mind, what does it matter. He believed it. Shall I tell you something, Englishman, shall I tell you a good joke? He is my husband."

One look at Granz's face was enough to tell Garden that this was true. The woman on the bed squealed with laughter. "Sophie Granz, that's the name, but I never use it. Sophie Petulik I call myself. If people knew I was married to him, it would hurt the *cause*." She took another drink. "Seriously now, Englishman, tell me what you think of this specimen. He makes love to a beautiful young girl, marries her, they live happily. He had nothing to complain of, believe me. I cooked and mended and scrubbed for him, and I was never too tired to make love. And how we made love! The undying love he swore to me, the things he promised. It would make you laugh if I were to tell you. Then there was the war and we were parted, but not for long. The army was finished, he came back, and where were the fine things he had said, that we should be together always and the rest? Now he told me something else. He was to go into the mountains, I was to stay behind and give information. There was no danger—and if there was some danger I should be pleased to run a risk for my country. I was prepared, of course I was prepared, not for my country but for him. Nine months I worked in the administration, passing on information whenever I could, like dozens of others. Nine months, before the Germans caught me. And when they did I was still lucky. The German commandant of this area, Colonel Welstein, dealt with my case himself instead of sending me to one of the establishments for the entertainment of the lower ranks. The Colonel had some unusual tastes, but what did that matter? For two years I lived with this man and —will you believe it, Englishman?—I heard nothing from my loving husband."

Granz made a weary gesture with his hand. "I have

told you so often, Sophie, that it was impossible then to send messages. We were fighting for our lives."

"You put it so clearly, Theo. Their lives, you see, were important, mine was, what shall I say, not so important. Perhaps one day I might be useful again, until then they didn't worry. But shall I tell you something extraordinary, Englishman? I became convinced that my life was important too. When Colonel Welstein was replaced by Colonel von Hopper and when von Hopper was killed in an ambush and replaced by Major General Stuttwitz I found that the one who looked after my skin best was the one who lived in it. Does that seem very strange? It did not seem strange to the Germans. Stuttwitz was delighted that I was able to satisfy his passion for very young girls, the girls themselves did not object. It occurred to him that it would be a fine idea if I ran for the benefit of high-ranking German officers a genteel and discreet establishment. Will you believe it, I discovered a great talent for the work? And I found out that houses of my kind are necessary always, whether men call themselves Fascists or Democrats or Communists. When the war was over and the heroes came down from the mountains—why, by that time I had my position in society well established. I offered to make Theo a partner, but he refused. So we parted, but on good terms I assure you, Englishman. I have helped him sometimes, and now he needs help again. Isn't it natural that he should come to his wife, who knows so well the value of patriotism?"

Granz had been walking up and down the room. "Come to the point, Sophie. What do you mean?"

She sat upright in bed now, and her voice rose to a scream. "I mean that you're not going to make a fool of me again, Theo. This time I shall help you on my terms."

Garden said, "What terms?"

She leaned forward and tapped him on the chest. Her

eyes were no longer hazy. "This is a matter of business. Your business is to make a revolution, mine to run this house without trouble. I manage my business better than you do yours. Theo comes here and asks me to take you all in. I am a fool, I do it. But Theo doesn't tell me that one of my guests is that sneaking old man, the traitor who has never caused anything but harm to his country. He knows that if he had told me I should have shut the door. Now was that honest, eh, Englishman? Was that a nice way for a husband to behave to his wife?"

"Perhaps not honest, certainly not nice. But I should be inclined to call it inevitable."

She mimicked the precision with which he spoke. "Perhaps not honest, certainly not nice. And if it was inevitable I will tell you something else that is inevitable too. I am going to give him up."

Garden had been prepared for this, but Granz looked utterly startled. He began to say something, but stopped when she lay back on the pillow and laughed at him.

"This time you will do what I say, Theo Granz. Listen to me. I was wrong when I said they would not search this house, I did not realize that this was an affair involving the Republic's greatest enemy. Baltnik tells me that they are searching this street late this evening. With the way they search they will find the little room. If they do that I am finished. But Baltnik also said to me this. He heard it from a man who is higher up among the black boys. It is Arbitzer they want. They want him badly and he must be alive and fit to stand trial. They want the Englishman too, but he is less important. About you, Theo, and the girl they are not very much worried. Now I must give them Arbitzer, and I must give him to them before they begin to search. After that it will be his word against mine, and I can pull strings to make sure that mine is believed." She stared hard at Garden. "I should give them you too, Englishman, but

I always was a fool for men. And to be frank, you are not so important."

Granz unclenched his great fists and moved away from her.

"What makes you think that we shall give you Arbitzer?"

Her smile was not pleasant. "You are not very bright, Theo. The Englishman has already understood that you have no choice. How are you going to get away without my help? Of course, if you all wish to stay that is your business. That would be truly heroic."

Casually Garden said, "What about this escape? Is it arranged?"

"Milo is arranging it. There is somebody he knows— he is very secretive about such things. But he has told me that it is fixed for eight o'clock."

"Eight o'clock!"

"That will be in time." She looked from one of them to the other.

Granz said slowly, "You are right, there is nothing we can do but give him up. The movement is more important than any one of us."

"Sensible." She yawned, looking somehow disappointed. "I shall speak to Baltnik again, tell him I may have news for him through an agent of mine at half-past eight. At eight o'clock you go, ten minutes before that you bring the old man down here. Milo and I will look after him. Agreed? Very good. You can go." She stared up at the mirror in the ceiling.

As they went up the stairs again Granz said, "He told her eight, he told us half-past seven. What's the trick?"

"I don't know. But if he keeps to the time he gave us we have no need to worry. If he doesn't, we go out over the roof on our own. That is why you agreed?"

"Of course."

Garden looked at his watch. The time was a quarter-past seven.

They entered the little room again, and several things seemed to happen at once. The girl came toward them saying something about the street. They heard voices shouting orders, a scream quickly stifled, feet racing up the stairs. Then the door opened, and a figure came in wearing police uniform. It was Milo. "Out of the trap-door," he said. "They are here."

Granz put the chair into place and pushed at the trap-door. It would not open.

"What are you doing in that uniform?" Garden asked.

"I have friends, didn't I say so? Be quick."

Garden got the rifle from under the bed and gave it to Granz, who pushed vigorously upward. The door gave suddenly. They saw the night sky. Granz jumped up. Milo followed, swinging himself up like a monkey. Garden made a gesture to Ilona, who stood on the chair. Granz stretched down from above and took her hands, her heels rested for a moment on Garden's shoulders, then she was up. "You now," Garden said to Arbitzer, who had got up stiffly from the bed.

The old man smiled. "No no. After you."

"Come on now, I can give you a hand."

"You first." Arbitzer smiled again. It was ridiculous.

Granz's head pushed through the opening. "What the devil are you waiting for? They're coming in."

"After you, please," Arbitzer said.

"All right." Garden stood on the chair, jumped to catch the edges of the trapdoor and was out on the roof. He looked into the room again and gave a cry. Arbitzer stood by the door. He waved his hand to Garden. The door closed. Garden understood.

"Theo, Theo, Jacob's gone to give himself up."

Granz had begun to move over the roof. He turned now, rifle in hand. They stood behind a chimney stack. The night was dark, but part of the scene below showed clearly in the light of two street lamps and a floodlight trained on the house. They could see the men round the doorway, the scurrying backward and forward of little black figures reporting to two men standing by a car. One of them was easily recognizable by the bandage round his head, the other was one of the army officers who had been with Peplov that afternoon. They stood motionless while the figures moved backward and forward like bees carrying honey, individualized for a moment as they came into the floodlit area, anonymous again as they hurried out of it. Then suddenly all the movement was checked, the two figures by the car stiffened. Even at this distance above the street they could feel tension. Granz breathed out deeply. *Ahhhh.* From behind them a voice called something.

Arbitzer came down the steps of the house. Two guards were holding his arms, but he shook them off with a gesture that held authority and advanced slowly toward the car. Peplov said something to the officer and began to walk toward Arbitzer with his quick, nervous step. Now Garden glanced sideways and saw that Granz had the rifle at his shoulder and was looking gravely downward along the barrel.

Peplov came into the floodlit area.

Granz's face, above the rifle butt cradled in his shoulder, was serene and almost compassionate.

Arbitzer stood still, waiting for the other to come to him. One hand was in his pocket, the other at his side. He appeared perfectly at ease.

Peplov came forward, head bent down a little, thoughtfully, his walk curiously plebeian and ungraceful. The two men were perhaps six feet from each other when Granz fired. Arbitzer spun round, crumpled slowly to the ground.

In a voice he did not recognize as his own Garden cried, "Theo," but Granz, bent low, was running now over the roof. Garden stayed a moment looking down at the street that was now filled again with hurrying figures. Arbitzer lay on the ground unmoving. Peplov and two other men knelt by his side. Some of the police were rapping on the doors of houses. Others were firing wildly into the air. Garden realized that they had little idea where the shot had come from, but even as he thought this Peplov said something to a man beside him, an order was shouted, and the floodlight began to play over the houses. Ilona's voice called him. Garden ran.

It was almost as easy as Granz had said, although he slipped a little on the roof. He heard Ilona's voice again saying, "Are you there? Why don't you answer?" Then he was by her side and had taken her hand. Beyond her loomed the shape of the fire escape. "The others went on. Why were you so long? Why are you trembling? Where is Jacob?"

"Later." He pushed her toward the fire escape and they began to go down. The descent seemed endless, and although they went as quietly as possible, the clatter of their shoes upon iron seemed tremendously loud. At last they reached the bottom—and saw nothing. In this narrow back street there were no lights, and darkness was complete. Garden heard footsteps approaching, with something decisive about their even beat. They edged along the wall, turned a corner, found a doorway and crouched inside it. Just beside them something moaned. The footsteps came closer. Garden put a hand over the girl's mouth and held his breath. Her hand clutched his. There was another moan. The steps came closer. A fork of light stabbed at the bottom of the fire escape, ran quickly along the wall revealing a man in police uniform lying in the gutter not two yards away from them. He stirred as the light flashed on him, and moaned again. The light moved on, picked them out in the doorway, and disappeared. Milo's voice said, "You've been long enough. Over the road. They're waiting."

Ilona asked, "Who is that man?"

"Guard. They've got one or two men along the back

here. I've been a guard for the last five minutes." Milo chuckled. "Now over the road, quick."

He took their arms and they hurried through the darkness, in which the little man seemed able to see without difficulty. They slithered down an embankment. Garden heard the slap of water on stone. "To the right, under the bridge," Milo said, and then, "Here." In the prevailing blackness something was a deeper black. Garden put out his hand and touched rough stonework. Milo said, "This way." His feet crunched on shingle and he stepped into the boat. They began to move, although Garden could not hear the splash of oars, nor distinguish any of the other people in the boat. No word was spoken until, after what seemed a long time but was perhaps only five minutes, they clambered up the ladder of the *People's Pride*. Here too nothing was said as they went down a narrow companionway and entered a small cabin with a smell of mingled engine oil and garlic. Now, at last out of the moleskin dark, they stood and blinked at each other beneath a lantern hanging from a hook in the ceiling. Granz still held the rifle. Milo had the happy smile of a conjurer who has brought off a difficult trick with particular neatness. The girl rubbed thoughtfully at a smear of dirt on her cheek and looked from one to another of them like a child who fears to ask a question. Garden caught sight of his reflection in a bit of cracked glass, and was shocked by the deep lines on his forehead, the weariness that showed in his faded blue eyes.

The girl said it at last, timidly. "Jacob?"

Milo shrugged his shoulders. Granz stood perfectly still, holding the rifle. Garden told her.

"But why?" she asked, turning from one of them to the other. A tear ran, as if by accident, down her cheek. She brushed it away fiercely, and the smudge of dirt lengthened. "Do you understand?" she asked Milo.

"I am not a politician. Of politicians I can believe anything."

She turned to Garden, "Do you? Couldn't you have stopped him?"

"I could have knocked his arm, but I thought he was shooting at Peplov. Oh no, he got the man he meant to shoot, don't imagine anything else. At the time I didn't understand, but now I know why he did it."

"Would you have done it?" She stared straight at Garden, as though much depended on his answer. And what did depend on it, he thought? Why nothing, nothing at all. Somewhere below them engines began to throb, voices murmured indistinctly. Milo undid the high neck of his jacket, pushed his cap to the back of his head, sat down and stretched out his legs.

"I don't know. A few years ago I would have done it, yes, certainly. Today, perhaps, if I were in Theo's position—I don't know, I can't tell you."

"But why, why?"

Garden waited for Granz to speak, but he stood in the little cabin, about which there was now a sense of movement, like a man made from wood. "I can tell you why Theo shot. Jacob was going to give himself up, he would have been put through the farce of a public trial, he would have confessed whatever they wanted. Don't argue about it, that is what would have happened. Perhaps Jacob thought he was saving us, perhaps he really believed Katerina was still alive and thought he might see her again; perhaps he simply did not care any more. But what Theo thought of was the effect of such a trial. To us it would be a farce, but people outside this country would say, 'There is something in it, perhaps.' And inside the country—cannot you imagine the effect of Jacob's confession that he was linked with foreigners to regain power? Could anything bind the people to a government they hate more surely than the threat of aggression from abroad? Could anything be more certain to ruin the cause?"

"Oh, the cause, the cause," she said sarcastically. "Are you saying what you think yourself?"

"I am telling you why Theo shot Jacob."

"And was he right?" she insisted. Garden turned away without answering, to touch the arm of an old leather armchair from which a spring ominously protruded, to run his finger along the rough grain of the wood, to peer out of the porthole at darkness. "He is a murderer," the girl said, with her arms hanging down in just that helpless fashion that Garden remembered from his first sight of her. And now at last Granz moved, putting down the rifle with a great thump in a corner of the cabin, throwing himself into the leather armchair, and speaking deliberately.

"You are a fool, little girl. Jacob's life was over, and he knew it. You saw him yourself, like a man who had lost his senses. If he had been able to think as he used to think, he would never have tried to give himself up."

"And because he was not very clever, that gave you a right to kill him?"

"Ah, be quiet." Granz shook his great head like a pestered bull. "Do you suppose I enjoyed it? Where's the captain? And what are you doing here?" he asked Milo.

"It's hot in here." The little man took off his black jacket, revealing a gaily colored shirt and braces. "Cigarette?" They lighted cigarettes. "The captain will be here presently. For half an hour he keeps a special lookout, but I think we are safe."

"What makes you think they won't realize we are on a boat?"

Milo chuckled. "In a car outside in the garage they will find food and drink prepared for a journey. In one of the pockets, not too obvious but not too well hidden, they will find also a map drawn by me which shows that we are making for the western frontier. They will find a note about the chance of bribing the frontier guards at one of the crossing points. No, I do not think they will suspect that we have gone down the river. We were going to get away by car, that is the idea, but they arrived too early for us. So how have we gone? On foot, in another car, by train? At any rate they will have no doubt that we are making for the western frontier. It is the logical thing to do, and they are very logical people." He laughed at the surprise on their faces. "You revolutionaries are clumsy conspirators. You need a reactionary to handle things for you."

"But Sophie knew, except that you tricked her over the time," Garden said. The little man nodded. "Won't she tell?"

"Warm in here, but my feet are cold." He took off his boots and spoke without looking at them. "Sophie was an intelligent woman, but she miscalculated. She thought that if she gave up Arbitzer she would be safe, she could use her little influence. Not so. This thing is too big for little influences. Sophie was finished. She could not have saved me, she could not have saved herself. She would have been off to a labor camp and she would not have liked that."

From the other side of the cabin Granz was glaring at him. "Say what you mean, man!"

Milo bent upon Granz the full light of his merry smile. "It was an act of mercy you carried out by shooting Arbitzer, was it not? I too have a merciful nature. I saved Sophie from the labor camps." He looked reflectively at hands that were remarkably large for so small a man. Garden remembered that single choking scream.

Was something discernible on Granz's face besides simple anger, Garden wondered—pity, remorse, a recognition of the power and inhumanity of the forces that had led Sophie Granz and Jacob Arbitzer to almost equally ironical deaths? Or were these merely the thoughts of an inveterate self-deceiver, grown too old and soft for his revolutionary trade? What Granz said certainly contained no hint of pity for the woman who had been his wife. "What are you doing here? There was no arrangement that you should come with us."

"Arrangement, no. But I had made up my mind. I should have been a fool to stay with Sophie. And have I not been useful? Aren't you glad I came?" His laughter at sight of Granz's scowl filled the cabin. "I feared you might not be. That was why I didn't tell you what I meant to do when you questioned my good faith back there. I shall come with you to England."

Garden shook his head. "I doubt if you would like it there. At the moment it's hardly the country for a man with your talents."

"Oh yes. It is the country—and the time. Tell me, Mr. Garden, have you seen Arsenal?"

"What?"

"Arsenal—Wally Barnes, Swindin in goal, Forbes the magnificent tackler, the little wizard Jimmy Logie. Would you say you have a center forward in England today to match George Camsell or Dixie Dean?"

"I've really no idea. I never go to football matches."

"Football is my passion." It was impossible to know whether Milo was joking or perfectly serious. "And England is the home of football. We have football players here also, but beside yours they are nothing. I would give much to see the match between Arsenal and Manchester United. Ah, hallo there, Captain."

The Captain was a villainous-looking figure with a black patch over one eye. He wore a dirty uniform, had a three-day growth of beard, and chewed continually at what was presumably a plug of tobacco. He looked reassuringly like a man who has little use for law and order, as he stared at them all with his one pig eye. "Where is the other?" he asked.

"He could not come," said Milo brightly. "No doubt you will not be sorry."

The Captain spat into the fire. Then he turned round and stood warming his backside at a miserable fire. "The money."

"It is in English pounds. One hundred and sixty."

"Two hundred."

"Two hundred was for five. Now we are only four. It is also true, as you know, that the fifth was the most important. The figure should really be one hundred and fifty, perhaps less, but we will say one sixty—"

The Captain's face turned red, and he gobbled furiously. "Two hundred."

Milo smiled up at him. "Come now, you are being unreasonable."

The Captain gobbled again. "You want me to put you ashore, eh?"

Granz spoke harshly. "He is a fool, take no notice of him. Pay the money."

Garden took out two of the packets that Arbitzer had given him, and laid them on the table. Captain Kaffel counted the notes carefully. He undid some layers of filthy clothing and came to a belt with a purse in it. He put the notes in the purse. Then, moving with great solemnity, he drew from a cupboard two small medicine glasses, a tooth-glass, two chipped cups, and a bottle containing a white liquid which Garden recognized as a national drink, in taste somewhere between vodka and slivovitz. The Captain filled the glasses and the cups, took the larger of the cups for himself, threw its contents down his throat, and poured some more. Milo's technique was similar, although a little less impetuous. Granz drank his medicine glassful in three great gulps, and Garden did the same. The drink was even more powerful than he had remembered. The first gulp made him feel as if the lining of his throat and the inside of his cheeks had been burned rapidly away. The second went down while his throat was still numb, and he felt the full force of it in a prodigious hiccough. The third gulp was comparatively pleasant, but it made him cough. The Captain slapped him on the back and roared with laughter. "Englishman, eh? Englishman they're looking for."

"Yes." There were tears in Garden's eyes, but good relations seemed to have been established.

"Another drink." The white liquid splashed into Garden's glass. "Remember you, fought with you up in Craska. Good days, eh, raiding the villages, always a full stomach, never known anything like them." He struck the great mass of clothing with his fist which rebounded as if he had struck a board. "Remember me, eh?"

"Yes," Garden said untruthfully.

"You looked different, younger, but I put two and two together. We all grow older every day, eh?" The Captain roared with laughter, clinked his cup against Garden's glass, and threw the liquor down his throat again. "Listen. We are running into fog, thick. Lucky for you if they are after you, but we must go slow, slow." His hand indicated the miserable speed at which they must proceed. "We reach Dravina perhaps in early morning. I set you down one mile, two miles this side of it. In Dravina is too dangerous. All right, eh?" He addressed Garden, who nodded. The little pig eye inspected him critically—or greedily, it was hard to know which. "Another thing. Your clothes are too English. I fit you up with real good stuff."

"Too English!" Garden stared in surprise at his shabby jacket and trousers.

"You come along with me, I fit you up," Captain Kaffel said. There could be no doubt this time about the gloating look with which he gazed at Garden's sports jacket. It did not seem politic to refuse. Garden went along to the Captain's cabin and exchanged his jacket, trousers and pullover for a collection of patched and greasy garments of indeterminate color and purpose. He also, more profitably, exchanged his raincoat for a kind of old duffel coat which, although somewhat filthy and ragged, was at least reasonably warm. The Captain was delighted. He slapped Garden on the back and gave him another drink. They returned along the deck, moving through layers of fog that seemed to swathe their bodies and make soundless their passage through the night. At sight of Garden Milo burst out laughing. The Captain was offended. "You do not like the clothes, eh?" he said menacingly.

Milo went on laughing. "I hope you paid him for them, Mr. Garden, though truly they are beyond price."

The Captain waved a dirty hand. "Between friends there is no bargaining. Now I shall lock you in. For your own good. Until the morning." The door closed, a key turned in it.

"Rats in a trap," said Granz, who had relapsed into gloom. "And it is what we deserve. To bring along a girl, what foolishness. She was bad luck."

Garden made a gesture of protest, but Ilona stopped him. "Let him talk, perhaps it is true. What have I been all through my life but bad luck to myself and others? Three people I loved, Jacob, Katerina and Nicko. Now they are all dead, I am alive. Isn't that bad luck?"

"I was a fool." Granz bent his great black head so that he was looking down at the floor. "I should have said 'Jacob yes, Charles yes, others no.' Then if he had not come it would not have mattered. Perhaps he was bad luck too. Now here we are in an old tub traveling with a reactionary aristocrat. What is the point of it all?"

There was a rosy flush now on Milo's cheek from close proximity to the fire. "The point is to get to Dravina, and then to England. I know a man in Dravina who might help." He chuckled. "At least he might help me. About the rest of you I don't know. You, Granz, I think he would draw the line at you."

"Do you suppose I care? Do you suppose I want help from your sort? I would as soon be dead."

Stockinged feet thrust out toward the fire, wholly at his ease, Milo said, "Ah yes, that is the sort of help you prefer, isn't it, the sort you gave to Arbitzer."

Granz's head jerked up. Then he was across the room and like a bull had bowled over Milo and his chair to the floor. His hands were on the little man's throat, he was muttering inarticulately. With an effort Garden dragged him off. "We're in this together," he said. "Keep your quarrels until it is finished." The schoolmasterish piety of the words sickened him, but what other words were there to use?

"You talk like a fool," Granz said. "How can it be finished now, except by our being caught?"

"We may get to England."

"And what do I care for England, land of bourgeois smugness? Better to die here."

"Nevertheless some of us would rather live in England."

Granz grunted. "Very well. But keep him away from me."

Milo was smoothing down his hair and rubbing his neck. He did not appear to be hurt. Garden extended his school activities to cover the role of dormitory prefect. "We'd better try and get some sleep. There will be work to do tomorrow. Ilona, do you want the chair by the fire or the sofa under the porthole?"

In a voice hardly audible she said, "The chair."

"Good. Milo can have the sofa. Theo, stay where you are." Garden turned out the lantern, pushed a small hard chair back against the wall, sat down on it, closed his eyes and tried to go to sleep. The chair was very uncomfortable. Images rose before his closed eyes, images that had the delusive clarity of a dream and yet were wholly conscious products of his waking mind. Little Mr. Hards leaned over and nipped the waitress's bottom, three figures, two short and one tall advanced across the shining tarmac and were replaced by another, a man of medium height with a plump friendly face, who moved with a nervous step across an invisible room. This figure faded and he saw Granz on the roof, rifle at shoulder, looking gravely down the barrel, down, down, down to the street below where—a voice whispered to him. Garden opened his eyes. In the firelight's flicker he saw Ilona's fair head near to his chair. "You jumped," she said. "What were you thinking about?"

"Jacob."

"So was I. Poor Jacob." She was silent. "What will you do if we get back to England?"

"I don't know. First I should like to clear up things."

"What things?"

"I don't know. There was something odd about the whole thing in England. I should like to see—" He paused. It would be wrong to mention Sir Alfred.

Milo said, "Very good advice that, about trying to get some sleep."

They were silent. Staring into the fire's flicker that slowly died, listening to the murmur of the engines, looking at Ilona's hand on the chair arm as it was revealed occasionally in a flicker of light, Garden wondered whether he was in love, moved his buttocks in a useless attempt to find a soft place on the chair, thought again of Jacob. He remembered how when he was a boy of six or seven their cat Timmy had trotted up the garden path and deposited a dead sparrow at a point nicely equidistant between the boy and his father. Mr. Garden had taken the occasion to read a brisk moral lesson to his pale and distressed son on the theme that it is the mission of the stronger to kill, of the weaker to suffer— that, he said, was natural selection. It was not in fact the dead unruffled body of the sparrow that had disturbed the boy, but the sudden revelation that the purring cat who never put out a claw in anger could kill so heartlessly, so casually. He cried out not for the sparrow, but for something in his own innocence that had been injured beyond repair. Why do I think of something so utterly irrelevant? Garden asked, and answered himself: if it were really irrelevant I should not think of it. He shifted again on the hard chair, and resigned himself to a sleepless night.

Something pressed his arm and he opened his eyes. Captain Kaffel blew a sour breath into his face, and moved on to the others. Granz woke immediately, Milo with a quick shrug. The girl curled up in the chair and muttered something. Garden said, "Ilona," and she opened her eyes, looked at him, and smiled. Getting up, stretching, Garden found his back and thighs aching from the night in the chair. He was conscious of a smell about the clothes he was wearing, a smell of drink and stale food, the captain's smell, that he had not noticed last night. This mingled unpleasantly with the smell of fog and human sweat in the cabin. Garden shivered. Captain Kaffel was solicitous. "A little drink, eh? To warm you up." Garden shook his head, and put on the duffel coat.

Granz placed a hand on the rifle and then took it off. "In Dravina, no, it would not do. It is yours," he said to the Captain, whose pig eye glinted approvingly. Now he positively would not be refused. The bottle of white liquid was produced and sloshed into the chipped cups and medicine glasses. "A safe journey, the best of luck," the Captain said as he tossed it back. He caressed the rifle affectionately, and suddenly dug Garden in the ribs. "We remember the old days, eh? Bang bang. When are they going to come back?" They all went up the companionway, shivering in the raw morning air. The Captain came with them in the boat. He took one of the oars and Granz another, and they moved slowly to the river bank. The fog was lifting slowly and the Captain said that in a couple of hours it might be clear. By walking for five minutes, he said, they would strike the road and could pick up a bus into the city. It was simple,

simple. He grinned a farewell with all his bad teeth and, bending over the oars, faded into the mist.

5

Kaffel's information was accurate. The fog lifted as they moved away from the river; they found the road and after walking along it half a mile were picked up by a bus which took them into Dravina. There was only standing room on the bus, which was crowded with men in shoddy clothes who gave the four of them no more than one incurious glance. To one side of them a man was reading the morning paper, and Granz from his great height rested his chin almost on the man's shoulder in his anxiety to see the news. Very deliberately the man folded the paper and put it in his pocket, growling a refusal when Granz asked to see it. Almost all of the men got out by the entrance gates of a big factory that was already belching smoke from two tall chimneys.

Dravina is divided into a new town and an old town, which is still enclosed by its original walls. The Street of the October Revolution, the conductor told them, was in the new town. The bus went within two minutes' walk of it. Part of the new town was built by the Austrians, who favored large square, vaguely classical buildings in fawn-colored brick. To this the Royalist government of the thirties added houses and offices in a kind of European Victorian Gothic, and since the war the Communist administration has contributed large blocks of flats and official buildings marked by a certain knobbly simplicity. In the Street of the October Revolution the three styles were all in evidence, with the effect of making it look curiously like a film set. The street was wide, and the buildings well kept. Number 14 was large and square, with many windows. They walked past the swing doors and looked casually inside. Nothing was visible but a wide and apparently empty entrance hall. Granz shook his head. "I don't like it. Who is this Lepkin?"

Almost opposite Number 14 there was a tiny bistro below a block of offices. They went in there, drank ersatz coffee with a flavor of nuts and goat's milk, and ate hard brown bread with a solid and almost tasteless jelly that was called marmalade. Milo asked the man who served them the name of the big building over the way, but got no intelligible reply. "Lepkin?" he asked. "Do you know Lepkin? Does he work there?"

This time the man seemed startled. He looked at them oddly. "I know no Lepkin." Then he walked away from them deliberately and went to the end of the room, where he stood in urgent conversation with a large woman who waddled from behind a counter to stare at them.

Ilona had reached over for the morning paper, which hung in a rack attached to a bamboo stick. She turned the front page and slapped down her hand suddenly. "A horse fly," she said, and pushed over the paper to Garden. A photograph of him stared up from the page. Beneath it in black type he read, "Watch for this man. He is the English saboteur and criminal pervert, ringleader of the dastardly assassination plot." No name was given. He recognized the photograph as one taken years ago, just after the liberation. It showed a remarkably youthful figure wearing a beret and making the V-sign. The picture had been touched up to make the smile on his face look like a triumphant and ugly leer. His first reaction was that the picture showed a man absurdly unlike the figure sitting in this bistro drinking ersatz coffee and eating hard bread. Or was that an illusion, a belief he held simply because the man in the photograph seemed so far away? If he could judge from the look of alarm in Ilona's eyes that must be true. He read the story carefully, and found that it gave no further important details of the "plot," and that there was still no mention of Arbitzer. He passed the paper over to Milo and Granz. After a minute or two Granz said, "Evidently it is necessary that we should see this Lepkin."

"Is the photograph like?" It was curious that he felt no alarm whatever.

"It depends on the keenness of your eyes. There is a great change, yes, but anybody who knew you in the past might recognize it. We must see Lepkin, there is nothing else for it."

"One of us should go over," Garden said. "The rest wait here. Since Peterson was my friend, and I have his diary, it had better be me."

"Madness," said Ilona, and the others agreed with her. "Your picture in the paper, your voice—you speak our language well, but there is an accent—"

"All the more reason for me to go. I have a friend here." He tapped the revolver. "If that photograph is really recognizable I must be caught very soon. Why should you be caught with me? If I don't come back or send for you in fifteen minutes' time you had better leave." The fat woman and the waiter were now engaged in a furious argument. She seemed to be urging him to some course of action. Garden got up.

Granz said doubtfully, "I do not think—" The girl said "No." Then he was out of the bistro and walking across the wide road. He pushed open the swing door of the fawn-colored building.

The entrance hall only appeared to be empty from outside. In fact a man sat in the middle of it at a glass-fronted inquiry box rather like the pay desk at a cinema. This cinematic impression was enhanced by the fact that the floor of the hall was some kind of black and white mosaic. Two or three other men stood unobtrusively within call of the inquiry desk at the entrances to corridors that led off the hall. Garden looked vainly for some sign that might indicate the nature of the business carried on here. Then he advanced to the inquiry box. "May I see Comrade Lepkin?"

Behind the glass a man raised sandy eyebrows. Garden felt that he had said something wrong. "An appointment?"

"I think he will see me if you give him this message." On a piece of paper torn from Peterson's diary he wrote: "I have an urgent message from Comrade Peterson or Floy." He folded the slip of paper and passed it under the glass. The sandy man pressed a button and one of the men at the corridor entrances walked briskly across the hall. Garden noticed that he wore a heavy brown belt with a pistol holster in it. The sandy man said something inaudible and gave him the note. The man with the brown belt went away down one of the corridors. Garden sat down on one of the benches that ran halfway round the hall, and waited, with a growing feeling of uneasiness.

He had not long to wait. A little figure wearing gold-rimmed spectacles walked quickly, almost trotted, out of the corridor and across the hall. Garden stood up. "Comrade Lepkin."

"No, no." The little man looked immensely amused. He had a happy expression, and looked slightly like Mr. Pickwick. "I will take you to him. Come along." They went across the black and white floor and down the corridor, which was flanked on either side by numbered rooms. Behind some of the doors came the sound of typing. At the end of the corridor the little man trotted down a flight of stone stairs. Here there were more doors on either side, but no sound of typing. Garden was beamingly waved inside one of these doors. He saw a desk and a man writing at it, head down. "Comrade Lepkin?" he said uncertainly. He heard the door close behind him.

The man carefully finished what he was writing, blotted it and looked up. He was in his late forties and the severity of his pale, strikingly handsome features was enhanced by a pair of rimless spectacles. He said in a cold voice, "District Commander Lepkin of the Special Section People's Police, yes." At the moment that these words were spoken Garden felt something hard sticking into his back. The voice of the little man, bubbling with suppressed amusement, said, "Please put up your hands." Slowly Garden raised his hands above his head and then, as he felt the other fumbling at his hip flung himself suddenly to the right and caught the little man's revolver hand with his arm. They crashed to the floor together and struggled there in a flurry of arms and legs. He heard Lepkin say, "Don't shoot," and then received a stunning blow on the side of the head.

He recovered consciousness to find himself sitting in a chair. His revolver lay on Lepkin's desk. The little man watched him carefully, still smiling, from one side of the room. Lepkin sat at the desk below two portraits, one of the President, the other of Stalin, looking calmly at him. The look was impersonal, directed less at a man than at an object. Lepkin was about to speak when the telephone rang on his desk. He picked it up, said, "Yes" twice, and then, "Yes, do that." He said to Garden, "You will be interested to hear that your friends over the road are being brought here. The woman reported their presence. She thought it suspicious that they wanted to know what this building was, and asked whether I worked here." The little man took off his gold-rimmed spectacles and polished them, smiling benignly to himself. "Prilit here can tell you that people do not often mention my name or ask for me. They think it does not bring them luck." Now little Prilit laughed outright. Lepkin's chilly gaze was transferred to him. "You realize who this is, Prilit?"

The little man tried to conceal an obvious bafflement. "A spy beyond doubt, a saboteur. Planning your assas-

sination perhaps. A madman. To ask for *Comrade* Lepkin indeed."

"I see that you do not realize." With a leisurely hand
Lepkin unfolded the newspaper on his desk and passed
it to Prilit, who looked at it, then at Garden, and back
again at the paper. "The Englishman!"

"Precisely, the Englishman. Now what we have to de-
termine is why the Englishman sent this note which you
very properly brought in to me, saying that he had an
urgent message from Comrade Peterson or Floy." With
cold politeness he asked Garden, "Who is Comrade
Peterson or Floy?"

"I invented him in the hope that you would see me."

"In that you have succeeded. What do you want to
say?"

Garden was silent. What could he possibly have to say
to District Commander Lepkin, of the Special Security
Section, People's Police? Lepkin touched Garden's revolver. "Search him, Prilit. I want everything that is in
his pockets. And let us have no more nonsense. I don't
want to kill you, but I should not have the smallest objection to crippling you." Prilit moved across and began
to search him. "Another point. Those are surely not
English clothes you are wearing. Where did they come
from?" Garden made no reply. "I can see that you are
going to be stupid. Surely, now that you have taken the
step of surrendering yourself to us it is pointless not to
answer questions. You don't agree? We shall see." He
looked at the collection of things that Prilit had put on
his desk. "English money, yes. Papers, very well. Keys,
English cigarettes—you did not play your part very
well, do you think our people would smoke filthy English cigarettes?—more money, a diary." Lepkin looked
through Peterson's diary, in which his own name was
noted down. Then he put his fingertips together. "Your
name, we have been told by headquarters, is Garden.
Come now Garden, why are you here?"

"I mistook the building." It did not seem to matter much what he said.

"I expect something better than that." Lepkin waited.

"Down below?" There was something fawning about little Prilit.

"You hear, Garden? Do not be deceived by Prilit's appearance, he takes great interest in the work that goes on down below. He is careful and thorough. You won't like it if I send you down with him."

"Can I take him?" There was no doubt now about Prilit's fawning eagerness.

"Not yet. Let us see the others first." Lepkin picked up one of his desk telephones and spoke a few words. Two men brought in Granz, Milo, and Ilona. There was a swelling on Granz's cheekbone and his coat was torn. Granz and Milo had their hands tied behind their backs. "Outside," Lepkin said to the guards.

Little Prilit almost bounced up and down with excitement. "Sir, it is about three of them that we had the urgent code message." His glance swept over Garden, Granz, and Ilona. "Should I not say that we have them safely?"

There was no change apparent to Garden in the icy calm of Lepkin's voice, but as the little man heard what was said he blushed as rosily as a schoolgirl whose secret diary is being read aloud. "Do you suppose that had not occurred to me? My dear Prilit, I am afraid you are a fool. What are you going to tell as your fine story of achievement? 'The man you were looking for has been in our town perhaps for a day or two. He obligingly came in here and gave himself up. The keeper of a bistro across the road came in and reported that the behavior of the others was suspicious, so we arrested them.' We shall appear marvels of cleverness, shall we not? The Director-General will be delighted when he learns that three of them were sitting at their ease on the other side of the road and we did not know it. You will obtain promotion, my dear Prilit, you cannot avoid it, and as for me I shall be made a Hero of the Republic." Lepkin bared strong white teeth in an unamused smile. Prilit stammered something, and Lepkin cupped hand to ear with a grotesque parody of courtesy.

"What's that? We need not tell that story to the Director-General? Bravo, little Prilit, a glimmer of intelligence is illuminating your brain. Now, shall I tell you what we are going to do? We are going to find out the exact background of these four, how they escaped from Lodno and Baritsa, how they got from Baritsa to Dravina, what they hoped to do here. Then it should not be beyond our ingenuity to think of some more romantic version of their capture, which will do us both credit, and may even bring you that promotion for which you are so eager. By the time we have done with them I do not think they will want to dispute our story. After all, what does it matter to them?" There was no hint of sarcasm in Lepkin's voice. "Am I making sense, Prilit? Do please inform me if I am not making sense."

The eyes with which the little man gazed at Lepkin were a dog's eyes, adoring. Granz said loudly, "If I have anything to do with it they won't pin any medals on either of you. I shall tell them we were sitting perfectly innocently over the road when your men came—"

Prilit ran across to Granz and smacked his face hard, once, twice, three times. Granz kicked him on the shin and Prilit howled with pain. Lepkin stood up, revolver in hand. He looked annoyed, and dangerous.

"That's enough. Prilit, you cannot even hit a man with his hands tied behind his back. I will see them myself alone, each in turn." He pressed a button, and the two guards came back. "Take those three next door and see that they do not talk to each other. Prilit, next door too. I will ring when I want you."

When they were alone Lepkin stared steadily at Garden, still with that air of one who sees something utterly indifferent to him. The pictures above looked down approvingly. Garden braced himself for an unexpected question as Lepkin put the tips of his fingers together, but he was still unready for the one that came.

"Have you read G. K. Chesterton's *The Man Who Was Thursday?*"

Garden was utterly confused. "I—why, yes. A long time ago."

"It is a foolish book, a feeble bourgeois fairy tale, but there is an ingenious idea in it. Chesterton wrote of a society of anarchists, all of whom turn out to be policemen. A bourgeois fairy tale, as I said, based on a belief in the stability of society. In our day the anarchists are not policemen, but it is possible that the policemen may be anarchists, or at least revolutionaries." Garden stared at him. "Come, come. This diary is Peterson's. I know his writing. How did you get it?"

What kind of game was Lepkin playing? In any case, it could do no harm to tell him the truth about Peterson. "I took it from his body. Peterson is dead."

Lepkin nodded. "Did you kill him? You can tell me, it does not matter. But we have little time for talking, it is essential that you believe what I say. You see this letter signed 'Rosa.' I am Rosa."

"I don't believe you."

Lepkin wrote a few words on a memorandum sheet and pushed them over to Garden, together with the letter from Peterson's pocket. He had written the same words in German, and even though the ink had run on the original letter it was obvious that they were in the same writing. "You believe now?" Garden nodded. Lepkin struck a match and carefully burned both letter and memorandum sheet. "That letter could have been the end of me," he said casually. "Now, listen, and speak only when I ask you questions. I believe you knew Peterson in Spain. He had been a revolutionary for many years and recently had joined our party, the W.U.S.R., that is the Workers for Universal Socialist Revolution."

"You are not an anarchist then?"

"I asked you to speak only when I asked questions," Lepkin said snappishly. "Of course I am not a romantic anarchist. I am a Universal Revolutionary. Peterson was one of us. He was in England trying to persuade Arbitzer to come out here. He was also keeping an eye on the Communists, who were playing some little game of their own. Who killed him I don't know, nor does it particularly matter. Peterson was romantic." Lepkin compressed his lips. It was obvious that he could offer no graver condemnation. "This ridiculous fairy tale about the fox and the tiger, that was typical. Our party was the fox of course, and he meant that we had to be cautious because we worked from weakness instead of from strength. But what a way to put it. Chestertonian!" Lepkin's eyes were cold. "We were cautious enough. Our plan was to help Arbitzer's Social Democrats to take power and then act as a group inside them. Within six months we would have ruled the country. There are not very many of us but we have determination and intelligence. The Social Democrats lack both. But something went wrong, the whole thing was given away to the Communists."

Garden had to stifle a sudden impulse to laugh. *I am a Universal Revolutionary*—he was back in the old days of the Spanish Civil War, the furious internecine struggles, the phrasemongering. "Supporters of Roosevelt are Labor Fascists," "Peace Front the road to War," "Treat the Trotsky-Anarchist as you would a Fascist." Absurd, absurd. Yet here and now, at this time and in this place, was it so absurd? Had it not, in the implacable, intelligent figure of Lepkin, a terrible plausibility?

"We have to begin again," Lepkin was saying. "Now what has happened to Arbitzer?"

"He's dead. At least I think so. He was going to give

himself up. Granz shot him so that he should not stand trial."

"So. Granz then is not such a fool as he looks. How did you get away from Baritsa? What is the little man doing with you, and the girl?"

Garden told him and described Milo's trick with the car. Lepkin shook his head. "Ingenious, yes, but it will not deceive Peplov. He is no fool." Lepkin made this remark, about both Granz and Peplov, in a tone of disdainful superiority, like a schoolmaster applauding the brightest in a class of dullards. "He may be tricked for a little. Then it will occur to him that the food in the car was a blind. If it was a blind, what does it mean? It implies clearly that you were intending to go to the western frontier. The conclusion is then that you mean to do nothing of the sort. What other possibility is there? Why, the river. Peplov finds out what boats were sailing down the Molna that night, and there you are. Your Captain does not sound like the kind of man who holds out under interrogation. The position is not comfortable. I will be frank with you, and say that my position is almost as uncomfortable as yours. You understand that?" Garden felt inclined to say that he was no fool, but he nodded instead. "Prilit is stupid. He is also devoted to me. I make him jump through the hoop, and he loves me for it. But he is not too stupid nor so devoted that he will fail to understand eventually that you came to me expecting help, and that my name is written down in these notes. Within an hour or two the obvious will occur to him, and he will get in touch with the Director-General on his own account.

"What is to be done, then?" Lepkin took a long-tipped Russian cigarette out of a box on the desk and lit it. Garden realized suddenly that the man was actually enjoying the situation. "Shall I give you up? In the case of Milo and Granz that would present little difficulty. They are small fish, nobody would pay much attention to the tale they told. But with you and the girl, who is Arbitzer's niece and also knew Peterson, the case is different. You will betray me under pressure, and that will be the end of me. That will not do. Besides, I should not wish to see you on trial. Your admissions would be damaging."

Lepkin blew a perfect smoke ring. "Shall I have you killed then, you and the girl? Nothing is easier, I assure you. You could be shot trying to escape, a little tablet could be forced down your throat, there are half a dozen other ways. Then I triumphantly present Peplov with Milo and Granz. But that does not solve my problem. If Arbitzer is dead—and if he were alive I should have heard something about his capture—you and the girl are the only ones of any use to them for a trial proving that they have checked an uprising backed by Anglo-American spies. A fine fool I shall look presenting Peplov with the two people he wanted—dead." Lepkin gave a bark of laughter, a logical unamused acknowledgment of comedy of the situation. "Besides there is something else. I wonder if you realize what it is?"

"Prilit."

"Precisely, Prilit." Lepkin looked vaguely surprised and not very pleased, as though a pupil had given a right answer at a wrong time. "There is that cursed Prilit who is going to say: 'Garden came to see District Commander Lepkin because he had his name written down in a little diary. I saw it myself.'

"Then what is the solution? How can I help you and the girl to get away—not because I love you, my friend, I assure you of that, but simply in my own interest?" The whole thing was settled in Lepkin's mind, Garden realized, and any suggestion or interruption would be pointless. "The key to the situation is Prilit. While he survives we are all in danger. Prilit, then, must be eliminated. Listen carefully. I shall give you back your revolver. I shall ask Prilit to bring in the girl. You will

shoot Prilit, and shoot to kill. The sound of a shot is
not unusual here, and there will be no investigation until I order it. This pass will take you out of the building,
together with the girl. Go left when you are outside the
building, and then left again. A hundred yards down the
road you will find the Seven Sisters Hotel. Say that you
come from Joseph and give him this card. He will look
after you until you hear again from me."

Garden took the pass and card. "What about the
others?"

"They must be left. Your escape can be blamed on
Prilit's stupidity, but I cannot let you all go. That would
be too much."

"No."

"Come, Garden, be logical. Have you any other plan
to suggest that will cover your interests and my own?
No? Then what are we arguing about?"

Garden hesitated. "All right. Give me the revolver."

"You are not thinking of playing some trick on me,
I hope." The impersonal eyes behind the rimless glasses
looked at him coldly. "Believe me, you are in no position to play tricks."

"I know that. Give me the revolver."

Still looking hard at Garden, Lepkin wiped the revolver and then handed it to him. Garden broke it, made
sure that it contained six cartridges, and pointed it at
Lepkin. "Tell Prilit to come in and bring all three of
them with him."

Lepkin stared at Garden. "You are a fool."

With a parody of Lepkin's didactic manner, Garden
said, "Not at all. You are mistaken, District Commander Lepkin, in assuming that we have identical interests. If you don't lift the telephone I shall shoot."

The President looked down on them, Stalin stared
across the room. "You are a fool," Lepkin said again.
He picked up the telephone and gave the order, Garden stood at one side of the door. Lepkin said in a stran-

gled voice, "It is essential, Garden, absolutely essential, that Prilit should be eliminated."

"Essential to your safety," Garden said. "But not to mine." It was very simple. When Prilit came in Garden knocked the revolver out of his hand and gave it to Granz. Prilit's mouth made an O of surprise. Without taking his eyes off Lepkin, Garden said, "He wanted me to shoot you, Prilit, while the girl and I got away. Don't worry, I have no intention of doing it."

Prilit seemed not to have heard. He was looking at Lepkin, and there was no change in the fawning devotion of his gaze.

"Prilit," Lepkin said sharply, "go and get him. It is your chance to be a hero."

The little man turned and then jumped without hesitation at Garden. As he did so Lepkin's hand moved to his desk and came out with something shining. Within the endlessly long moment of Prilit's jump there was a fraction of time in which his body was interposed between Lepkin and Garden. This was the moment at which Lepkin shot, throwing himself sideways in the following instant so that he was behind the barricade of the desk.

Prilit gasped, clawed at the air and came down to the floor with a hole in the back of his head. His eyes, open, showed no change in the devotion that had moved him to obey his master's voice. He had died with his illusions about him like a cloak which, Garden reflected afterward, is perhaps as good a way as any to die.

At the moment Garden was conscious only of unreasoning anger. A shot hurriedly fired by Granz at Lepkin had struck the President's picture, which clattered to the floor. Splinters of broken glass covered the carpet. Lepkin was half-hidden by the desk, and as Garden stepped round it he made no attempt to shoot again, but began to say something. Was it another plea for reason and logic? Garden never knew, for he shot Lepkin, as Lepkin had shot Prilit, neatly in the head.

6

There is no chaos like that of a bureaucratic organization deprived of its chief. Had Lepkin been alive he could have picked up the telephone on his desk and ordered their arrest. In that case they would probably never have reached the outer hall. With Lepkin and Prilit dead, there was nobody to issue orders. Garden showed the pass and they strolled calmly out under the eyes of the guards.

"We have a minute or two before they give the alarm," Garden said. "And even then they don't know who we are. We have a chance, especially if we split up. Ilona and I, Theo and—" He looked at the other two, remembering the scene in the cabin.

"That is all right," Granz said. He patted Milo's shoulder. "But we must have a place to meet."

"Three miles from here on the coast, a fishing village called Zeb." Milo chuckled at the surprise on their faces. "I told you I had a friend. A real friend, not like your Lepkin. He is a fisherman named Poltzer, he lives in a pinkwashed house on the left-hand side at the end of the village furthest from here. I have a little idea this Poltzer may help us."

"A boat?"

"Perhaps, perhaps. Who knows but he might be our pilot, if we paid him enough. He too would like to see Arsenal play Manchester United. Meet there tonight at nine o'clock."

"Tonight, nine o'clock, the village of Zeb, at the house of Poltzer the fisherman."

"Until then, good luck." For a moment they were all standing on the corner of the Street of the October

Revolution, the decorous shabbily dressed crowds eddying round them. For a moment Garden saw their faces, fixed in expressions that he remembered ever afterward, Milo's nut brown and wrinkled, set in his determined smile, Granz with thick brows drawn together over dark and puzzled eyes. Then they had crossed the street and were walking away together, a big lumbering man and a little perky one, looking like thousands of big and little men all over the world. As they went the overcast skies broke. Rain spattered down in large drops, making dark blobs on the pavement.

"What are we going to do now?" Garden noticed absently that some of the old hostility was back in the girl's voice.

"I don't know. I'm not sure that we ought to get out of here. That's just what they'll expect us to do. Within a couple of hours they will realize just who it was that escaped from police headquarters. They will expect us to leave the town. It might be a good idea to stay if we can find a bolt-hole." He stopped outside a shabby building with dirty windows. It was the Seven Sisters Hotel. "Lepkin told me to come here. Do you think we should take a chance on it?"

She shrugged her thin shoulders. "Why ask me? You were very good at shooting Lepkin back there. You will know whether to take his advice about a place to stay."

The immediate past had already become utterly remote in Garden's mind. Was it really true that, for the first time in years, he had killed a man? Why had he done it? For reasons that had seemed extraordinarily cogent at the time, but were now as fantastic as the whole scene in the office. It was in a dream, surely, that all these things had happened. Or was that dream, as he had been told very long ago, reality itself, a terrible rending of the veils of falsity through which we generally look at life? And in the dream that was reality, surely the death of Lepkin had been urgently necessary?

Out of such reflections he produced the words, "It was necessary."

"It was necessary," she mocked him. "To you killing is always necessary. I said nothing would come of this but killing."

Garden came back suddenly into the world in which he was being hunted by the People's Police. A voice boomed his Christian name. Turning round, he saw Trelawney. His hand was vigorously pumped.

"Haven't seen you for years, old man. What are you doing? Marvelous country, isn't it? But what filthy weather. This your wife? Come along and meet the boys and girls." Garden allowed himself to be borne along on what he remembered as a typically Trelawneyan flood of ejaculatory eloquence into a building three doors away which had once been a church and was now, he saw, the local Museum of Revolutionary History. Inside two or three small knots of people, each piloted by a voluble English-speaking Dravinian, looked at relics of the new history—the paper once edited in exile by the President, the letters exchanged by the Foreign Secretary and Stalin on the Nationalities question, a reconstruction of the President's escape from a Royalist prison in the thirties, a great mass of material about the Peasant Rising of 1875 when thousands of countrymen armed with clubs and farm implements had been mowed down by a crack Guards Division. The history of the last few years remained undocumented, no doubt, Garden thought, because it was subject to such a rapid process of change. He reflected also that in a sense the Museum of Revolutionary History had changed its religious character remarkably little. The relics were here, although they were not the same relics; and, as always, the older they were, the safer and the more holy. As always, too, the relics produced a strong emotional effect—voices were hushed, the demeanor of the worshipers had a proper reverence. The enthusiasm of Trelawney, however, was only slightly damped by the reverential atmosphere. In a loud whisper he told Garden of the splendid tour they were having under the auspices of some Friendship Society or another, of the enthusiasm of the workers, of the new housing projects, and the spread of education.

In an anteroom they drank glasses of lemonade and ate little cakes. Trelawney talked on with undiminished zest, blowing a fine spray of spittle toward them. How was it possible to make use of Trelawney? Garden remembered him as a kind of ideal Left Book Club figure of the thirties. He was a tall, thin, raw-boned man with a prominent Adam's apple, who always wore sports jackets with sleeves that were slightly too short. In moments of excitement, and Trelawney was often excited, the sleeves shot up to show hairy reddish wrists. Trelawney was an accountant with a passion for statistics. He read almost all of the Left Book Club publications, but the ones he enjoyed most were those that told him by what percentage Russian production of pig iron had increased in the past year or how quickly the Soviet transport system had been unified. "I like something I can get my teeth into," Trelawney would say with a grin that showed great horselike yellow fangs that could champ through an economic survey or an analysis of the Corporate state in a couple of hours. Trelawney was also interested in art and literature. "A fine old argy-bargy we had the other night," he would say, puffing at his pipe. "Social realism versus formal expression. I don't pretend to be an artistic chap, but I can see what they mean about the decadence of formalism. Take Eisenstein now—" Or Trelawney would take Stravinsky or Proust or Joyce or Swift or Michelangelo, and repeat the latest judgment on them that he had been reading in *International Literature* or *Left Review*. Perhaps he had never read a page of Proust or Joyce, never looked at a Michelangelo reproduction (for art, as he readily admitted, was not really his cup of tea); that was of much less importance to Trelawney than getting the right outlook on books and pictures. And once you had the right outlook, once you had realized that Proust and Joyce were typical figures of the bourgeois decadence, why then there was no point in reading them anyway.

Trelawney, in fact, was a perfect specimen of his kind. He was just good enough to be true. And with it all, Trelawney was really rather a nice fellow, generous and often spontaneously kind. Spontaneous kindness, however, would hardly extend to helping the enemies of the Republic. If Trelawney saw that photograph, would he recognize it?

How was it possible to make use of Trelawney? Garden tapped his bony knee. "I'm here on a sort of semi-official mission," he said. "The name's Charles Rose."

Trelawney gave a great horselike guffaw and a prodigious wink. "I understand, old boy. Gone native a bit in dress, hasn't he, Miss—"

"Just call her Ilona," Garden said.

A formidable-looking gray-haired woman with a large flat white face advanced on them, preceded by breasts that jutted forward and upward rather like a large sloping shelf. This was Lady Violet Wythe-Watling, secretary of the Friendship Society and in charge of the touring party. Trelawney introduced Charlie Rose, an old friend of his, a progressive here for a holiday.

Lady Violet listened, frowning. "A *holiday*," she said with some disgust. "Alone?"

"This is my fiancée Ilona. She is Rumanian," Garden added, to avert awkward questions about nationality.

Lady Violet thawed perceptibly. A Rumanian girl, in these circumstances, was obviously a good card to play. "Not much point in going round on your own. That's what *he's* been doing the past day or two, seeing friends in the north." Her frowning gaze was bent upon the impervious Trelawney. "Bit antisocial. Better join our party, guinea a day all found, and see everything." She whisked out like a conjurer three typed sheets which, Garden saw without surprise, covered every hour of the day for a three weeks' tour. "Might help to keep Trelawney in line. He's got no more sense of direction than a child, missed a splendid performance of local ballet last night."

Trelawney wriggled uncomfortably. "What time's lunch, Lady Vi? I'm so hungry I could eat a horse."

Lady Vi fixed him with a steely glance. "Breakfast was perfectly adequate for those of normal appetite. Lunch will be at one o'clock."

"Roll on, one o'clock," said Trelawney. To Garden he showed a characteristic officious friendliness. He arranged about rooms for them at the hotel, lent Garden his razor and a new blade, and looked critically at his clothes. "A bit Bohemian, old man," he said. "You look as if you'd just changed clothes with the captain of a tramp steamer. Haven't you got anything else?" Garden said that their luggage was following.

When they were upstairs Ilona said, "I hope you know what you're doing. If one of them recognizes you from that photograph—"

Garden was slightly irritable. "Of course I don't know what I'm doing. It takes us off the streets, that's all, and gives us the cover of a crowd. We have to take a chance on the photograph." He smelt himself disgustedly. "I wish I had some different clothes."

They ate lunch with the rest of the party at the Traveller's Hotel. The meat was unidentifiable, but it was well cooked. It was served with salad, and followed by a good local cheese. Trelawney created a stir by demanding potatoes. There were hurried consultations at the back of the room. At last potato salad was offered to him.

"I wanted fried potatoes," Trelawney shouted. He seemed really annoyed.

Lady Violet called sharply across the table, "Trelawney. You know what the harvest figures were like here last year."

Trelawney snapped to, as it were, emotional attention at this mention of scarce *figures*. "The harvest figures, yes. Very bad because of the drought. The number of hectares of—"

"Precisely. The harvest was the worst for many years. All the crops suffered. Potatoes are reserved for heavy workers."

Trelawney subsided. Amused glances were cast up and down the table. The little man with buck teeth and horn-rimmed glasses on Garden's right said, "He really is a card, you know. Never minds speaking out, always says what he things. We all of us do that, of course, don't think I mean anything else, but Trelawney—well, he's a card and that's all there is to it." The little man launched on a sea of personal reminiscence. His name was Dwiggins, and he was a chemist in a large engineering works just outside Manchester. He had come on this tour with Mrs. Dwiggins—here a little woman in a peasant smock sitting on Dwiggins's right suddenly revealed herself, smirked, and disappeared again behind Dwiggins—for educational purposes. They had come to see revolutionary socialism in action. Garden nodded.

"But have we seen it? I'm rather doubtful. Do you read the papers?"

Garden felt a chill of alarm. "Just a few words."

"My wife has a certain—ahem—proficiency in the language." Mrs. Dwiggins appeared again, smirked, bowed her head slightly in ladylike acknowledgment of this recognition of her accomplishment, and disappeared. "Only one or two others in our party have it. She has been reading the reports of this rising, this conspiracy against the government. Lady Vi insists of course that it is nothing, the plot of a handful of bandits, but I'm not so sure. We've seen things even here in Dravina that, quite frankly, I didn't like." Very solemnly Mr. Dwiggins said, "I wonder whether we are not being influenced by propaganda."

They drank coffee, real coffee, Garden noticed. But it was quite natural—even a good thing perhaps—that real coffee should be offered to tourist parties. Dwiggins leaned over and whispered in Garden's ear. It was plain that he was anxious not to be overheard. "I am convinced that there is a kind of—State police. The country seems in fact to be a sort of—dictatorship."

Garden said nothing. At his left side he could sense Ilona sitting up straight, tense with alarm.

Trelawney pushed his long neck across the table. "Dwiggins, old boy, there's a treat in store for you. Inspection of the Dravina Car Works this afternoon. Got the details here. Working from an American Ford prototype, they've produced a car which—"

Dwiggins coughed. "Not quite in my line, I'm afraid. I'm a chemist, not an engineer."

"Good for you, old man." Again Trelawney showed his strong yellow teeth in a great laugh, as though this were a tremendous joke. Then he became intensely serious. "But my word, whatever you are, it's grand to see a real constructive job going on in a socialist country, isn't it?" There was a murmur of agreement with these unimpeachable sentiments from those still at the table. "At the end of the war the factory started production. Now just listen to these figures. Take 1946 as the norm and the production in 1947 was a hundred and eighty per cent of the norm, in 1948 three hundred and fifty per cent, in 1949 seven hundred and seventy per cent. Do you know what it is now? *Over three thousand five hundred per cent.*"

A round-faced man smoking a pipe and wearing baggy plus fours said, with a trace of Yorkshire in his speech, "Depends a bit on the original norm, doesn't it?"

"There's too much emphasis always, in my humble opinion, on the American prototype, as though people here had to rely on the Americans for construction of their cars." This came from a tall, thin, nervous man with a face furrowed by years of agonized thought. A chorus of "Hear hears" went round the table, but they seemed somehow not quite wholehearted.

Trelawney was delighted. "But the whole point is how much improvement has been effected on the prototype. This car does fifty-three miles to the gallon with a maximum of sixty-three miles an hour, an increase on the prototype of thirty per cent in m.p.g. and forty-seven per cent in—"

"I stick to the point," said the thin nervous man. "To talk so much about the prototype is virtually to accuse the people here of lacking original engineering capacity."

"I'm only quoting the figures they give themselves, old man," Trelawney said mildly.

"And I say that the emphasis on the prototype is an insult to national prestige," said the thin man. A slight hubbub ensued through which there emerged the voice of the man wearing plus fours:

"I still say it would be interesting to know the original norm of 1946." Nobody took much notice of this, but his next words produced a sudden silence round the table. "And it would be interesting to know the effect on production of all the recent arrests that we have seen."

"Hear hear," said Dwiggins unexpectedly.

The thin man turned on him savagely. "If you are referring to the recent attempt by bandits to sabotage socialist production I must say that I am surprised you should think—"

"Come on now, Moxon," said the man with plus fours. "That was no sabotage. You saw what happened as well as me. Men taken away from their homes, beaten up by the police, wives and children crying."

"I suppose saboteurs don't possess wives and children, Bridgewater?"

"Course they can do. But these were ordinary workers, pulled out of their beds in the middle of the night. They weren't plotters."

Moxon put his thin head on one side. "You speak the language here, I suppose, Bridgewater?"

"You know I don't, any more than you do. Don't need to when you see police using force on workers. I know which side I'm on then, Moxon. I'm with the workers. What about you?"

Moxon hunched his shoulders, rolled his eyes alarmingly, and murmured "Petty bourgeois opportunism."

"Call it what you like. Shall I tell you what I think?"

"Oh, by all means tell us what you think. I am sure it will be most instructive."

"I think this is nothing more nor less than a police state." Bridgewater knocked out his pipe defiantly. "And I should very much like to know the actual production figures in 1946 of this factory we're going to see. But I doubt they'll be available."

Trelawney made uneasy flapping gestures with his long arms. The sleeves of his sports jacket shot back showing the hairy red wrists. "Moxon and Bridgewater, break it up now. There's nothing I like more than a good old argy-bargy, but you can go too far. Here comes Lady Vi," he said with relief.

Lady Vi surged forward, booming out suggestions that had the force of commands. "Three o'clock at the Dravina Engineering Works. The Tourist Bureau has thoughtfully provided a coach. Just twenty minutes to spare, time for a wash and brush up."

"Lady Vi." The voice belonged to little Dwiggins. "My wife has rather a headache. We've done a lot of sight-seeing in the past week. We should like, if you don't mind, to be excused this afternoon."

"Say it out straight, man," said Bridgewater encouragingly. "You don't want to see this factory, that's it, isn't it? And I must say I agree with you, I'm not much inclined for the trip myself. All right then, we're all paying our way and there'll be no offense taken. Isn't that so, Lady Vi?"

Lady Vi, however, seemed to think that offense would certainly be taken, and that even if it were not taken an undoubted slight would have been put upon their hosts. Her flat face showed some sign of emotion as she spoke of the trusting confidence with which their hosts had made these arrangements, of the modest pride they had felt in showing the achievements of their people to friends from another country. And now what happened? A slap in the face from a section of the party (for half a dozen others had now indicated that they would prefer to walk about the town, or even sit in their rooms, rather than look at the factory). Their hosts extended the right hand of friendship, said Lady Vi, and received a slap in the face by way of return. Some people were too tired, or too bored, or too little interested in the achievements of a socialist country, to be able to spare time to look round a factory working in the service of the people instead of for private profit. . . .

As Lady Vi waxed strong, so the resistance of her listeners wilted. At last only the Dwigginses and Bridgewater remained recalcitrant, and determined to spend the afternoon on their own. Garden wondered why Lady Vi was so concerned that everybody should visit the factory, and decided that it was because of the recent troubles. The seeds of disaffection were obviously present in the party already, and one or two more incidents might mean the failure of the tour.

"Mr. Rose." Garden came out of his reverie with a jerk. "You and your friend are not, strictly speaking, members of our party, but if you would care to take two of the vacant places—"

Garden hesitated. By going with the party they would

preserve their cloak of collective anonymity. By staying at the hotel they would obtain seclusion and a precious rest, but they would offend Lady Vi. He was about to say that they would go, when Ilona decided for him.

"If you please, would you excuse us. I am so tired— we traveled most of last night and had very little sleep. And I am sure Charles is tired too. It is not that we lack enthusiasm." She gave a shy smile to Lady Vi, who received it with comparative graciousness, and to Trelawney, who responded with a toothy grin.

Five minutes later they were in Ilona's bedroom, which was large and furnished with light oak furniture that bore a strong resemblance to English utility. A private bathroom was attached. "I found this on my plate while we were having coffee," she said.

It was a slip of paper, printed in capitals, which said: DO NOT GO TO THE FACTORY. STAY IN THIS AFTERNOON. WAIT FOR INSTRUCTIONS.

Garden read it with astonishment. Someone in the party, then, knew their identities and was prepared to help them. "How did it get on your plate?"

"I don't know. A waiter must have put it there I suppose. I saw it suddenly, a little screwed-up piece of paper. Or it could have been flicked across somehow. I don't know and I don't much care. I'm going to have a bath." She went into the bathroom and came back in a moment wrinkling her nose in disgust. "I might have known it. The water is not hot. In hotels like this it used to be hot."

Garden was quite unreasonably annoyed. "Since then they have had a war and a revolution. You might remember that."

She shrugged her thin shoulders. "The water used to come out hot, steaming hot, the moment you turned on the tap. Now it is filthy tepid stuff that leaks out thinly and meanly. There's your revolution, that's what you've been working for all your life—no hot water and an efficient secret police." She began to laugh.

"Stop it," Garden shouted. "Stop it." In a paroxysm of anger and love he gripped the shoulders that seemed to melt into nothingness under his large hands. They fell heavily onto the bed together and he saw her face beneath him pale and bloodless, eyes closed, mouth like a red flower. She remained in this passive attitude, allowing him to do whatever he wished, during the moments that followed. It was like making love to a statue, Garden thought, and tried furiously to bring the statue to Galatean life. But in this he failed, except that once she moaned faintly and passed her hand over the short crisp hair at the back of his head; and at last she subdued him (as he felt) to her own passivity and he lay quietly on top of her, a mere weight. Her eyes opened and looked at him with no expression.

"That wasn't very good. I'm sorry," she said, and slid herself away from beneath him. Her body, half-dressed, looked unformed and childish as she walked to the bathroom. Garden heard the sound of running water. Then her head peered round the door, suddenly gleeful. "The water's hot."

"The water's hot," Garden echoed.

"You don't know what a difference it makes. I was dying for a bath." She came up to him and put her hands on his shoulders. "I really do care about things. And about you too. Who do you think sent that note?"

"I think Milo or Theo must have got it to us from outside, through a waiter. Otherwise it was somebody in the party, but goodness knows who." Garden stifled a yawn. He felt immensely tired.

"Go and lie down in your room. I'll come to see you when I've finished."

His room was next door to hers, with a communicating door. It contained exactly similar furniture, two single beds, a wash basin. He crossed to the window, pulled up the Venetian blinds, and looked out upon the Bay of Dravina, with a few fishing boats in harbor, and the water gray and desolate under slanting rain. In a full-length glass on the wall he saw his own reflection, and laughed aloud. This clownish figure in a seaman's cast-off clothes certainly looked quite unlike Garden the night watchman, or for that matter Garden the guerrilla fighter in the photograph. "Garden the knock-about performer," he said, pulling off his boots, taking off the dirty wadded coat. "Garden the hunted man." He sank onto the bed, which was cool and comfortable, and a phrase came into his mind. He stretched to grasp it, but could never quite manage to do so. The phrase turned strangely into something tangible, something opalescent and shining, a stone perhaps, in whose depths could be discovered an image of satisfied desire. He remembered, or imagined, some lines of poetry lucidly burning:

> This image salvaged from futility,
> A warm bronze body by a waveless sea.
> Breasts, belly, tapered legs fulfill a dream
> Of sensuality, the red lips seem,
> Though silent, to be moving longingly. . . .

"The waveless sea," he said, "The waveless sea"; and sank down into it.

7

He woke feeling cold, and with a sick certainty of catastrophe. At first it seemed this was connected with his own body—he was paralyzed, perhaps, or tied to the bed. Staring up at the white ceiling he cautiously moved arms and legs, and was happy to find them in working order. Something pressed urgently against the small of his back—what was it? He flung himself to one side and

clapped one hand to his back. Of course, the revolver!
Still only half-awake he rolled off the bed and sat on the
edge of it, rubbing his eyes with his fists. His watch said
six fifteen. He had been asleep for more than three hours.

The note lay underneath the door, at the edge of the
thin carpet. It was typed on a sheet of ruled lines, perhaps torn from an exercise book, and it said: "Go with
the party this evening to the Cultural Reception. Leave
at ten o'clock. Go with the girl down to the Riva Dock.
A man wearing a yachting cap will be waiting. Say to
him in English, 'A fine night.' He will reply, 'The water
is smooth.' Then follow his directions."

Garden stared at the note, unable to take in its meaning. Obviously it came from a friend—anyone else would
simply have turned him over to the police. But what
stopped this friend from revealing himself? Since so
many conflicting interests were apparently at work,
could this be some kind of trap to place him in the
hands, say, of one of Lepkin's associates? Holding the
note in his hand he went over to the communicating
door and turned the handle. It was locked. "Ilona," he
called. There was no reply. He knocked gently, but
heard nothing. He ran out into the corridor and opened
the door of her bedroom from there. The room was
empty.

Advancing into the room with the probing step of one
who looks for a mine under every floorboard, Garden
went into the bathroom, opened a cupboard, even
peeped under the bed. Ilona was not there, and it was
as though she had never been there. The room, bare
and cold, contained no trace of her presence—but what
could she have left, when she had brought no luggage?
Something, surely, he thought as he looked round the
empty room, something should remain to record the fact
that only a few hours ago in this room they had argued
and he had pushed her onto the bed and they had made
love. But the bed cover was smooth, no pots stood on

the dressing table, there was nothing to say whether she had gone of her free will or been taken by force.

He stepped out into the corridor again and came face to face with a dark paunchy man who had been sitting near to him at luncheon. The man smiled, showing a set of perfect false teeth, and stuck out his hand. "Ah, we met at lunch. My name's Belton, John Belton of the A.G.W.P." There was a kind of nervous expectancy about the man. Garden nodded and moved to return to his room. "Ah, could I have a word with you privately." His false teeth clicked decisively. Unwillingly Garden led the way into his bedroom, putting the note into his trouser pocket.

The man offered a packet of cigarettes with a hand that shook slightly. He seemed at a loss how to begin. "What is the A.G.W.P.?" Garden asked, and it was as though a floodgate had been opened.

"The A.G.W.P. is the Amalgamated Groups for World Peace. Don't confuse us, please, with any of these so-called 'Peace Movements' which are really Communist organizations. We believe in world peace through absolute nonresistance to aggression on the part of all who are called to fight. My position with the party here is a semiofficial one. The group sent me to report on the situation in this country, and the chances of establishing a Peace Group here which could work effectively with Peace Groups in Western Europe." He gulped and then said with a sudden clash of teeth, "They chose me, you see, because I speak the language. And of course I am one of our permanent officials."

Garden said nothing. Belton puffed quickly at his cigarette. "I speak the language." He puffed again. "I read the papers."

"What are you trying to say?"

"They say in the papers that an Englishman is behind this, ah, plot. A guerrilla leader during the war, or as they say now a spy who was placed in the guerrilla organization. They are looking for him."

Garden said impatiently, "What has all this got to do with me? My name is Charles Rose, and I am on holiday here with a friend."

There were beads of perspiration on Belton's forehead. His teeth clicked so loudly that they seemed about to fall from his mouth. He said apologetically, "No. Your name is Charles Garden. We met several times at Victims of Fascism Committee meetings before the war. You don't remember me, perhaps, but I knew you as soon as I saw you. I never forget a face." The man said proudly, "Although I shouldn't have recognized that photograph in the paper. And I was over here just before the end of the war driving a Peace Ambulance. I heard a good deal about you then."

The Victims of Fascism Committee—had this man been on it? Well, perhaps. It was all so long ago. Looking at the weak and nervous face which seemed to him perfectly unfamiliar Garden said calmly, "You've made a mistake. My name is Rose. I don't speak the language. And I don't understand at all what you're getting at."

"Garden is the man they're after. I knew that as soon as I read the papers, and then there's the photograph. They haven't named him yet, but that's because they never do name people until they've got hold of them. They want him for trial. Tortures, intimidation. They'll make him admit things." Belton crushed out the stub of his cigarette. "I recognized you the moment I saw you. And it's obvious anyway as soon as you put two and two together. Those queer clothes you're wearing, and no luggage."

Belton might be highly nervous, but he was not unobservant. "Our luggage is following on," Garden said, but the words so easily accepted by Trelawney sounded altogether false. "Supposing this fantastic story of yours were true, supposing I really were the man Garden, what then?"

"Then don't you see, you must go away at once."

"But we've only just joined this little group. I'm going to stay for a few days."

"I won't permit it." The teeth clicked, Belton's eyes watered with indignation. He dabbed at them hastily with a handkerchief. "They'll arrest you, within a few hours they are certain to find you, and then they will arrest us too. We shall be subjected to indignities, brutalities, perhaps torture. Innocent people, you are sacrificing them—us. Why should we be a sacrifice to your lust for power? I won't permit it, I say." The teeth clattered, the thin voice rose. "You will leave today and this woman of yours too, or I shall—I shall—"

Why, Garden thought with a shock of surprise, the man's afraid for his own skin. "You will inform the People's Police, will you, and give me up? That would be an act in the interest of peace, no doubt, a perfect example of nonresistance to aggression."

"You think I'm a coward, well perhaps I am. I've got a wife at home, she's delicate, any shock to her—if I were arrested—I couldn't afford to risk it. But it's in your own interest too. It's no good staying here. If I've recognized you somebody else will too. What about that man Trelawney? Surely he remembers you."

"He remembers that my name is Charles Rose, and you would be well advised to remember it too." Garden deliberately took the revolver out of his pocket and balanced it on his palm. "I may have some kind of unofficial mission over here. Trelawney believes that, I don't see why you shouldn't believe it. If, on the other hand, you insist that I am the man Garden, I should think you would feel rather uncomfortable. From what you tell me, Garden must be desperate. I doubt if he believes, like you, in absolute nonresistance to aggression."

"You think I'm a coward." Belton put both hands over his paunch. "But I'm thinking of others, I tell you, not myself."

"If I were really Garden, do you know what I should do?" Garden pulled Belton forward by his shirt. Belton's body quivered with fear. His arms hung down by his side. "I should hit you over the head with this revolver, knowing that you would offer no resistance. Then I should break your neck, which is a simple trick taught to every young soldier in unarmed combat training. Then I should toss your body over the balcony there, thirty feet down to the paving stones. I doubt if the doctors here would feel fussy over the means by which an English member of the A.G.W.P. met his death. Isn't it lucky for you that I am simply Charles Rose, a harmless tourist. Don't you agree?" He released Belton, who staggered back against the wall and stayed there, tie pulled to one side, presenting an appearance at once pitiable and unpleasant, like a half-crushed spider. "To relieve your anxiety, let me say that I have changed my mind about staying with this band of brothers. You and I are—what shall I say?—not in perfect sympathy. By tomorrow morning I shall be gone." If one was going in for this kind of cloak and dagger stuff one might as well, Garden thought, do it wholeheartedly. "I needn't say that a man like Garden has his friends. Anyone who informed on him would be a bad insurance risk." The revolver was still in his hand. He looked at it absently and put it back in his hip pocket.

Cautiously Belton straightened his tie and, skirting Garden, moved toward the door. Two feet away from it he stopped. "I have your word that you will leave by tomorrow morning?"

Garden nodded. Feelings of sickness and self-disgust overwhelmed him.

"Then I shall do nothing. Please don't think I'm intimidated by your words. I know my duty, I hope I know my duty, and if it were necessary I would pass on the information in my possession to the authorities. But I have no wish to injure anybody in your difficult position."

"Get out."

"I wish I could convince you that I have at heart only the communal interest—"

"Oh, get out, get out." Garden stood up. Belton had the door open, and was outside it in a moment. Garden began to laugh. He stopped when he reflected upon his own behavior. Could he have done anything more foolish than to frighten Belton, and then let him go free? Was not the course of action with which he had threatened him a perfectly logical one? What foolish vacillation, what imaginary moral barrier, had led him to watch Belton walking out of the room carrying his destructive germ of knowledge, when he had justified the hole made in Lepkin's head with three simple words: *It was necessary?*

And where was Ilona? As this thought throbbed in his mind, Garden became aware that he was not alone. Trelawney stood in the doorway, teeth drawn back in a grin, long arm extended toward the light switch. The room was bathed in mild yellow light and Trelawney advanced toward him arms swinging. "What's wrong, old man? You look a bit down in the mouth. Luggage not got here yet?" Trelawney's eyes, which somehow gave the impression of being set very loosely in his head, looked curiously round the room. "Been to the station?"

"I've been asleep. How was the factory?"

"Terrific, wonderful spirit the workers have got. Another year or two, and they'll really have the cars rolling off the line." Trelawney spoke a little absently. "Lady Vi wasn't too pleased by the absenteeism this afternoon. Solidarity's the thing, you know. Crack solidarity and you've got a split, and we all know what a split means. You'd better come to the reception tonight."

"All right."

"Trouble is, clothes. Frankly, old man, you can't come in those things. They just wouldn't understand, they attach a lot of importance to these dos, there might be an incident. Anyway Lady Vi would bite your ears off. Hate dressing up myself, but I shall have to wear my one and only suit. We'd better try and do a spot of borrowing." Trelawney hesitated. "Nothing else worrying you, is there, old man? If it's the old incog, don't disturb yourself. Mum's the word as far as I'm concerned. I remember you were over here doing a job years ago, isn't that so? Of course, any beans you feel you can spill without upsetting the apple cart . . ."

Garden felt somewhat cheered. Trelawney was really such a very fine specimen. "I'm sorry," he said solemnly. "If I could tell you anything I would. Officially I've got no standing at all, I don't exist. But there are occasions, if you understand me, when an unofficial figure is less compromising than an official one if things go wrong." All this had its miserable truth, he reflected.

"Yes." Trelawney leaned forward, eyes rolling.

"This spot of bother has messed things up a bit." With astonishment he heard himself using such Trelawneyan language. "It's made my position a bit awkward in one way and another. Frankly I was pretty glad to join up with you and no questions asked."

"I get you, Charles."

Garden warmed to his work. "I'm expecting a message from someone connected with the Foreign Ministry here—let's call him X. If everything goes well he will arrange a meeting with his superior—and I'll leave you to guess who *that* is."

"A nod's as good as a wink to a blind horse," said Trelawney.

"And when I get the signature of the gentleman concerned on a piece of paper, I shall go back by private plane." Garden wished this were true. "Lord knows what it may mean in the way of additional productive capacity if *certain things are agreed*," he added, with what he felt immediately as too high a comic flight.

It seemed that no flight could be too high. "Old man, I appreciate your confidence." Trelawney's horse face was preternaturally solemn. "And if there's anything I can do I shall be proud."

"If I have to leave suddenly I may ask your help."

"Anything, old man, anything."

They should have clinked glasses, Garden felt. Instead they shook hands.

The door opened and Ilona came in with a large parcel in her arms. "Clothes, clothes, any old clothes for the rag and bone man," she called. Then she saw Trelawney and her face went crimson.

"I've told Trelawney about our mission," Garden said hurriedly. "He's going to borrow some clothes for me."

"Not necessary," she cried triumphantly. "I got some. I even got some brown paper, which was more difficult. Look." She took out of the parcel a shoddy-looking new brown suit, a striped shirt, and a blue frock.

"Where did you get them?" Garden asked sharply. "What about coupons?"

She snapped her fingers. "Money talks louder than coupons, here and everywhere else." She held up the brown suit against Garden. "I had to guess your size, but it's not bad. What's the matter?"

Trelawney said heartily, "You've saved me from doing a borrowing act. We're all meeting downstairs in half an hour to go to the reception. See you then."

"Just a minute." Trelawney turned at the door. Garden hung the trousers of the brown suit against his legs so that they looked inches short. "Will you see if you can do that borrowing act after all? I think I'm going to look a scarecrow in these clothes. I'm six foot tall, thirteen and a half stone."

"I'll see what I can do." In Trelawney's glance there

was something shrewd, appraising, or perhaps approving. Then he was out of the door and the girl was in tears, beating at him with her fists, asking why he would not wear the clothes, crying out that he wanted to humiliate her.

Garden caught hold of her hands. "You've been very foolish. Listen while I try to explain. Why did you go out alone without saying anything to me?"

"You were asleep. I knew you needed fresh clothes, and so did I. I wanted to surprise you."

"Don't you realize that they're searching for us throughout this town? That one of the things they'll look out for is that we may need some new clothing? It would have been risky enough to buy clothes if you had got hold of some coupons. To go into a national store and pay double the price—is that what you did?" She nodded. "You must have been crazy."

She began to cry again. The door opened, a hairy arm was thrust round it, a voice said, "Togs." The togs were a gray suit with a chalk stripe and a plain blue shirt, both unmistakably English. Garden tried them on and found that they fitted him fairly well. He rolled up the brown suit and put it in a cupboard.

Ilona stared with longing at the cheap frock. "Am I not to wear the frock? It is a standard production, many thousands like them."

"No."

"Then I cannot go. These are filthy and there is no time to wash them." She fingered the blouse and skirt distastefully. "I should look more conspicuous in them than in the frock. But you say no. Very well, I stay here."

"You know damned well you can't stay here. All right, wear the frock, perhaps it doesn't matter. It's really me they want, not you."

"Thank you, thank you." The sudden gaiety of her mood delighted him. He showed her the note which had been pushed under the door. She was utterly bewildered by it. "Then there must be somebody else who is trying to help us. Who can it be?"

"Some British agent, perhaps. Or more likely one of the little sects like Lepkin's, who'd like to use me as some kind of lever against the government."

She slipped the new frock over her head. "How do I look?"

"Delightful."

"But what shall we do? Meet Milo and Theo at nine o'clock or these people at ten?"

Garden told her.

8

The reception given by the Dravina Trades and Artists Co-operative was held in the Union Hall. It followed a well-known pattern. First the introduction of local figures, and conversation through interpreters. Trelawney was particularly strong here, pouring out a barrage of the right kind of questions. It seemed that there were now twenty-seven literary societies in the province compared with five before the Revolution, eighteen ballet companies instead of two, thirty-five dramatic societies instead of six. Nearly a thousand poems had been submitted from the province for the great national poetry awards. "Song of the Socialist Fatherland" and "Hymn to the Revolution" had been awarded prizes. Trelawney grinned round triumphantly with his yellow teeth, and the rest of the company were plainly impressed. They were right to be impressed, Garden thought, and wondered why he was not more impressed himself. This was part of the ideal for which he had worked, a people's spontaneous expression of feeling about the new society they had created. There could be no doubt of the enthusiasm and sincerity of the prize-winners, who talked volubly in a manner that received scant justice from the translators, who rendered a three-minute speech with the phrase "I agree with you entirely," or "I wanted to express the feelings of the people in our beautiful valley." What was it that made the proceedings seem somehow a travesty of all that he believed in? Or was it simply that he no longer believed?

After the conversation the younger of the two poets, a young man with a fine leonine head unsupported by a chin declaimed the "Song of the Socialist Fatherland" for nearly half an hour. This time there was no translation, and some of the company showed signs of restlessness. This poem, again, was like many Garden had heard before. He translated passages in his mind:

My comrades, when the iron heel of the invader
Pressed deep upon our country mercilessly crushing
Our youth, our children, mothers of unborn socialist
warriors,
Who was it said: "They shall not conquer, they shall
never conquer"?
When bosses and landowners ran away
Who stayed to fight?
Who but the people, the real people of our country,
Trodden by the jackboot, beaten by whips,
Imprisoned, enslaved.
Who but the people broke the iron shackles,
Rising triumphant and glorious at last?

Garden thought, I seem to perceive traces of nationalist deviation. Then he reproached himself for cynicism. Ilona stood stiffly by his side.

After the recital a buffet supper, which Garden saw with relief was ample. He ate three different kinds of salt fish, a plate of cold meat, and what appeared to be hot chicken patties with cheese. Then he felt very thirsty and, with an awareness of his own unwisdom, drank several glasses of sweet, strong local wine. Lády Vi came up to him. "Magnificent, our poet, was he not?"

Garden gulped chicken patty. "Superb."

"Such feeling."

"Such power."

"—rhythm—"

"—sincerity—"

Lady Vi looked at him suspiciously. *Sincerity*, plainly, was a thing she preferred to have taken for granted. "We missed you this afternoon. I hope you will be with us tomorrow."

Garden bowed his head graciously. He felt a little drunk. He made his way across the room to where Belton stood sipping uneasily at a glass still almost full. "Belton!" Garden dug him suddenly in the stomach. "I am still here, you see. Have you denounced me yet?" Belton looked terrified. Garden wagged a finger. "You have not. My agents have reported half-hourly on your movements. Your word is your bond, Belton. And so is mine. Your sinister slogan is safe with me. Do you know what it is? It's a wise peacemonger who knows his own slogan. Your slogan is *Peace through Nonaggressive War*. Let nonaggression be victorious, eh, Belton?"

After supper there was a cinema show. They went into another room and sat down on hard chairs. A newsreel showing Soviet athletes was followed by a historical film about the lubricous lives of monks and nuns in prerevolutionary days, and the power insidiously exercised by the Catholic Church. Garden closed his eyes, then opened them and looked at his watch. The time was half-past eight. He pressed Ilona's arm. She got up and went out. After a few seconds Garden followed her. He tripped over a foot on the way. It was Trelawney's.

"Old boy," a voice hissed in the darkness. "Where are you going?"

"Out for a leak, old boy."

"Oh ah."

Ilona was waiting outside the Union Hall. They boarded a tram that took them to the outskirts of the town, within half a mile of Zeb. It had been, after all, perfectly easy to get away. But sitting in the tram as it jolted through the old city over cobbles, past drinking shops in dimly lighted streets, Garden was aware of a profound unease. The people in the tramcar sat silent, almost unmoving. The friendliness he remembered in them seemed to have gone. Fear was here, sitting next to everybody, ready to place a tight hand on a reluctant arm.

> *Who but the people broke the iron shackles,*
> *Rising triumphant and glorious at last?*

Had the word-intoxicated young poet ridden in many tramcars lately, he wondered?

The tramcar jolted to a stop. Two People's Police got in and checked papers. It was an everyday matter, Garden saw, perhaps something that might happen two or three times in a day. Hands were dug into pockets, grubby papers looked at and handed back. Garden showed his own papers and launched into an explanation about Ilona leaving hers at the hotel. The policeman looked at him sharply, then scribbled a note instructing Ilona to present papers at the local station within twelve hours. Two stops later the policemen got off again. By the time they had reached the terminus the tramcar was almost empty.

Just outside the town the metal road ended and became dirt. It was quite dark. By his side Ilona spoke:

"Do you think they will be there?"

"Yes. You know Milo. He has a great many friends."

"If not, what shall we do?"

"We can get back by tram and keep the other appointment."

"I do not think they will be there. I think they are caught or have got away."

"I don't think they would leave us."

"I don't think they would leave us," she mocked him

savagely. "Of course they would. Anyone with any sense would leave Milo and Theo to look after themselves and keep the other appointment. That must be a friend, or he would have given us away."

"I've told you, we can still keep it."

"And if Milo and Theo are here and have no plan of their own you will take them with us, yes?"

"Yes."

"And if our friends, the people who have arranged things for us, will not take them, what then?"

"We'll meet that when it comes." Spacing his words like a man talking to a child he said to the invisible figure by his side, "Try to understand, Ilona, that it is important for people to behave decently toward each other. If we fail in that, how can we hope to succeed in anything?"

Her voice was shrill. "You make me sick. Do you think Milo is anything but a pimp?"

"Be quiet. This is Zeb."

Now they could see the outlines of cottages on either side. Here again there was a silence that Garden found ominous. Nothing moved in the village street, doors were closed, there was no sound of voices. They could hear, not far away, the lapping of water. Garden took a torch which he had found in the pocket of his duffel coat and flashed it briefly up and down. The street seemed absolutely deserted. His apprehension of disaster grew stronger. They went on walking up the street. Once Ilona's foot slipped in a rut and she caught his arm. Every twenty yards Garden flashed his torch. It showed nothing but blank houses.

"We are getting near to the end of the village." Garden drew in his breath. His torch had picked out a small cottage, unmistakably colored pink. It looked as dead as the rest. There was a door and a curtained window. Recklessly he played the torch over the cottage, up and down the road.

"They are not here."

"We shall soon see." Garden took three steps to the door and knocked.

The door opened almost at once. A burly figure stood there. He was wearing a jersey. Inside a light glimmered, not enough to show through the curtains. "You are the fisherman Poltzer?"

The man said in a deep voice, "I am the fisherman Poltzer."

"Is Milo here?"

"He is here." The man stood aside and they entered. "Why is the village so silent?" Garden asked as he went in. Then he stopped. There were several people in the square, low, dim room. In one corner a woman sat, heavy-faced and sad, with two boys perhaps seven and five years old, and a baby wrapped in a shawl. The other figures in the room, who now crowded round Garden and Ilona, searching them for weapons and then briskly pinioning their arms, all wore the black uniform of the People's Police. They had been everywhere—standing behind the door, crouching by the open fireplace, sitting at the deal table. No doubt there were more of them outside.

"You are always wrong," Ilona said. Her voice was bitter and loving at once. "And now you are wrong for the last time."

The man in the jersey had gone over to stand by the woman. His arms were folded, his face had a somber dignity and strength. "You are really Poltzer?" Garden asked, "Was Milo here?"

"He is here," the man said with no change in his deep voice. "Inside."

Their captors jerked them forward, and opened the door of an inner room. In the right-hand corner of this room there was a large bed, above it a crucifix. On the bed lay two bodies. A voice said, "Let them look," and the grip of hands was removed. Garden went over to the bed and stood looking down. Milo lay there, a nut-brown man brightly smiling as he had smiled in life, and by his side gigantic Theo, his face a mass of blood and bruises, clothing torn, jaw hanging open. Ilona buried her face in Garden's coat. Her body, touching his, was racked with sobs. It was strange, Garden thought as he looked down dispassionately at these two who had so recently been alive and were now dead, that she should be moved so much and he so little. Yet it was she who had been prepared to let Milo and Theo look after themselves, he who had insisted on walking into a trap.

The voice that had spoken before said, "Three of you stay here, the rest outside." There was a clatter of feet. The door closed. Garden turned slowly to see the figure he had expected. At the other side of the room, round-faced and genially smiling, Peplov sat on a rickety chest of drawers, swinging his leg.

He said in perfect English, "So it is all over, Mr. Garden. In a way you must feel almost as relieved as I do. Have a cigarette?" He offered a case with a smile so warm and friendly that it was hard for Garden to resist smiling back. Hard for Garden but not apparently for Ilona, who launched herself at Peplov like a large cat. He ducked aside and one of the police caught her. "Tie her hands," Peplov said. "I have suffered enough from her tantrums. That damned dog." He rubbed his ankle ruefully, with an air of appealing for sympathy which was again extremely engaging.

"Why did you have to kill them?" She flung her head up. "But I had forgotten. It is your trade."

"My dear girl, I can assure you that such stupid remarks do not serve your purpose of annoying me. They are merely a waste of time, and we have not"—Peplov looked at a wrist watch—"very much time to waste. I did not kill these two men—some overenthusiastic subordinates did so before my arrival because they offered such persistent resistance, and were so troublesome. I can assure you that I would much prefer Granz to be alive. Granz alive might have been of some use. Granz is like the rest of us when we are dead, something that needs quick burial."

"They admitted nothing. Then how—"

"How did I know about you? Poltzer. They had made a plan for escape in his motorboat, and had told him of the two friends who were joining them. We picked up their trail in Dravina and followed them out here. They did not talk. Neither did Poltzer, when he was simply threatened. I gave him promises instead of threats and he talked. He has a wife, you see. That is bad. And children. That is worse. I promised that he would continue to live here unharmed, even receive certain fishing concessions. He talked."

"He will find out what your promises are worth," Ilona said.

Peplov looked surprised. "But I shall keep my promises. Why not? Do you think I make a profession of breaking promises? I am not so foolish. But that is all of little interest. You were in the hands of Lepkin at H.Q. here, isn't that so? Then somehow you managed to shoot Lepkin and his assistant, and walked out. You must have acted quickly and resourcefully. On the other hand, Lepkin must have been very careless. That is odd, because Lepkin was efficient. I respected him. What happened?"

The smoke rose from Garden's cigarette and curled in the lamplight. "Just what you said. Lepkin was careless and I took advantage of it."

"I doubt very much whether you are telling the truth. There is something I do not understand about it. No matter." Peplov's smile broadened. His head was no longer bandaged, but there was a big patch of plaster above one eyebrow. "Then you separated. Granz had the idea of getting help from a comrade in Dravina, and it happened that the comrade was one of my agents.

He reported immediately, and I had Milo and Granz followed here in the hope that they would lead us to you. The people of the village shut themselves in when they saw what was happening. It is strange that they don't love us when we are their protectors. We were less successful in tracing you. A shop manager reported that a woman whom we identified as Miss Arbitzer had bought some clothes from him. We were looking out for those clothes. I see that Miss Arbitzer is wearing the frock she bought, but yours is not a new suit, Mr. Garden. At the same time you are not wearing the easily identifiable fisherman's clothes in which you were dressed this morning." Peplov crossed the room and felt the cloth of Garden's jacket. "Not good quality, but English I should say. Now, where would you have been able to get English clothes in Dravina? You wouldn't care to tell me, I suppose? It is a matter of almost idle curiosity. After all, we have you." Peplov looked at Garden quizzically, with his round head on one side.

"But not my friends."

"We shall have them soon." There was a touch of complacence about Peplov. "But I can see that you are determined not to talk. Very well. I, however, am not so taciturn. Is there anything you would like to know during the next"—Peplov looked again at his watch—"ten minutes?"

Ilona asked, "What has happened to Jacob?"

"Arbitzer?" For the first time Peplov looked a little surprised. "He is dead. One of you shot him and he died within five minutes. It was Granz, I suppose? You won't say? Well, there again it is not of much importance."

Garden stubbed out his cigarette. "Why haven't you announced his death?"

"We waited until we had caught you. That, now, *was* a matter of some importance."

"Why?"

"Because you will be able to confirm the confession

made by Arbitzer in the few minutes before he died, that he had been induced to come here by the Anglo-American Imperialists, who wished to replace a people's government by one that would serve their own ends. For this purpose you, as a notorious spy and agent-provocateur, were an ideal instrument. That is what you will say at your trial, Garden. You, Miss Arbitzer, will give general confirmation of the plot. It is a pity that Arbitzer himself cannot testify, but fortunately you will give ample confirmation of his verbal confession. And there will be plenty of support in the testimony of the members of the committee arrested at Lodno." The merry eyes twinkled. "You have caused me a great deal of trouble, the pair of you. Had everything gone as we intended I should have been arrested and put on trial with the others, and any remnants of your organization that still existed would have found it difficult to trace their failure to its source. As it is you have changed my sphere of usefulness. But I forgive you. After all I have you, in the end."

"And if you hadn't got us?" But Garden knew the answer.

"Then no trial—what is the use of a trial with the principal defendants all dead or missing? Perhaps rapped knuckles for Peplov, perhaps worse." Outside Garden heard a car stop. "Time is up."

Garden leaned forward. There was a question to which the answer seemed desperately important. "Peplov, you worked with the people you call conspirators for months, perhaps for years. You know that their motives were not as you describe them. You know that Arbitzer's motives and mine were not as you describe them."

"Time is up," Peplov repeated. His smile had gone. His look was cold and withdrawn.

"You know that if there is hope for this country and for the world it lies in us," Garden cried. He waved an arm wildly. "Admit it, Peplov, admit it once and save yourself. These men won't hear you, or if they hear they won't understand."

The door opened and two men came past the guards. Both were very tall, and woodenly handsome. One of them carried a machine gun. "It is useless for you to talk to these men," Peplov said. "They are deaf and dumb." He wrote on a sheet of paper and held it up so that they could read: "Handcuffs. Deliver them *unharmed.*" One of the men nodded. Garden felt the cold steel on his wrists.

"Peplov," he shouted. "You have not answered my question. You said you would answer all my questions."

"There is only one answer for you," Peplov said. He came close to Garden and spat in his face. "Spy! Saboteur!"

They began to hustle Garden out. He backed against the wall so that they had to drag him. While they dragged he shouted: "Listen, Peplov, you are infected, do you understand, you spent too long with those conspirators, their ideas have eaten into your beliefs. You will be in the dock soon after us."

"Stop him," Peplov screamed, his face a mask of rage. Garden had a glimpse of Poltzer's hand raised in a kind of feeble protest. Then they had dragged him outside and pushed him into the car.

9

He moved uneasily on the seat of a car that was sliding over a wet ribbon of road. His head ached violently. "Did they hit me?"

"A little tap." Ilona's voice sounded almost cheerful. "You made Peplov angry."

Garden opened his eyes and saw that one of the men was driving. The other had turned round in the front seat to look at them, revolver in hand. "My word, they take good care of us, don't they? What a tribute to our escaping powers."

"It's no good," she said. "No fear they'll give anything away when they're dumb."

"They may be dumb, but I'm not so sure they're deaf. They can probably lip-read." Experimentally he said, "Why not take us back to Dravina? We have friends there who will pay you well or get you out of the country if that's what you want." The man beside the driver leaned over and crocked Garden playfully on the knee with his revolver. The blow was painful. "Hold on, now, I'm a valuable property. You know you were warned to deliver me in perfect condition."

The mute grunted, waved the gun warningly at Garden. Ilona repeated, "It's no good."

"Stop saying that. There are advantages in being handcuffed, and in being a kind of sacred cow who mustn't be damaged." Garden jumped forward suddenly with the cuffs raised ready to bring down on the driver's head. The other man gave him a push in the chest which sent him sprawling back on top of Ilona. Before he could get up again the car had stopped and the two mutes were communicating with each other in grunts. They got out and took lengths of rope from the luggage boot. While they were doing this Garden scrambled over into the front seat and tried to turn the engine key with his handcuffed hands. The mutes grunted with alarm. They pulled him out of the front seat, tied the rope round and round him so that his arms were tight at his sides, and thrust him into the back again. Then they did the same to Ilona. The man beside the driver continued to give them his exclusive attention.

"Our last state is worse than our first," Garden said. "But our future state is likely to be worse still. Don't tell me that it's no good, I'm beginning to understand that." He managed to sit up, and moved around in the hope of finding some projection that might loosen his ropes, or some sharp surface that might cut them. He was still engaged in this vain project when he noticed a car moving slowly just ahead of them. They pulled out to pass it and then the mute driver gave a high-pitched cry as he saw the two vans standing together across the road. The brakes screamed as they came to a stop a yard from one of the vans. The two mutes opened the doors and dived out. Garden was aware of the car they had passed rushing up beside them. He remembered the machine gun and thought, "They'll never do it." But instead of the spatter of machine gun fire he had expected, there came a terrible long-drawn wailing cry, like nothing he had ever heard. A moment later the car that had rushed up beside them crashed into the van, making a tremendous noise. From this side, the left, he heard again the wailing cry, a shot and then silence. From the other side there were several shots and the sound of running. Then somebody said in English, "All right, got him." Garden could see nothing at all of what was going on.

The front door of the car was opened, and then the back one. A light played over Garden and Ilona, a voice said, "Trussed up like a chicken dinner. Half a jiffy." Their ropes were cut. Stiffly Garden got out of the car. He looked closely at his deliverer in the darkness, but could see nothing except that he was apparently youthful. "Come on now, come on, over to this van." The night seemed alive with dark figures.

"Who are you?" Garden asked.

"Nobody you know. Over to the van, quickly, the one we haven't bashed up. We'll clear up this mess."

Garden found that he had been steered dexterously over to the van. "Lend a hand there," somebody said. Ilona disappeared inside. He put a leg up on the footboard and winced as his leg muscles refused to obey him. Hands from outside lifted him up, hands from in-

side received him. Inside the van it was quite dark. A
voice that seemed familiar called "Ready." The engine
revved up, they moved away, made a turn, and were
going back on the road to Dravina.

The same voice said, "Cigarette?" A lighter clicked
and a small flame lit up the face of Trelawney. Garden
saw it with a certain slight shock which was somehow
remote from surprise. Ilona gasped.

"Well, old man, you made a pretty fair mess of that,
didn't you? Why the devil didn't you keep the date we
fixed instead of haring off to Zeb?"

"I don't know. It seemed important. Perhaps it
wasn't." He thought of the two bodies on the bed, the
big man and the little man.

"I'll say it wasn't. The only important thing as far as
you're concerned, old man, is getting out of the country.
I got the willies when I found you'd popped out of that
film show for good. Luckily, one of our boys was hanging about outside and saw you board the tram. Then
we had another bit of luck. A lad of ours in the People's
Police saw you on the tram and reported it. We traced
you as far as Zeb and then set a little ambush on the
main road. It worked." Trelawney chuckled. The tip of
his cigarette moved in the darkness. "Pity about those
dummies. They often use 'em for important jobs. Safe,
you see; can't give anything away."

"What do you mean, a pity?"

"Car ran over one—didn't you hear him squeal?
Didn't have any option, he was going to machine gun
us, another half-minute and we'd have been for it." Unreality again oppressed Garden. This was Trelawney,
quite recognizably the loud-voiced Trelawney who uttered progressive clichés at every opportunity, the man
who was just good enough (or was he just too good?)
to be true, the Trelawney to whom Garden told his
fantasies about a mission. But the body of this Trelawney with its rolling eye, stringy neck, and hairy red

wrists was now understood to be the home of a quite different inhabitant. That was not precisely what disturbed Garden. What seemed incongruous and terrifying was the fact that the two Trelawneys were one, that this new Trelawney spoke with the other's coarsely confident voice. They turned a corner sharply and Garden clung to one of the struts on the side of the van. Trelawney spoke again. "You saw Peplov, I suppose? Did he tell you anything?"

"Jacob Arbitzer is dead. They were going to use us as the show witnesses for a State trial."

"Of course they were. Lord, man, you were the best bit of propaganda that had dropped into their lap for years. We simply had to get you away."

"Now that you've done that, what's going to happen?"

"Anybody's guess, old boy. I doubt if they'll hold a public trial—not much point in it without you or Arbitzer to testify. Peplov will get demotion if he's lucky, if he's unlucky he'll find himself on trial too. That's my guess, but I can be as wrong as the next man."

Garden had almost forgotten Ilona's presence when she spoke: "Who are you? Some kind of special agent?"

"Call it that if you like, my dear. Kind of general dog's body you might say. Secret dog's body, with secret the operative word. At least it was. That's why I passed those notes through to you anonymously. The less people know about this kind of thing the better. I've been doing it for years."

"A spy."

"Call it what you like," Trelawney said impatiently. "Most of it's routine stuff. Two of us came over here specially to keep an eye on friend Garden and see he didn't get into mischief. The little chap in plus fours is the other one. I was going to push off on my own, but I couldn't do much of that. Lady Vi got pretty touchy when the trouble began, didn't want any of her lambs to stray. Now I've had to come out in the open much more than I like. There's still a bit of the resistance movement left here that we're in touch with, otherwise we'd never have got you out of trouble tonight. But I shall have to think up something for Lady Vi when we get back, and it will have to be good."

There was an injured note in Trelawney's voice. Garden felt constrained to say, "I'm sorry to have given you so much trouble."

Trelawney responded handsomely. "That's all right, old boy, all in the day's work. But shall I tell you what I think, as an unprejudiced observer. I think there was something phony about the whole thing."

"Peplov—" Garden began.

"Yes, I've heard about Peplov. I've got a feeling there was something more than that. I'm only a small cog in a big wheel, mind you, but to me the whole thing smells uncommonly fishy."

"How are you going to get us away?"

"All laid on, old boy. We're a bit late, but they'll wait. At least I hope so."

"Suppose they don't."

There was a short silence. "Then we'll have to think of something else. But we shan't have to. A boat will take you over the straits—you should be across before daylight. The skipper's got a fix with the harbor authorities here. A dozen people have come out this way in the past month. Once you're across the straits, out of the country, you make your own way home. I shall send a message through to say mission accomplished as far as I'm concerned, V.I.P. on his way home. Somebody at H.Q. seems to be taking an awful lot of interest in you."

"Very nice of them. What about money?"

"All fixed with the captain."

The van stopped. Trelawney moved up to the front of the cab and held a consultation in murmurs. Then he came back. "This is the place. Come on." The back of the lorry dropped with a rattle. They jumped down to the road. It was very dark. They could hear the sea's suck and roar. A voice Garden recognized as Bridgewater's said, "Over the road."

A dozen steps took them to pebbles. A hand, cool and small, groped for Garden's. A fresh wind blew in from the sea. They crouched behind rocks, Trelawney and Bridgewater with them. The noise of the sea was loud. The lights of the lorry flashed on and off. They flashed on again, more lengthily, and then off for a moment. Short-long-short, short-long-short, the lorry's lights repeated three times. Garden looked out to sea and saw no answering signal. "They don't reply."

"Too dangerous. They'll put a boat out."

"If they're still here," Bridgewater said in an unfriendly voice. "We're three-quarters of an hour late." They waited in silence. A few feet away the waves rushed up the beach and back again, with a sound like tearing fabric. This was repeated over and over. Time passed. Ilona's hand grasped Garden's with convulsive tightness.

"Shall we signal again?" Bridgewater was fidgeting.

"No," said Trelawney decisively. They crouched and waited. Bridgewater began to swear quietly.

Ilona said, "I can hear something." Garden listened and heard nothing but the sea. "A boat."

Bridgewater said contemptuously, "You're daft. You couldn't hear a boat over the sound of—"

"Quiet," said Trelawney. They were quiet, they listened. Was there a sound over or inside the sea's suck and roar? At times Garden thought so, and then he could not be sure. Then Ilona cried sharply, "Over there." Garden heard the scrape of a boat a few yards away from them on the beach. Trelawney left them, and came back jubilant. "Looks as if we've done 'em in the eye this time. Come on, you two."

There were two men in the boat. "Good-by and thank you," Garden said to Trelawney.

"All right, old man. Into the boat."

Ilona said, "Thank you for—"

"Yes, yes. Into the boat."

They moved away from the shore, and instantly the two figures merged in blackness. "Good luck," Garden called, but the words were lost utterly, swallowed up in the surge of the sea. And suddenly there was something disquieting, disturbingly familiar and yet strange, in this passage over the waves. "How far?" Garden asked, but the men in the boat did not reply. Something shapeless loomed in the darkness, they clambered up a ladder— and about this too there was something familiar. Then a heavy hand thumped Garden's shoulder, a thick voice said, "The Englishman, eh. My friend the Englishman and his little girl."

"Captain Kaffel." Garden understood what he had found familiar.

The Captain's laugh rolled richly on the air. "And my little friend Milo and the big fellow, they are not with you?"

"They are dead."

"It is the lot of man," the Captain said philosophically. "Come and have a drink." They went down the companionway and into the small cabin that had housed them before. The filmy white liquid went into the same glasses, but there were two less of them this time.

"I didn't know you were connected with our friends on the beach."

"I have many connections, I take many risks, I earn much money. What else is in life?" With appalling gallantry the Captain bowed to Ilona and took off his filthy cap. "I had forgotten. There is also woman. But is she not the biggest risk of all?"

"No," said Garden. "The biggest risk of all is faith."

The Captain's one small eye stared at him blankly. "Of that I know nothing. I believe in myself, Captain Kaffel, in the cunning that lies here and the strength that lies here." He tapped his head and his arm. "Everything else is nonsense. Good health." The Captain downed his second glass.

"You're probably perfectly right. How long will it take us to get across?"

"Four hours, perhaps five, no more. Then I set you down in safety and you will have something to thank me for, eh? You will say afterward, 'That Captain Kaffel, he was an old scoundrel, but he had it up there.'" He tapped his forehead. "I have made this trip a dozen times, twenty times, with no trouble. Why? I know people, I am useful to people, I use my head."

"One of these days you'll lose your head."

The Captain guffawed. "One day perhaps. And then what shall I say? It is the lot of man. Now I must go. Five hours remember, no more."

In fact it was nearly six hours later when they stood on deck and saw land appear like a smudge in the pale light of dawn. Ilona put her arm through his. "It is all over. We have come back."

"Yes."

"And you love me? You have never said that you love me?"

"I love you." He turned away from the land they were approaching to look back at the country they had left. But there was nothing except sea, glassy and bluish-green, and a cold pale sky.

"I love you also. And I am not such a miserable creature as you think me. I have lost an aunt and an uncle and a dog. Do you wonder that things have been no good? But they will be better later on. I promise it. Shall we get married?"

"Yes." Garden stared at sky and water.

Looking back, looking at the lost country shaped like a broken penny which was now no more than sea and sky, Garden felt that something in his life had ended forever, that there was some fundamental innocence of the heart which he had betrayed.

III

RETURN

1

The sun began to shine as they passed through the
Customs at Newhaven, explaining to a surprised Customs officer that they had lost their luggage. It continued
to shine as they came up in the train, an English October sun lacking in warmth but lending a clear light to
the unimpassioned countryside, and filling Garden with
a curious sense of peace. He felt a melting sentimental
contentment with everything, the grubby magazines on
station bookstalls, the benevolent silence of the middle-
aged matron knitting in the railway carriage, the over-
cooked expensive food in the dining car.

Trelawney had been right, he saw as he read *The
Times*, in which news of the rising had dwindled to half
a dozen lines near the bottom of the foreign news page.
Order had been completely restored, and it was not now
considered likely that the great public trial mentioned
by the Ministry of Home Security would take place. In
particular, *The Times* correspondent noted, there was
now a complete absence of official interest in the mysterious Englishman who had been mentioned earlier as a
leader of the revolt. Another note said that there was
no further news of Professor Arbitzer, who had disappeared from his home at Brightsand just before the pre-
sumed rising. His disappearance had apparently no political connection with the rising, and there was no
indication that he was in government custody. Well that

was fair enough, Garden thought, very fair and very English. He settled down to enjoy the mild pleasures afforded by cows, the pattern of fields, rolling downs. Then to the pleasures of London—how quickly the train flashed past Clapham Junction and the delicious sight of Battersea Power Station. Victoria Station, when it came, overwhelmed him with its barracklike simplicity and its nostalgic names—Haywards Heath, Three Bridges, Worthing, Brighton. "Here is my home," he said to Ilona with a sweep of the hand as they stood by a Smith's bookstall. She smiled uncomprehendingly.

"You are going to telephone your friend?"

"Latterley? Yes." No doubt Latterley knew all about the failure of their mission. He was presumably the H.Q. to which Trelawney had reported. The whole thing was over. But a feeling of responsibility remained with Garden, and a feeling too that something remained to be cleared up. Somewhere there had been betrayal, someone in Latterley's organization had told Peplov to expect both Arbitzer and Garden. It was perhaps merely an academic exercise now to discover the traitor's identity, yet Garden found himself anxious to do it. He telephoned Latterley at the Central Liaison Organization from a box in Victoria Station, and spoke to a girl who said that he was on a few days' leave. She had no idea where Garden could get hold of him. Yes, she agreed politely, it might be a good idea to try his home. She gave him the number. Garden telephoned, and learned that Mr. Latterley was away.

They took a bus to the big white building, and went up to the third floor. Garden rattled the handle of the door that said THE NEAR-EASTERN, EUROPEAN AND BRITISH GENERAL SECURITY COMPANY LIMITED. The door was closed. The liftman said that nobody had been in now for three days. If Garden asked him, they had skedaddled because they were behind with the rent.

Garden telephoned Multiple Steel, and asked to

speak to Sir Alfred. A voice, secretarial, male, urbane, murmured the word unavailable. Garden gave his name, but it made no impression. In a slight variation of the formula the voice murmured *out of town*.

By this time Ilona was becoming impatient. She wanted a bath, she said, she wanted to do some shopping. Garden took her back to his room in the Brixton Road. "There's only one bathroom for seven people, and they're all individualists who don't believe in queueing," he told her. "We're in a vantage spot, though, only two doors from the bathroom, and at this time of day most of them will be at work. Still, it will give you a glimpse of what life on my income is going to be like."

But in fact Ilona had very little chance to see that, because when Garden opened the door of his room they saw Latterley inside. He sat in Garden's battered easy chair nodding gently, with *The Charterhouse of Parma* on his lap. Garden's first reaction on seeing him was annoyance at the negligently self-indulgent comfort of his attitude. "Hallo," he said, and Latterley stretched. "What are you doing here? How did you get in?"

"I convinced your landlady I was respectable and she unlocked the door. That was ages ago. I expected you early this morning. Good Lord, I'm hungry. There was only a bit of moldy bread in the larder." Latterley got up and patted Garden's arm. "Good to see you again, Chas my boy. You too, Miss Arbitzer. It was touch and go for a bit, but we knew you'd got out. We heard about Jacob too. That was a bad bit of organization those boys did over there. They were so sure everything was sewed up tight." He said to Ilona directly, "We were all really very sorry about Jacob, and we blame ourselves very much."

"It's too late to be sorry," Ilona said flatly. "I want a bath." The bathroom was unoccupied, the water surprisingly hot. Garden gave her a towel and returned to Latterley, who regarded him quizzically.

"Have you formed an attachment?"

"Ilona and I are going to be married," Garden said stiffly.

Latterley rocked with delight. "My dear old Chas, you really are a sweetie." What was there, Garden wondered, funny about that? And he was conscious again of irritation, although many years ago he had tried to reconcile himself to the fact that he would never understand Latterley's sense of humor.

Latterley said more seriously: "A nice girl but sulky, or that's what I thought when I went down to Brightsand. And not quite in sympathy with a salmon-pink idealist like you, I imagine. You'll have to watch her carefully, Chas. But that isn't why I'm here. The chief wants to see you."

"And I want to see him." Garden told Latterley about his telephone calls. When he said that he had telephoned Multiple Steel, Latterley's head jerked up.

"You know it was agreed you shouldn't get in touch." Garden protested that no harm had been done. "How do you know? You mentioned your name, you provided a link that somebody may remember one day."

"It doesn't need me to provide links. Somebody's doing that already." Garden told Latterley of his certainty that there was a spy inside the English organization who had revealed their plans to Peplov. He was aware while he talked of Latterley's bright, mocking look. When he had finished Latterley positively clapped his hands.

"Bravo, my Chas, brilliantly deduced. You must tell it to the chief."

"You don't think I'm serious," Garden said half-angrily.

"Serious? I've never known you anything but serious in your whole life."

"You don't take me seriously then."

It seemed only by an effort that Latterley restrained the laughter present in the glance of his eye, quivering in the light tone of his voice. "You know me. I never take anything seriously except my own comfort and the things that are said by very young girls. And Stendhal, of course, I take him very seriously." He patted the volume of *The Charterhouse of Parma*. "Here's Ilona. Let's go and get some lunch. Then we'll go down and see the chief. He wants to hear exactly what happened from both of you. He's down at the Multiple Steel factory just outside Maidstone. I'll give him a ring while we're having lunch. And now we must get away from here as quickly as possible. The air of Brixton is quite unsuited to a man of my fine susceptibilities. It's only tough, coarse figures like you, Chas, who can stand up to it."

2

A car met them at Maidstone and took them out into a countryside that showed as yet hardly a trace of autumn. As they approached Maidstone in the train the flow of Latterley's sprightly conversation abruptly ceased. He was silent as they got out of the carriage, nodded curtly to the little man who sprang forward to open the door of the car, and looked moodily out of the window when they were in the car. Phrases, sentences, almost whole eloquent paragraphs formed themselves in Garden's mind as he thought of the coming meeting with Sir Alfred. Green fields, oasthouses, tidy orchards unrolled themselves before his unregarding eyes. Ilona looked from Garden to Latterley as though she expected to find in their relationship the answer to some baffling question.

The car stopped with a jerk. Latterley said, "What's this?" Ilona gave a stifled scream. Garden brought himself back from his imaginary exposition and saw with surprise that the driver was talking to a dozen men in uniform. They were all wearing what looked like a new type of service respirator, some carried small revolvers and others Sten guns. Their leader, who had a blue star pinned on his jacket, held up a gloved hand to stop them.

"We got a pass out," their driver was saying indignantly. "You got no call to stop us."

The leading figure came up to the side of the car. The driver held out the pass. The man's voice came through the respirator, disembodied and almost without inflection, yet thinly clear. "Very good. Pass approved. Go ahead."

They moved on slowly. More khaki-clad figures appeared, running clumsily over fields, all of them wearing respirators. Few of the men seemed to know just what they were doing. Incomprehensible orders were being shouted. Garden became aware of the buzz of training planes and helicopters overhead.

Their Cockney driver grumbled back at them. "Some kind of damn silly exercises going on. Barmy if you ask me, playing at soldiers. Exercises!" He spat contemptuously out of the window.

Nobody replied to this. One of the hovering helicopters came down very low, evidently to have a look at them. "You can see the factory across there, to the left," said Latterley. "Bensley, where the workers live, is just beyond it." Garden had a glimpse of long low silvery buildings, with a high square tower in the middle. Then the car was surrounded by men waving to them to stop. One of them wearing the blue star, and blue tabs on his shoulders, said through his respirator, "Out at once, all of you. You're contaminated."

"Now look 'ere," said the driver, "we got a pass. You give us the pass yourself."

"I did nothing of the kind. Let me see the pass. Just as I thought. This was issued by Livingstone, who was contaminated half an hour ago, when we took the farmhouse. I cannot regard it as valid."

The little driver shook his fist out of the window. "I don't bleeding well care if it was Doctor Livingstone who issued it. I was given a pass for the works, and that's where I'm going."

"Indeed you're not. You're in charge, and what's more you're contaminated. Take him off to Receiving Station Two."

"Just a minute." Latterley got out of the car and addressed the man with the blue tabs. "I'm Geoffrey Latterley of Central Liaison. I take it you're in command here."

"Correct, Mr. Latterley." The voice through the respirator was thin but clear. "I'm Captain Foskett, Ninth Gas Artillery. Sorry to cause you trouble, but we're carrying out special gas exercises here, and G.H.Q. orders are pretty strict. We've laid down gas artillery fire over half a square mile here, and anything within that area is judged contaminated. You're inside it now, and we'll have to take you off to Receiving Station."

"I appreciate you've got to do your duty, Captain."

"Quite so, Mr. Latterley, quite so." The thin voice said suddenly, "Harbord, Gravelney, and Waterlow, cover those fields as far as Pinney's Bottom." Garden saw that they had pistols containing little colored streamers which they fired as they ran. "Streamers indicate contaminated area," said Captain Foskett.

"But we have an urgent appointment on government business."

"Can't help that, I'm afraid. You'll have to go through the decontaminating process. G.H.Q. are very anxious to know how many people we can pass through the receiving stations."

"How long will that take?"

"Can't say. Half an hour perhaps, or a couple of hours. Depends whether they can revive you."

Latterley looked urbane but perfectly serious, and even grave. Garden admired him for it, knowing that he would have lost his own temper long ago. "Frankly, I'm concerned on your account, Captain. This is a very important conference." Latterley brought his head down to the Captain's ear and lowered his voice.

"Can't hear you. Speak up."

With finely controlled anger, or a good simulation of it, Latterley said very loudly, "I'm certainly not going to bawl this out for everyone to hear. If you don't want to pull the biggest boner of your life you'd better take off that respirator so that we can talk properly."

"Not really supposed to remove them during exercise," Captain Foskett said, "but exceptional case I suppose—" The respirator, removed, revealed a red-faced perspiring man with ginger mustaches and an anxious eye. Latterley took him by the arm and they moved away together, with Latterley talking rapidly. Whatever tale he told plainly impressed Foskett, for when they returned he was feebly servile. "Mistakes will occur even in the best regulated families. My apologies, sincere apologies." His voice without the respirator had an incoherent quality, as if he found it difficult to speak at all.

"All right." Latterley was not too obviously pleased, still inclined to be a shade severe in fact. He motioned to the driver to get in. Suddenly another group of soldiers, all wearing respirators and led by a man wearing a green star and green tabs came down the road. "Oh damn," said Captain Foskett. He made frantic efforts to adjust his respirator.

The green-tabbed figure spoke. The effect was eerie, for behind the respirator his voice had exactly the same thin and colorless tone as Foskett's. "Got you all. I declare you prisoners of Green Defensive Force. As for you, whoever you are, you're under arrest," he said to Foskett. "You know it's an offense to remove respirators during an exercise."

Foskett pulled off his respirator again, defiantly.

"Now look here, don't talk a lot of cock. I had to take it off—"

Green Tabs laughed. "That's what they all say. Anyway, I'm not talking to you, you're dead."

"If you'd read Orders properly you'd know that casualties are listed as contaminated, not dead. If they're got down to the Receiving Station quickly enough it may be possible to decontaminate them."

Green Tabs laughed again. "Come on then, let's have you down at the Receiving Station. You too," he said to Garden and Ilona. "Out of that car please. You've got no business in an exercise area." They got out. A helicopter came down low to have a look at them, and ascended again. The blue-starred men, accepting capture most willingly, all took off their respirators.

Latterley and Foskett both began to explain things to Green Tabs, who waved them aside. "Got no time for all that nonsense. You can complain to the Colonel afterward. I'm trying to stop Kent from being overrun by gas artillery groups."

At this Latterley did lose his temper, and caught Green Tabs by the arm. He was seized instantly by two of the soldiers. Garden looked across the fields. The factory was plainly visible, tantalizingly near, separated from them only by a five-barred gate and a field. He pressed Ilona's arm and looked meaningfully over the field. She nodded.

Foskett had put on his respirator again, and motioned his men to do the same. They did so unwillingly. His voice, when he spoke again to Green Tabs, was transformed accordingly. "Look here, old chap, how did you come down this road? I thought we had it covered."

"Came along through Simley—"

"Through Simley, yes old chap."

"—took a short cut by Haddocks Wood, if you follow me—"

"I follow you perfectly, old chap. A short cut by Haddocks Wood. And what then?"

"Over Double Bottom bridge and down this road."

"I thought so," said Foskett, "I thought so." A note of triumph could be heard in his voice, even inside the respirator. "Double Bottom bridge was atomized early this morning."

"Nonsense. There's no atomization tag on it."

"Then someone's taken it off. Atomized early this morning, I assure you. There's no way you can get through to this road from Haddocks Wood, no way whatever. You'll have to go back."

"Now look here—" Green Tabs pulled out a map. The two officers bent over it. "*Now*," said Garden to Ilona. Two steps brought them to the five-barred gate. Garden lifted her and swung her over, then vaulted over himself. Latterley saw what they were doing, and made an unsuccessful attempt to wrench himself free. Some of the men began to climb the gate in a half-hearted way. By the time they had done so Garden and Ilona were halfway across the field. At the other side of it a stile led into the main road. Just across the road stood a gate above which the words MULTIPLE STEEL appeared in a great glittering horseshoe. The gate was closed, but a small gatekeeper's house stood by it with a bell push and a notice above it, WHEN GATE IS CLOSED PLEASE RING. Garden rang this bell.

3

A door of the gatekeeper's house opened, and there appeared the peroxide curls and enameled cheeks of Miss Fanny Bone. She looked at them, a little disconcerted. "Where's the car?"

"It got mixed up with some gas exercises. So did Latterley and the driver."

"Oh. Well, I'll just say you're here." She vanished again, came back within a few seconds and opened the gates. "Over to the big building. The lift will be waiting for you. Go up to the top floor."

Garden stared round him with interest. What had looked from a distance like a tower was, he saw, simply a central administrative block from which long low workshops radiated off in all directions. The place was as silent as the deserted playground of a school. "Nobody working," he said to Fanny Bone. "Is there a strike or something?"

"Don't you know what day this is? It's Saturday. Multiple Steel works a five-day week."

"How long have you been gatekeeper?"

She gave him her varnished look. "Go right across. The lift will be waiting."

They walked together slowly across the gravel and she stood watching them, hands on hips, a spot of radical color in her yellow blouse and red skirt against the prevailing silver and gray of the workshops. Walking across the gravel, Garden wondered what he was reminded of? Schooldays? Then he remembered the airfield and the wet tarmac and the three figures advancing briskly to meet them. The end of that had been disaster. But this, he reminded himself, was a traditional England in which the routine of life remained undisturbed. Then he thought of the men in respirators running about with their toy pistols, dealing an imaginary death with colored streamers, a death rendered somehow indifferent by its reduction of human beings to the status of mere contaminated things—and he was not so sure.

The high glass doors of the square building opened at a touch. They stood in an empty hall, with murals on every wall showing the development of man through the power of steel. Or did they show only the place of steel in the life of man? The floor was of foam rubber. They moved over it noiselessly to a lift at one corner,

above which a red light glowed. Garden closed the doors
behind them and pressed a button numbered 8. Gently
the lift whirred upward.

What had he expected to see when the lift stopped,
and the doors opened? There was a pleasant sense of
light and air, explained by the fact that no brick but
only glass was visible on this top floor. And there was
Sir Alfred facing him, hand outthrust, bald head jutting forward, tie a little on one side, chunky body
formidable in its ash-stained suit. He did not smile—
the occasion was too serious for that—but the grip of
his hand was reassuringly firm. To Garden he said nothing, to Ilona only the words, "You're the niece, yes. Very
glad to see you."

He led the way into a large glass-walled room in which
the illusion of space was even more marked. There was
a comfortable fitted carpet, a desk with papers, half a
dozen chairs, and nothing else. A door stood open onto
a large sun roof. They went out with him and saw the
works below them, absurdly squat and small. Beyond lay
wooded country, the small town of Bensley built by Sir
Alfred for his workers, the sports grounds and swimming
pools he had provided, on which tiny figures now dis-
sipated energy innocently by kicking large balls, striking
small ones, jumping into water, or running round a track.

"I like to stand out here and look at it," Sir Alfred
said in his thick voice, hands gripping the guard rail, eyes
staring round at village and country, pressing shops,
and furnaces. "Makes me feel I've done something more
real than talking. People make things here, things that
get used, things you can touch and hold. Stand here on
a workday and you can see what you're doing is adding
something to the world's wealth. That's more important
than talking, eh?"

Garden stared down at silver workshops and green
fields and the little figures going through the formal mo-
tions of Saturday afternoon. It all looked more remote

even than it was. "I used to think so. Now I'm not so sure."

"To build a world," the other said with no sign that he had heard Garden's words. "And to build it *right*, that's what's important. But can you make them see it? They're born fools, and that's how they die." The reference of his words was not clear. A cloud obscured the sun, dulled silver, darkened green, cast its shade upon the tiny figures. Sir Alfred turned abruptly, went back through the window into the room, flung himself down in the chair behind his desk. Garden realized that this was in fact an old man. The temples were marked with the peculiar white of age, the hand that played with a paper knife on the desk was beginning to shrivel.

"You have come back, Mr. Garden. I congratulate you on that, and you too, Miss Arbitzer. But there congratulations must end."

"We were betrayed," said Garden. Ilona stared from one of the men to the other.

"You were betrayed," Sir Alfred repeated heavily. "By Peplov."

"And over here." Outside the lift whirred faintly. Now Garden spoke logically, eloquently, in the phrases he had planned. The arguments ran as he had intended, he spoke plainly of his suspicions that little Mr. Hards had killed Peterson, he told of his own earlier knowledge of Peterson, he mentioned barely admitted doubts about Bretherton and Colonel Hunt. One of these, he said, had told Peplov that Garden and Arbitzer were on the plane. There was no other way in which he could have been certain of it.

The paper knife tapped on the desk. "What happened over there?"

Garden told him the whole story. Sir Alfred put on a large pair of horn-rimmed spectacles, and made notes. Once or twice Garden shifted and saw Ilona's gaze upon him, fiercely protective and pitying. The sun shone again.

"You have told nobody else this story since your return to England?"

"Nobody."

"Good." Sir Alfred took off his glasses, put away his pen, and spoke with an uncomfortable kind of joviality. "It is your opinion, then, that you were betrayed by a traitor in the organization?"

The question seemed somehow faintly ridiculous. "Yes."

"Let us see." Perhaps he pressed a bell. Garden was aware of other people in the room. He turned and they stood looking at him like monsters in a dream, the red-faced Colonel, the pale and pimply Bretherton, and dapper little Hards with his umbrella. Garden stood up. Ilona also got up, and ran over to him.

"You have heard the indictment," Sir Alfred said in a voice which was now openly mocking. "Mr. Hards, I am bound to ask you whether you killed the man Peterson, alias Floy."

Mr. Hards raised his umbrella and in a moment sunlight flashed on a thin, beautiful blade. With a low comedian's bow the little man replaced the blade in his umbrella.

"I take that gesture to indicate assent. Why did you kill him?"

"Orders." Mr. Hards jerked his thumb at the Colonel.

"Why did you give orders that Peterson should be killed, Hunt?"

Colonel Hunt's fingers combed his bald head. "Discovered he was passing information back to some little group abroad. Wormed his way into our team. A spy."

Sir Alfred put his fingers together in a gesture that, again, reminded Garden of something he had seen recently. "You see, Mr. Garden, that the Colonel regarded this man as a spy. Naturally, therefore, he had to be eliminated. Are you satisfied?"

It was Lepkin who had put together long thin fingers a few minutes before he died. "I don't understand."

"Let us see if we can make things perfectly clear to you. Bretherton, what was Garden's position inside our organization? A brief general recapitulation might be in order."

Bretherton's voice was a little bored. "The position abroad was a difficult one for the government—"

Sir Alfred broke in heavily. "Bretherton, you understand, is not referring to the government of this country, but to the government of the country you visited."

The pale man ignored the interruption. "There was a widespread plot involving several groups ranging from dispossessed aristocrats and members of the officer caste to liberal idealists and Social Democrats. Very fortunately, Peplov was on the inside of this conspiracy from an early stage. He fostered it carefully, and made himself the conspirators' chief agent in the north. He passed on all information he received, including the fact that the conspirators were able to use very effectively the so-called incorruptibility of the bourgeois liberal politician Arbitzer. Peplov was responsible for the suggestion that Arbitzer should be persuaded to return, so that he could be arrested on arrival and placed publicly on trial. The people could then understand precisely the nature of this savior whose name they invoked so hopefully.

"It proved difficult, however, to persuade Arbitzer that it might be to his advantage to return, even when we tried to make him believe through Latterley that his return would have unofficial backing from the British Government." A shade of contempt now colored Bretherton's voice. "We had made little headway when there occurred to Latterley what he personally described as a brainwave. He offered to enlist the services of a disreputable down-at-heel adventurer named Garden, who had

had some past connection with Arbitzer. He thought that Garden might be able to persuade Arbitzer that their mission would be successful. If Garden accompanied Arbitzer it would be very easy, in view of Garden's past activities, to implicate the British Government at the trial. At the same time, to supply additional pressure, Peplov persuaded the conspirators' committee to send over Granz. At this end the plan was carried out. At the other end—" Bretherton shrugged his shoulders.

"You see," Sir Alfred said in his thick voice. "You see. From Bretherton's point of view there is no traitor here except you, Mr. Garden."

Tentatively Ilona put out her hand and touched Garden's arm. He got up, walked over to the side of the room, and stood staring out at a landscape that showed no slightest sign of change. Inside the room nobody spoke. Without turning round Garden asked, "What are you going to do now?"

"You know too much, Mr. Garden. Our organization lost track of you after you escaped from Peplov. Had you gone to a certain branch of Scotland Yard you would have caused a great deal of trouble. Not to me, you understand. I should simply have denied knowledge of you. I am untouchable." He said this with a kind of solid and terrifying assurance. "But to my friends. They hastily dissolved their little organization which you visited, in case of trouble. But Latterley said that there would be no trouble, that you would have no suspicions, that you would play the game to the end. He was right, as he very often is."

"What are you going to do?" Garden asked again.

"We shall do what is necessary, if you understand me."

It was necessary, Garden thought. "And Ilona?"

"And Miss Arbitzer, yes. There is no other way. I hope you will accept that. Believe me, I greatly regret the necessity." Sir Alfred expressed his regret in the formal, unembarrassed voice that he must often have used in Parliamentary answers. Something in that voice made Garden angry. He whirled now upon his heel, abandoning the outer world of green fields and happiness, confronting their hostile or indifferent faces with the shreds of his own belief.

"And will you *greatly regret the necessity* when your own time comes, and half a dozen people decide that you have played your part and are no longer required by the strategy of power?" He brushed violently aside the response that the other seemed ready to make. "You work in the shadow of deceit and by the force of violence. You organize the masses to behave like violent delinquents while you encourage them to believe in a world where delinquency will not exist. Why should you hope that the world you create will do anything but destroy you? You are merely the weak precursors of the truly inhuman man of the future. That is something which must be secretly known to you all. And since it is known, why should you work for your own destruction?"

Bretherton shifted restlessly. Hards tapped his jaw politely to conceal an enormous yawn. Sir Alfred, however, twirled his horn-rimmed spectacles and leaned forward with every appearance of interest. His thick voice was muted to almost wooing tones. "But, Mr. Garden, were you not also committed to deceit and violence when you supported Arbitzer? Were you not attempting to seize power by a conspiracy?"

"In a different interest. Only force can answer force. Arbitzer was not a man who would have tolerated personal dictatorship." Even as he spoke these words Garden felt doubt. Was not the Arbitzer who had gone out with him the perfect figurehead for a dictator?

"Ah ah." The great head was pushed forward. "You base your claim, then, upon the superior virtue of your liberal friend. You believe in force just as we do, but you think that there is some quality in the candidate you support which would permit him to apply his power with divine wisdom. But that is a matter of opinion, is it not? I may attribute that very quality of divine wisdom to the candidate of my own choice. And as to which of us is right—that again is simply a question of personal preference."

"As much a matter of personal preference as whether Marcus Aurelius was more intelligent and civilized than Nero."

Outside the lift whirred faintly. "Latterley," Bretherton said. The sun disappeared behind cloud again. The room seemed to become dark and slightly chilly.

Now Sir Alfred stood up behind his desk and spoke in a voice of thunder. "I tell you that I know these liberal politicians and that whatever coat they wear— whether they call themselves progressive Conservatives or good trade union men—the reality of power lies behind their fine words about freedom and democracy and self-determination. I have worked with them for years, I have seen them crush projects for social reform in Britain and the colonies. They use nothing so harsh as a heel, you understand, the good weight of their broad bottoms is enough. The time, they will tell you, is not ripe for action. I answer that the time is never ripe except when men make it so. Oh, let me tell you, those men know the realities of power, Garden, only they never admit it. They deny the power by which they live. Upon their atomic destruction they drop the balm of crocodile tears. With the words *honor* and *morality* upon their lips they are busy making a shambles of the world. We acknowledge the reality of force, we say that lip-service to the sacredness of human life, yours or mine, is sentimental. We announce the truth that without power there can be no place for pity." With finger outstretched, great head thrust forward, the Minister asked, "Do you prefer their morals, Garden, or ours?"

"What does it matter?" said Bretherton.

The door opened and Latterley stood there looking at them. His hair was ruffled, his face pale. Almost reluctantly Sir Alfred lowered his finger. "Geoffrey. You are late."

Slowly, with the exact step of a somnambulist, Latterley walked into the room. On his face was a look which might have expressed anguish or despair; and then again, so doubtfully does the human face indicate human feeling, that look might have been one of joy or resignation. Behind Latterley there appeared, like a clue to the ambiguity of his expression, four men. Three of them were unknown to Garden. The fourth man had the slightly popping eyes and the handlebar mustache of the man who had been fishing off Brightsand pier.

The men already in the room stayed quite still for a moment, as if stunned. Then Sir Alfred said with elaborate patience: "Kind of you to bring back my friend Latterley. I suppose all this is something to do with the exercise."

The man with the handlebar mustache said, "It has nothing to do with the exercises. Look outside of your sun roof."

Sir Alfred deliberately put on his great horn-rimmed spectacles. "I shall do nothing of the kind. Who the devil are you?"

"Name's Pressway, Special Security," Handlebar said, and at that moment Mr. Hards acted. Even Garden, who was behind the little man, could hardly follow the speed with which he drew the blade from his umbrella, flung it across the room, and with his left hand brought the revolver from his hip. But quick as Hards was, he was not quite quick enough. There was a crack and a cry of pain. The revolver clattered to the floor. The swordstick went through a cushion in one of the armchairs and stayed there, quivering. And there, Garden saw with a sense of anticlimax, the little flurry of violence was ending. Bretherton and Colonel Hunt had plainly no thought of resistance, and Latterley stood in the middle of the room in his private dream.

"That's no use. Nothing is any use," Handlebar said as though he were demonstrating an academic point. He said to Sir Alfred with a certain deference, "Just take a look outside and you'll see that this building is surrounded. We picked up the trail of Latterley and our friends here soon after they left London."

Sir Alfred walked with a firm tread to the sun-roof door. He opened it and stepped out. They watched him move slowly round the roof, looking down. Then he nodded, came back to the doorway, and stood looking at them with his head hunched forward on his shoulders. "I congratulate you," he said to Pressway. "Very efficient. But you won't find it easy to identify me with whatever these fellows may have been up to."

Handlebar coughed. "That won't be difficult, sir. We have Latterley, you see, who was your link with what you might call the active side of the organization. A born squealer if ever I saw one, Latterley."

"Oh, Latterley," Sir Alfred waved a hand dismissively.

"And then Miss Bone. You were very unwise to carry on a little affair with her, if I may say so. Never trust a woman. I dare say you expressed yourself pretty incautiously to her from time to time in what you might call the heat of the moment." Garden suddenly remembered little Hards's remarks about Miss Bone's one particular friend.

Sir Alfred's head seemed to be shrinking back into his shoulders. "A jealous bitch. She can be discredited."

"And more important than Latterley or Miss Bone—" Handlebar looked at Garden. "You won't find it easy to discredit him. An honest man."

"An honest man, yes. They are always dangerous." Sir Alfred's head was now completely hunched into his great shoulders. "All this would mean a trial, something of that sort. They would never be prepared for that."

Handlebar tugged reflectively at his mustache. He seemed to choose his next words with painful care. "If necessary—I am instructed to say—yes. The necessity, of course, would be much regretted." An irony involved in the use of these words escaped Garden at the time. More painfully still Handlebar said, "It is hoped—that the necessity—may not arise."

"I see." Sir Alfred's next remark was apparently irrelevant. "These walls are a kind of perspex, not glass. You couldn't put your fist through them. Have to cut." Handlebar nodded intelligently. "So that if I lock this door—" He walked out to the sun roof and did so. Then he stood looking at them all with a heavy but not unfriendly gaze. The barrier between them was invisible, and yet impenetrable. Out there on the roof he was living in the world he had created, the world of which he was supreme ruler. He took several steps to the edge of the roof, and stood again looking down. Then, taking care to avoid the flowering shrubs in pots that had been planted by the safety railing, he clambered awkwardly over to the foot-wide parapet beyond it. Inside the room they stood intently, spectators watching the last act of a drama in which their own parts had ended, and only the final catastrophe remained to be enacted.

He stayed for perhaps a minute holding the safety rail behind him, looking out over his empire. Hards began to laugh. "He's windy. What a joke when he climbs back." But at that moment Sir Alfred let go of the safety rail, and stood there in the darkened afternoon with his arms spread like a bird about to fly. He seemed to sway for a moment as though uncertain of his direction, half turned, and fumbled in a pocket as though there were some last message that might be scribbled to change the course of the world. Then he jumped.

4

"The best thing you can do about all this is to forget it," Pressway said to Garden and Ilona. They sat in his uncomfortable clean aseptic office. A dejected-looking old man came in with a tea trolley. "Have a cup of char. It comes in the category of army tea, hot water browned off, but at least it's liquid. Sugar?"

Garden stirred his tea round and round. "What happens now?"

"Nothing much. What do you expect?"

"When will that lot—Hards and Bretherton and the Colonel—come to trial?"

"They won't. Do you think we want them blabbing out their connection with our late respected Sir Alfred, and saying an ex-Minister was engaged in a treasonable plot? No, my lad, we've got this nicely settled as a case of suicide while balance of mind was disturbed, and it's going to stay that way."

"What's going to happen to them?"

"Nothing. They're not even in custody." Pressway raised a hand. "It's no use you riding your high horse about it. The big fish was the one we wanted to get. The others aren't important or dangerous, but he was a dangerous man." He sucked up tea through his handlebar mustache. "Dangerous to his country, I mean. Which is your country, and mine too."

"And Latterley?"

"He's resigned his job. Nothing else will happen to him. Might have a future in public relations. He's a small fish too."

"If you knew all about this plot, why didn't you stop us from leaving England?"

"Wanted to get the big fish. Besides, we only knew the general outline, couldn't think what they were playing at trying to get you and Arbitzer out of England, except that it must be a bit of no good."

"What happened to the man who helped us to escape?" Ilona asked. "Trelawney."

"Oh, Trelawney's all right. Back in England as a matter of fact. Rather a good story." Pressway began to laugh. "Peplov put two and two together and deduced that it was someone in the English party at Dravina who'd helped you. Wanted to arrest 'em all. But Peplov's bosses thought he was pulling a fast one to cover up for himself, and wouldn't have any of it. They arrested him instead. I doubt if there will be any more news of Peplov." Pressway began to push tobacco into a pipe bowl with a stubby finger, looking shrewdly at Garden. "What are you going to do now?"

Ilona said, "We're going to get married."

Pressway put a match to the pipe. Smoke drifted up. He was still looking at Garden. "You're not thinking of going back?"

Garden thought of Theo's face in the bungalow at Brightsand, dark and eager, and then of Theo as he had last seen him in the fisherman's cottage. It seemed to him that all the past had turned to ruin in his hands. He thought of that country shaped like a broken penny as he had last seen it, a shadow on the blue horizon. "No, I shan't go back."

"Good. It really would be awkward for us if you tried to go back. We should have to do something about it." Pressway laughed heartily to show that this was a joke. "You've quite made up your mind."

"Yes. You heard Ilona say that we were going to get married."

"Congratulations. I'll send you a present. Anything else I can do for you?"

Ilona said hesitantly, "My uncle. He left some money. It would come to me as his nearest relative. We shall need it now that Charles is going back to his job as night watchman—"

"Night watchman!" Pressway began to laugh.

Ilona looked at him in surprise. "What's the matter? Of course he hopes to get a better job later on."

"Nothing at all. Got a crude sense of humor, I'm afraid. Go on."

"If you are not making any announcement about Jacob's disappearance the authorities will not pay me the money. Isn't that right?"

"Um, yes," Pressway made a note on a pad in front of him. "I'll contact the appropriate department and get them to put a special confidential clearance through. Glad to. Anything else?"

There was nothing else. As they rose to go Pressway tugged at his handlebar mustache. "Just one thing more, old man. Take my tip and don't get mixed up in this cloak and dagger stuff any more. Not your cup of tea. Stick to being"—here Pressway's handlebar mustache curled upward, his face reddened and he repressed laughter with difficulty—"a night watchman."

5

"So you want your old job back, eh?" said Mr. Goldblatt. "The holiday's over and you've brought back a little woman and you've come to see old Goldblatt, who's the wickedest skinflint that ever threw his money about like a man with no hands."

"That's right."

"And how's the state of the world? Did you put that right while you were away, or couldn't you manage it?"

"I couldn't manage it."

"And you didn't try, don't tell me, or you wouldn't have brought back a little woman. Politics was it you were going in for, I never believed a word of it, do you see any green in Ike Goldblatt's eye? But I'll tell you something about politics now, about all the war, murder, lynching, bloody revolution we got today. Do you know how we could stop it? Get all the politicians into one big room and knock 'em all on the head, bang!" Mr. Goldblatt drew a deep breath. "Eh, how sweet the air would smell afterward."

"You're not a conservative, you're a natural anarchist."

"A natural anarchist, hear what he's calling me. Now I'll tell you what Ike Goldblatt's going to do with you, Ike whose heart is tender so that if you tried it against cast iron in a furnace the cast iron would melt first. He's going to raise you from five pound ten to seven pounds a week. How's that, eh? Can you live on it?"

"Many live on less."

"Many live on less, some live in Park Lane, that ain't what I asked you. Can *you* live on it, eh?"

"Yes. And thank you."

"Don't thank me, thank the Lord who gave me that much brains that if I had a few more I'd be half-witted. That's one thing. Now you bring your little chicken down here to the warehouse and I let her choose a wedding present there. Anything she likes." Mr. Goldblatt's arm moved outward in an extravagant arc.

"It's very good of you."

"When I say anything, you know what I mean." Mr. Goldblatt tapped his nose. "A nice fox cape, a good beaver, lamb, even a muskrat maybe. But ermine, sable, mink—pfui! Leave them for the snobs. It's the snobs we live on."

"Of course. I'll bring Ilona down tomorrow. Shall I come back next Monday?"

"Next Monday, yes. Now, can you say Ike Goldblatt didn't treat you square. You can't, my boy, no more can anyone else. Go ahead and get married, and may all your troubles be little ones."

Garden walked slowly down the street to the café where he had left Ilona. Children, he thought—there will be children who grow up to hate me or love me, if they grow up at all. And what shall I say when they ask, as every new generation asks its elders: "What do you believe in"? And because he could no longer answer such a question, his eyes filled with tears.

He stood in the doorway of the café. Ilona got up and came to him. "Was it all right?"

"Was what all right?"

"The job. Did he give you back your job?" He nodded. "Oh, that's good isn't it, that's very good."

He took her hand. "Ilona, I hope that when we are married—when we have children—they will be ready to fight for the things they believe in."

She said impatiently, "Always thinking about fighting. You are too old for that now, leave it to the fighting men."

"I expect you're right. What do you believe in, Ilona?"

"Trying to be happy," she said laughing. "Not worrying about the future, not thinking too much about the present."

"I expect you're right," Garden said again.

"There's a cinema just down the road. Gary Cooper, my favorite actor." She pulled his arm. "Come along."

They walked down the road together and went into the cinema.

THE PERENNIAL LIBRARY MYSTERY SERIES

Gavin Black

A DRAGON FOR CHRISTMAS
"Potent excitement!"
—*New York Herald Tribune*

THE EYES AROUND ME
"I stayed up until all hours last night reading *The Eyes Around Me*, which is something I do not do very often, but I was so intrigued by the ingeniousness of Mr. Black's plotting and the witty way in which he spins his mystery. I can only say that I enjoyed the book enormously."
—F. van Wyck Mason

YOU WANT TO DIE, JOHNNY?
"Gavin Black doesn't just develop a pressure plot in suspense, he adds uninfected wit, character, charm, and sharp knowledge of the Far East to make rereading as keen as the first race-through."
—*Book Week*

Nicholas Blake

THE BEAST MUST DIE
"It remains one more proof that in the hands of a really first-class writer the detective novel can safely challenge comparison with any other variety of fiction."
—*The Manchester Guardian*

THE CORPSE IN THE SNOWMAN
"If there is a distinction between the novel and the detective story (which we do not admit), then this book deserves a high place in both categories."
—*The New York Times*

THE DREADFUL HOLLOW
"Pace unhurried, characters excellent, reasoning solid."
—*San Francisco Chronicle*

END OF CHAPTER
"...admirably solid...an adroit formal detective puzzle backed up by firm characterization and a knowing picture of London publishing."
—*The New York Times*

HEAD OF A TRAVELER
"Another grade A detective story of the right old jigsaw persuasion."
—*New York Herald Tribune Book Review*

MINUTE FOR MURDER
"An outstanding mystery novel. Mr. Blake's writing is a delight in itself."
—*The New York Times*

A QUESTION OF PROOF
"The characters in this story are unusually well drawn, and the suspense is well sustained."
—*The New York Times*

THE SAD VARIETY

"It is a stunner. I read it instead of eating, instead of sleeping."

—Dorothy Salisbury Davis

THE SMILER WITH THE KNIFE

"An extraordinarily well written and entertaining thriller."

—*Saturday Review of Literature*

THOU SHELL OF DEATH

"It has all the virtues of culture, intelligence and sensibility that the most exacting connoisseur could ask of detective fiction."

—*The Times* [London] *Literary Supplement*

THE WHISPER IN THE GLOOM

"One of the most entertaining suspense-pursuit novels in many seasons."

—*The New York Times*

THE WIDOW'S CRUISE

"A stirring suspense....The thrilling tale leaves nothing to be desired."

—*Springfield Republican*

THE WORM OF DEATH

"It [The Worm of Death] is one of Blake's very best—and his best is better than almost anyone's." —Louis Untermeyer

E. C. Bentley

TRENT'S LAST CASE

"One of the three best detective stories ever written." —Agatha Christie

Andrew Garve

A HERO FOR LEANDA

"One can trust Mr. Garve to put a fresh twist to any situation, and the ending is really a lovely surprise." —*The Manchester Guardian*

THE ASHES OF LODA

"Garve ... embellishes a fine fast adventure story with a more credible picture of the U.S.S.R. than is offered in most thrillers."

—*The New York Times Book Review*

THE CUCKOO LINE AFFAIR

" ...an agreeable and ingenious piece of work." —*The New Yorker*

THE FAR SANDS

"An impeccably devious thriller....The quality is well up to Mr. Garve's high standard of entertainment." —*The New Yorker*

MURDER THROUGH THE LOOKING GLASS

"...refreshingly out-of-the-way and enjoyable...highly recommended to all comers."
—*Saturday Review*

NO TEARS FOR HILDA

"It starts fine and finishes finer. I got behind on breathing watching Max get not only his man but his woman, too."
—Rex Stout

THE RIDDLE OF SAMSON

"The story is an excellent one, the people are quite likable, and the writing is superior."
—*Springfield Republican*

Michael Gilbert

BLOOD AND JUDGMENT

"Gilbert readers need scarcely be told that the characters all come alive at first sight, and that his surpassing talent for narration enhances any plot.... Don't miss."
—*San Francisco Chronicle*

THE BODY OF A GIRL

"Does what a good mystery should do: open up into all kinds of ramifications, with untold menace behind the action. At the end, there is a bang-up climax, and it is a pleasure to see how skilfully Gilbert wraps everything up."
—*The New York Times Book Review*

THE DANGER WITHIN

"Michael Gilbert has nicely combined some elements of the straight detective story with plenty of action, suspense, and adventure, to produce a superior thriller."
—*Saturday Review*

DEATH HAS DEEP ROOTS

"Trial scenes superb; prowl along Loire vivid chase stuff; funny in right places; a fine performance throughout."
—*Saturday Review*

FEAR TO TREAD

"Merits serious consideration as a work of art."
—*The New York Times*

Cyril Hare

AN ENGLISH MURDER

"By a long shot, the best crime story I have read for a long time. Everything is traditional, but originality does not suffer. The setting is perfect. Full marks to Mr. Hare."
—*Irish Press*

WHEN THE WIND BLOWS

"The best, unquestionably, of all the Hare stories, and a masterpiece by any standards."
—Jacques Barzun and Wendell Hertig Taylor,
A Catalogue of Crime

Arthur Maling

LUCKY DEVIL

"The plot unravels at a fast clip, the writing is breezy and Maling's approach is as fresh as today's stockmarket quotes." —*Louisville Courier Journal*

RIPOFF

"A swiftly paced story of today's big business is larded with intrigue as a Ralph Nader-type investigates an insurance scandal and is soon on the run from a hired gun and his brother....Engrossing and credible." —*Booklist*

SCHROEDER'S GAME

"As the title indicates, this Schroeder is up to something, and the unravelling of his game is a diverting and sufficiently blood-soaked entertainment."

—*The New Yorker*

Julian Symons

THE BELTING INHERITANCE

"A superb whodunit in the best tradition of the detective story."

—August Derleth, *Madison Capital Times*

BLAND BEGINNING

"Mr. Symons displays a deft storytelling skill, a quiet and literate wit, a nice feeling for character, and detectival ingenuity of a high order."

—Anthony Boucher, *The New York Times*

THE COLOR OF MURDER

"A singularly unostentatious and memorably brilliant detective story."

—*New York Herald Tribune Book Review*

THE 31ST OF FEBRUARY

"Nobody has painted a more gruesome picture of the advertising business since Dorothy Sayers wrote 'Murder Must Advertise', and very few people have written a more entertaining or dramatic mystery story."

—*The New Yorker*